ALL TO HERSELF

"It's really very simple." Luck curved a hand under her chin and turned it toward him. "I want to kiss you. I've been wanting to do it all evening, but I never found the opening. So I was trying to make one."

Her heart fluttered at the hint of desire in his blue eyes. Luck had finally said "I," and her senses were on a rampage, wild with the promise that the word held. With a total lack of concern for the deliberateness of his actions, he took the coffee cup from her hands and set it on the stone hearth beside his.

Her composure was so rattled that she wondered how Luck could go about this all so calmly. Anticipation had Eve trembling on the brink of raw longing for his embrace.

BOOK YOUR PLACE ON OUR WEBSITE AND MAKE THE READING CONNECTION!

We've created a customized website just for our very special readers, where you can get the inside scoop on everything that's going on with Zebra, Pinnacle and Kensington books.

When you come online, you'll have the exciting opportunity to:

- View covers of upcoming books
- Read sample chapters
- Learn about our future publishing schedule (listed by publication month *and author*)
- Find out when your favorite authors will be visiting a city near you
- Search for and order backlist books from our online catalog
- Check out author bios and background information
- Send e-mail to your favorite authors
- Meet the Kensington staff online
- Join us in weekly chats with authors, readers and other guests
- Get writing guidelines
- AND MUCH MORE!

Visit our website at
http://www.kensingtonbooks.com

JANET DAILEY

Eve's Christmas

ZEBRA BOOKS
KENSINGTON PUBLISHING CORP.
http://www.zebrabooks.com

Chapter 1

"Sure you don't want a ride home?" Reverend Johnson asked. "If you can wait a few minutes, I'd be happy to drive you."

He didn't look like a minister in his plaid shirt and khaki-colored pants. In fact, Fred Johnson resembled a fisherman who had strayed into church by mistake. He was an older man and a lifelong angler, overjoyed that his Wisconsin parish was situated in an area with so many lakes, streams, and rivers.

"No, thanks, Reverend," Eve Rowland said. "It's nice out, even if it's cold."

"Not too bad for early April," Fred said. "But it really wouldn't be a problem."

"I'll enjoy the walk. It's good for my character."

"As a minister, I can't argue with that," Fred said.

Eve slipped on her coat. She was waiting until the January sales to buy a new one. This one was a serviceable dark beige that didn't show stains— but it did absolutely nothing for her brown hair and pale skin. "Besides, it isn't that far, really."

"No, but I don't like the idea of your walking alone after dark."

"This is Cable. Not Minneapolis or Milwaukee," she laughed. There were times when she even forgot to lock the front door of her parents' house, but she didn't worry much about it when that happened.

"True enough. Guess I shouldn't worry." He shook his head ruefully. "Hey, thanks again for filling in for Mrs. Alstrom at the organ tonight. It was nice to have a rest from crashing chords and the usual all-stops-out finale. You're a lot easier on the ears, Eve."

Eve smiled. Mrs. Alstrom was the regular church organist. A minor crisis at home had kept her from attending Sunday evening choir practice and Eve had been asked to substitute for her.

"I hope we didn't upset any of your plans," Fred continued.

She shrugged. "I didn't have any plans," she said. Or a date. Or an anything. The social whirl in a little town like Cable was pretty much nonexistent.

"That's a pity." The minister's eyes darkened with sympathy, even as he changed his expression to give her an encouraging smile. "You should. Maybe I should whisper in the ears of the eligible male members of my congregation."

He meant to be kind but his offer had a demoralizing effect. A lineup of the single men who made it to church on Sunday appeared in her mind. The guy from the gas station. The post office clerk who collected Hummel figurines. The classic-car buff who spent all of his free time polishing chrome.

Eve fixed a quick smile in place to hide her reaction to his attempt at matchmaking. "That's a nice thought, but most of them are, uh, already semi-attached to someone else. But thanks anyway." She started to leave. "Good night. And I'm glad I could help out."

"Okay then. See you in church on Sunday." Reverend Johnson lifted his hand in a saluting wave.

"Not this Sunday," she said. "My parents and I are going to open our summer cottage on the lake early this year, so we won't be in church."

"Oh? Which lake?" His fishing curiosity was awakened.

"Namekagon." Which was only a few miles east of town.

"Great fishing there," he stated.

"I know. It's Dad's favorite. He even got into ice fishing last year. That's why we had the cottage winterized." She glanced at her wristwatch, a utilitarian piece with a plain leather band that made no pretense of being decorative. "I'd better be going. Good night, Reverend Johnson."

"Good night."

Leaving the church, Eve buttoned her coat against the cold night air. Spring in Wisconsin took its sweet time to arrive, that was for sure. She added a warm muffler and gloves that matched her coat, and a handknit hat with a rolled brim, also in brown. The hat let her glossy, thick hair frame her face, which had nothing to do with vanity and everything to do with covering her ears.

The sky was crystal bright with stars, hundreds of thousands of them lighting the heavens. The moon, big and fat, competed with the stars, its silver globe like a spotlight shining down on the

earth. The streetlights along the main thorough-
fare were almost unneeded.

As she walked along the sidewalk, her mind
kept returning to the matchmaking offer the minister had made. Having lived in Cable for all of her
twenty-six years—with the exception of four years
spent at college in Madison—Eve knew virtually
every single man in the area. There were others
who didn't go to church, of course, but those she
might have been interested in never noticed her,
and those that noticed her she wasn't interested
in. It wasn't a question of being too particular;
there just wasn't anyone who could be considered
a remote possibility.

Her mother was afraid that Eve would never find
a man, but unfortunately, Teresa Rowland wasn't
afraid to say so. Repeatedly. She kept reminding her
only daughter not to be so picky. Eve had given up
hope long ago that Prince Charming would ever
come this far north, but she wasn't going to get
married just for the sake of being married, no matter how nice and safe and ordinary a suitor might
be. She didn't intend to marry unless she felt
something for the man.

Passion would be nice, everlasting love even better. Warm affection might have to do, but so far no
one had aroused even that. There had been boy-
friends now and then. Most of them she genuinely
liked, but not with any depth. It seemed she was always attracted to men who weren't attracted to her.

It wasn't because she was homely. She was attractive, in a plain sort of way. With brown hair and
eyes, she had a flawless complexion, but her features were unassuming. Her figure was average,
neither thin nor plump. She wasn't too tall or too
short. She simply didn't stand out in a crowd. In a

sea of pretty faces, hers would be the last to be noticed.

Eve was just as realistic in her assessment of her personality traits. She was intelligent, basically good-natured and possessed a good sense of humor. As a music teacher, she appreciated music and the arts. But she tended to be quiet and not quick to make friends. Her childhood shyness had lessened, but she still wasn't crazy about going to parties and things like that. She preferred celebrating with a few close friends to attending a large social function.

A few relatives—not her mother or father—suggested that, at twenty-six, she was too old to be living at home. When Eve added up the cost of living alone plus the cost of owning her own car and subtracted it from her salary, it became a matter of sheer practicality. Besides, she and her parents were good friends. She was just as independent as she would have been living in an apartment or a rented house.

With all her thoughts focused inward, Eve didn't notice the tavern she was approaching. The neon beer signs in the window cast jewel-toned shadows across the dark sidewalk. Her footsteps sounded lonely in the cold, empty night.

Despite the temperature, a window was open to let out the smoke and let in fresh air. Inside, a jukebox was loudly playing a popular song. Eve didn't hear it or the laughter and spirited voices. Her gaze was on the sidewalk in front of her feet. She stepped carefully around an uneven spot in the concrete.

Suddenly a man walked directly in front of her. Eve didn't have time to stop or step aside. Her hands came up to absorb the shock of the collision. He evidently didn't see her, either, as he took a step forward and they collided. In a reflex action his arms went around to catch her, while his forward progress carried her backward two steps.

Dazed by the total unexpectedness of the accident, Eve lifted her head. No telling who was at fault, but he had knocked the breath out of her. Too stunned yet to speak, she stared at the stranger she'd bumped into—and vice versa.

The light from the window signs fully illuminated his face. Nearly a head taller than she was, he had dark hair that waved thickly, falling at a rakish angle across his forehead. His eyes were blue, very blue, and he was tanned, even though winter had barely ended.

Skiing vacation, she thought. Farther west and at a higher elevation. She had a habit of filling in the blanks when life got confusing. The snow around Cable, a cross-country mecca, was mostly gone, but he could definitely be a downhill skier—he had an athletic build that she couldn't help noticing. And he was handsome in a hell-raising kind of way. His reckless smile did something to her.

"Hey. I caught something. Hmm. Let's see. What is it?" There was a laughing glint in his gaze as it moved over her, taking in the brown of her hair and eyes and the brown coat. "I believe it's a brown mouse."

The stranger was undoubtedly teasing, but given her mood, the remark didn't amuse her. Her gaze dropped to the cream-colored pullover that fit his muscular chest well, and the puffy outside of the down jacket over that. He wasn't wearing a hat or a muffler, so maybe he wasn't feeling the cold.

Since he had obviously just left the tavern, Eve

wasn't surprised that there was liquor on his breath. He'd been drinking, but he wasn't drunk. He was steady on his feet, and there was no glaze of alcohol in the rich blue of his eyes.

"I'm sorry," Eve apologized stiffly. "I was trying not to trip. I really wasn't looking where I was going." Then she realized his arms were still holding her and her hands were flattened against his chest—a very solid chest. Her heart began to beat unevenly.

"I wasn't looking where *I* was going, so it seems we were both to blame, brown mouse. Did I hurt you?" It was more disturbing to listen to the low pitch of his voice without seeing his face, so Eve looked up. His half-closed eyes were difficult to meet squarely.

"No, you didn't." When he showed no inclination to release her, she said, "I'm all right. You can let go of me now."

He sighed deeply. "Do I have to?" His hands moved, but not away from her. Instead they began roaming over her shoulders and spine in an exploring fashion, as if testing the way she felt in his arms. "Do you know how long it's been since I held a woman?"

"Huh?" Eve squirmed. That was definitely not a question she wanted to answer. Just her luck. Her thirty seconds of bliss in the arms of a handsome stranger were over and it was back to reality. She looked around to see if there was anyone else in sight, but the two of them seemed to be the only people out tonight.

The well-shaped line of his mouth held a latent sensuality that unnerved her. Eve could guess what he was thinking about. His hands were exerting a slight pressure to inch her closer to him. They were standing on the sidewalk of a main street a few feet away from a tavern full of people.

Surely he wouldn't try anything when help was so near. She wanted to struggle, but she was afraid he might view it as provocation rather than resistance. Maybe he was just a friendly guy who'd had a few too many beers and was ready to throw his arms around anyone, but right now Eve felt the situation was uncomfortable, bordering on dangerous. She kept her body rigid.

"Please let me go," she asked.

"I'm frightening you, aren't I?" He tipped his head to one side, regarding her lazily, while his hands stopped their movement.

"No, not at all," Eve lied. She didn't want him to think she could be easily intimidated, even though right now her heart was beating a mile a minute and her throat felt tight.

He let his hands slide away to let her stand free. She had expected an argument. It was a full second before she realized he was no longer holding her. She brushed past him and was a step beyond him when he reached out to catch her arm.

"Don't scurry off into the dark, brown mouse." His voice was gently chiding, not scary at all. But she still didn't like what was happening. "Stay a minute."

"No." His hand brought her to a stop, and she tried to pull free. She couldn't, not without using all her strength. Eve held still.

"What's your hurry? Are you meeting someone?" The question sounded friendly enough and lightly curious but Eve was confused and wary. He wouldn't release her, but he was making no move to do more than keep her there. "No," was all she said.

"Then where are you going in such a rush?" Shadows fell across his face and heightened the angles and planes of his features. The effect enhanced his rough virility, adding to his attractive aura.

"I'm going home," she stated, and immediately regretted it. What if he followed her? She should have said she was going inside the tavern and then made a call from there for her dad to come pick her up.

"I don't have anywhere to go but home, either," he said. "So why don't we go someplace together? Then we won't have to go home."

"Look, we bumped into each other and now we're going to unbump." She wondered why she'd said that, not sure how he would interpret her made-up word.

"Unbump." He thought that over. "I'm not sure what that means but whatever you want is fine."

"It means we're going to go our separate ways. This discussion is over," Eve said firmly. A faint quiver was spreading up her arm from the restraining touch of his hand.

"Guess I'll have to let go of you." He did, giving her a wistful look instead. "Hey, tell you what. We could talk inside. It's cold out here. And kinda lonely." He gave her an engaging grin that almost melted her. Almost.

But she wasn't going to walk in on his arm and have the patrons think she was his date. Anyway, she had difficulty imagining a man like him ever being lonely. It was obviously a line. She wasn't going to be strung along by it.

"Let me put it another way: I don't want to go with you."

"I think I'm giving you the wrong impression." A bigger grin, boyishly disarming, curved his mouth. "And besides, this is the wrong place. The tavern is too damn noisy and if the guy who's glued to the jukebox plays that Shania Twain song one more time, I'm going to lose my mind. I want to go someplace where we can talk."

Another line, Eve guessed. "I doubt that you're interested in talking," she returned with a tinge of sarcasm.

"It's true," he insisted, looking hopeful. "You know, I think I've seen you before."

Eve shook her head. "No, we've never met."

He looked her up and down. "I didn't say that. Just that I've seen you. Just before last Christmas, at the tree lot next to Moore's Hardware. The snow was coming down, but I'm pretty sure that was you." Why that memory had stayed with him for so long, he didn't know. He'd only glanced at the glowing, bright-eyed young woman with her parents, but she'd made an impression on him. He had been tying the biggest tree in the lot to the top of his car, busy with his young son, and trying to keep his mind on everything that needed to get done around the holidays.

"I don't remember it."

At least he was keeping a safe distance. Her every instinct told her that he really was an okay guy who'd just overdone it and was being a little too friendly.

But Eve had never been one to trust her instincts. She stared straight ahead in an effort to ignore him and the strange leaping of her pulse. Suddenly his other hand moved to touch the side of her silky brown hair. Instinctively she jerked away from the soft caress, feeling the slight brush of his fingertips on her cheek, and turned her head to stare at him.

When she met his eyes, Eve realized he was a man who communicated by touching—with his hands and his gaze . . . or his mouth and his body. Unbidden, her mind had added the last. She didn't doubt his expertise in any area. Her calm facade began to splinter a little, undermined by her unexpectedly wayward imagination.

"Hey," he said. "Don't you know that a man can talk to a brown mouse?"

The comment was hardly flattering, considering her own low opinion of her attractiveness. "Would you please not call me that?" Irritation flashed through her—partly at him for saying it, and partly at herself for caring.

"Sorry. Guess you're not as timid as you look."

Eve had had enough of this odd chitchat. It was freezing, and it was getting late and she was arguing with a stranger over whether she was or was not a—

"A brown mouse," the man said again. "That's what you are, you know. With your brown hair and your brown eyes and your brown coat."

Maybe he would stop if she pretended to humor him. "Okay, but this brown mouse really wants to go home, so would you let me go?" She injected a weary note into her voice, as if he was being just too annoying for words. Which he was. If humoring him didn't work, she might have to push him down on the sidewalk and run inside the tavern for help after all. Fleetingly it occurred to her that she wouldn't be in this situation if she had accepted Reverend Johnson's offer of a ride.

"If you insist that's what you want to do, I'll walk with you to make sure you arrive safely and no cat pounces on you on the way home."

"I can think of only one cat that might pounce on me and that's you," Eve retorted.

"Good comeback!" He laughed, and she was upset with herself for liking the sound of it.

She faced him directly. "Listen, if you don't leave me alone, I'm going to have to scream."

"Mice squeak," he corrected, but his gaze had narrowed on her, judging to see how serious she was about her threat.

"I scream," she insisted.

She could, and if she felt sufficiently threatened, she would. It hadn't reached that point yet, but this conversation had gone on long enough.

"I believe you," he agreed after a second had passed. He lifted his hands in a mocking indication that he wouldn't touch her again.

"Thank you." Eve wasn't sure why she said that. She spotted two police officers on patrol half a block away—they looked familiar and there wasn't a chance that she wouldn't know them in a town as small as Cable. Whoever they were, she was thankful that, true to their training, they seemed to be checking out her overly friendly companion. A man with no hat and no gloves standing outside a tavern on an unseasonably cold spring night in Wisconsin was worth investigating, apparently. She breathed a sigh of relief and immediately began walking away, trying not to walk too fast.

Still, she could feel the stranger watching her with those magnetic blue eyes. It was an unnerving sensation. "Good night, brown mouse," his low voice called after her, a hint of regret in its tone.

She didn't answer him. For another ten feet, Eve wondered if he would start following her and told herself that help was only half a block away if he did. There was no law against talking to a girl or standing on the sidewalk, but it was clear, even from a distance, that he'd had a few, and conscientious cops wouldn't dream of letting him get in a car.

A few seconds later she heard the tavern door open and close. She glanced over her shoulder, but he wasn't in sight. Since no customer had come out, he had obviously gone back inside. The patrol officers reached the door of the tavern and one gave her a wave, while the other rubbed his hands and blew clouds of warm breath into the frosty night. Ray Braun and Kyle Dobbs. She recognized both of them from high school, and knew they'd stick around long enough for her to get on home.

Eve didn't have to wonder anymore whether the stranger would come after her. Instead she found herself wondering who he was.

It was after ten when she reached her home. Both her parents were in the living room when she walked in. Like their daughter, they weren't particularly striking in terms of appearance. Her father was a tall, spare man with hazel eyes and thinning brown hair, while her mother was petite, with graying brown hair and brown eyes. One look in the hall mirror as she pulled off her knit hat and muffler, and Eve was reminded that she'd inherited her looks from both of them—and that the DNA was not movie star material to begin with. Oh, well. There were worse fates.

"Choir practice must have run late," her mother observed. It was a simple statement of fact, not a dig about Eve's lateness in getting home.

"A little." She shrugged out of her dark beige coat and wondered if she would ever wear it again without thinking of herself as a brown mouse. "The minister offered me a ride home, but it was a nice evening, even though it was really cold. So I decided to walk and it took a little longer."

"Oh, okay. Well, we'll be taking the last carload of stuff out to the cottage tomorrow morning. Think you'll be up in time to help?"

"Sure. I always get up early. Even though I have Monday off."

"So you do, now that I think of it," her mother said absently. "You can catch up on your beauty sleep."

"Yup." She looked at herself in the mirror and rubbed her not-very-glamorous nose, still pink from the cold outside. She decided not to mention the stranger outside the tavern. They were still her parents and Eve didn't want to worry them. It had been a harmless incident anyway, not worth recounting.

In the middle of the night Toby McClure rolled onto his side. His long, little-boy lashes fluttered, his sleep disturbed by familiar footsteps. He slowly opened his eyes, focusing on the door to his bedroom, which stood ajar. The hall sconce cast a faint light over his racetrack carpet and the small cars he'd left on it.

Listening, he heard hushed movement in another part of the house. A smile brightened when he heard someone bump into a chair and curse beneath his breath. Only his dad would ever use that mix of four-letter words and only when he thought his eight-year-old son wasn't listening.

Throwing back the covers, Toby slipped out of his single bed and walked to the hall door. His bare feet made no sound on the carpeted floor and he carefully avoided the cars. He opened the door wide and waited until he saw the towering frame of his father separate from the darkness. A tall man, he was walking unsteadily, trying too hard to be quiet.

The light from the sconce provided soft illumination in the hallway where Toby stood. The instant he saw the boy, Luck McClure stopped abruptly and swayed, bracing a hand against the wall to steady himself. A frown gathered on his forehead as he eyed his son.

"What are you doing out of bed? You're supposed to be asleep," he said in a low voice that had a trace of a slur.

"You woke me up," Toby replied. "You always do when you try to sneak in."

"I wasn't sneaking. I was dancing with a chair. It stepped on my feet." He winked at his son and waved in the general direction of the living room downstairs. "Where's Wanda? Isn't she supposed to be babysitting you?" His tone was joking. Not for one minute did he imagine that she'd left the house, although he hadn't seen her when he'd come in. Maybe she was in the family room watching TV with the sound off and had fallen asleep. He'd go down and check just as soon as he got Toby back to bed.

"She was going to charge double after midnight, so I paid her off and sent her home. You owe me twenty dollars."

"Excuse me? You did what?" Luck McClure could not believe what he was hearing.

"I don't like her, Dad. She yaks on the phone with her stupid girlfriends the whole time she's here and she rips the bread when she makes peanut butter sandwiches. I can make my own but she won't let me, because she says I'll mess up the kitchen. I told her you'd called on my cell phone and said you'd be right home and—"

"She believed that?"

"Yeah. I think she wanted to go out."

Luck compressed his lips and said nothing, trying to control his anger at a babysitter who would let a kid tell her what to do—and then leave said kid alone. Wanda Jackson hadn't struck him as being all that bright, but she'd seemed responsible enough. Clearly, she was anything but. He carefully raised a hand to cradle his forehead. "We'll talk about this in the morning, Toby," he declared.

"Okay, Dad. I'll remind you if you forget," he promised. A mischievous light danced in his eyes. "You owe me twenty bucks."

"That's another thing we'll discuss in the morning." A wave of tiredness washed over him. "Right now, I'm going to bed."

Luck pushed away from the wall and used that impetus to carry him to the bedroom door opposite his son's. Toby watched him open the door to the darkened room and head in the general direction of the bed. Without much light to see by, Luck stubbed his toe on an end post. He started to swear and stopped sharply when Toby came into the room to flip the switch, turning on the overhead light.

"Why aren't you back in bed where you belong?" Luck hobbled around to the side of the bed and half sat, half fell onto the mattress.

"I figured you'd need help getting ready for bed." Toby walked to the bed as his father sat down on it. The two McClures exchanged looks of approximately equal concern, but Luck felt a flash of guilt, wishing his son hadn't woken up. All Luck wanted to do was fall asleep. The day had seemed endless and he didn't remember too much about how he'd spent his evening.

"For an eight-year-old kid, you figure out a lot of things," Luck observed with a wry sort of affection. While he unbuttoned the cuffs of his shirt, Toby unfastened the buttons on his shirtfront.

"You gotta admit, Dad, I did you a favor tonight," Toby said as he helped pull his father's arms free of the shirt. "How would it have looked if Wanda Jackson had seen you come home drunk?"

Given that Wanda was probably having a high old time at the tavern he'd just left and buying beers with Toby's twenty dollars, Luck didn't much care. "I'm not drunk," he protested, keeping on his pants and letting himself fall backward into the pillows. "I just had a few drinks, that's all. There's a difference."

"Sure, Dad." Toby reached over and dragged a folded down comforter from the foot of the bed. It didn't take much persuasion to get his father under it.

"It feels so good to lie down," Luck groaned, and started to shut his eyes when Toby tucked the comforter around him. He opened them to give his son a bleary-eyed look. "Did I tell you I talked to a brown mouse?" The question was barely out before he rolled onto his side, burrowing into the pillow. "You'd better get some sleep, son," he mumbled.

Shaking his head, Toby walked to the door and paused to look at his already snoring father. He reached up to flip off the light.

"A brown mouse," he repeated. "That's another thing we'll discuss in the morning."

Back in his dimly lit room, Toby crawled into bed. He glanced at the framed photograph on the table beside his bed. The picture was a twin to the one on his father's bureau. From it, a tawny-haired blonde with green eyes smiled back at him: his mother. She was beautiful. Not that Toby remembered her. He'd been a baby when she died—six years ago today. His gaze strayed in the direction of his father's bedroom. Sighing, he closed his eyes.

Shortly after eight the next morning, Toby woke up. He lay there for several minutes before he finally yawned and climbed out of bed to stretch. Twenty minutes later he had brushed his teeth, washed and combed his hair and found a clean pair of jeans and a yellow T-shirt to wear.

Leaving his bedroom, he paused in the hallway to look in on his father. Luck McClure was sprawled across the bed, the spare pillow clutched by an encircling arm. Toby quietly closed the door, although he doubted his father would be disturbed by any noise he made.

In the kitchen, he got the coffeemaker filled and pressed the on switch, then pushed the stepstool to the counter and climbed it to reach the juice glasses and a cereal bowl in the cupboard. Positioning the stool in front of another cupboard, he mounted it to take down a box of cornflakes. With orange juice and milk from the refrigerator, Toby sat down at the kitchen table to eat his breakfast.

By the time he'd finished, the coffee was done. He glanced from it to the pitcher of orange juice, hesitated, and walked to the refrigerator to take out a pitcher of tomato juice. Climbing back up the stepstool, he took down a tall glass and filled it three-quarters full with tomato juice. When he returned the pitcher to the refrigerator, he took out an egg, cracked it, and added it to the tomato juice. He stirred that mixture hard, then added garlic and Tabasco to it. Sniffing the end result, he wrinkled his nose in distaste.

Taking the glass, he left the kitchen and walked down the hallway to his father's room. Luck hadn't changed position in bed. Toby leaned over, taking care not to spill the contents of the glass, and shook his father's shoulder with his free hand.

"It's nine o'clock, Dad. Time to get up." His statement drew a groan of protest. "Come on, Dad."

With great reluctance, Luck rolled onto his back, flinging an arm across his eyes to shield them from the brightness of the sunlight shining in his window. Toby waited in patient silence until he sat up.

"Oh, my head," Luck mumbled, and held it in both his hands, the bedcovers falling around his waist to leave his torso bare.

Toby climbed onto the bed, balancing on his knees while he offered his father the concoction he'd made. "Drink this. It'll make you feel better."

Lowering his hands partway from his head, Luck looked at it skeptically. "What is it?"

"Don't ask," Toby advised, and reached out to pinch his father's nose closed while he tipped the glass to his lips. He managed to pour a mouthful down before his father choked and took the glass out of his hand.

"Gah," Luck said disgustedly, wiping his mouth with the back of his hand.

"Dad, it's good for you."

"What is it?" Luck coughed and frowned as he studied the glass.

"It's a hangover remedy." And Toby became the recipient of the glowering frown and a raised eyebrow.

"And when did you become an expert on hangover remedies?" Luck challenged. "How do you even know what the word means?"

Toby shrugged, his small shoulders almost coming out of pajamas that were still a little too big for him. "Like you're always saying, I watch too much TV."

Luck shook his head in quiet exasperation. "I should make you drink this. You know that, don't you?" he sighed.

"There's fresh coffee in the kitchen." Toby hopped off the bed, just in case his father intended to carry out that threat.

"Go pour me a cup. And take this with you." A smile curved slowly, forming grooves on either side of his mouth, as he handed the glass back to Toby. "I'll be there as soon as I get some clothes on."

"Want some orange juice instead, Dad?"

"Just straight orange juice. Don't put anything else in it."

"I won't." A wide grin split Toby's face before he turned and scampered out of the room.

With a wry shake of his head, Luck threw back

the covers and climbed slowly out of bed. He paused beside the bureau to glance at the photograph. *Well, Lisa, do you see what kind of boy your son has grown into?* His tired face had a pensive expression as he left the bedroom.

Chapter 2

"Your coffee is cold," Toby said accusingly when his father finally appeared in the kitchen. Dressed in worn blue jeans and a gray sweatshirt, Luck had taken the time to shower and shave. His dark brown hair gleamed almost black, combed into a careless kind of order. He smiled at the reproof from his son.

"I had to shower and shave," he defended himself, and sipped at the lukewarm brew before topping it off from the hot coffeepot. He sat down in a chair opposite from his son and rested his forearms on the table. "Okay. Tell me again what happened with Wanda Jackson last night. I want to hear your side of it before I call her up and yell. She should not have left you alone, not for any reason."

"She said something to whoever she was yakking with about charging you double for staying after midnight. So I paid her and sent her home," Toby said, repeating his previous night's explanation.

"And she went—just like that," Luck replied

with a wave of his hand to indicate how easy it seemed to have been.

"Well . . ." Toby hedged, and squirmed in his chair.

"Was that the only reason she left?"

"Like I said, I told her that you were coming home and I think she, um, was going to meet a girlfriend or something anyway."

"Was that the right thing to do?" Luck vowed to have it out with Wanda, for what it was worth. Not that he'd ever hire her again. He didn't like the idea that she spent hours on the phone, and he couldn't rely on a sitter dumb enough to assume a headstrong eight-year-old boy would always tell the truth.

"I'm too old to have a sitter, Dad," Toby protested. "I can take care of myself."

"In some ways, yeah. But when I go out, I want to know there's an adult here. A bad peanut butter sandwich isn't the worst thing that could happen to you. If there's an emergency—if you got sick or hurt or something like that—or God forbid, a fire—there has to be someone here with you to help," he explained firmly. "Do you understand?"

"Yes." Toby's voice was low but not sulky or disrespectful.

"When I go out for the evening, you will have a sitter and she will stay here until I come back. Is that understood?"

"Yes."

"Good." With the discussion concluded, Luck raised the coffee cup to his mouth.

"What about the twenty dollars?" As far as Toby was concerned, the discussion wasn't over. "It's from the money I've been saving to buy a mountain bike."

"You should have considered that before you spent it."

"Da-ad! That's what you would have had to pay her if I hadn't," Toby reasoned with childlike logic. He did a little fast mental arithmetic. "No, you would have had to pay her that and more. So I actually saved you some money."

"I'll give you the twenty dollars back on one condition," Luck replied. "You apologize. I haven't heard you say 'sorry' yet, even though you know you did wrong."

"Wanda did wronger."

Luck frowned. "There's no such word. But you're right about that, and she's not coming back. You're still responsible for telling fibs to get rid of her. I don't need the aggravation, kiddo. Or the worry. You're all I've got."

There was a long sigh before Toby nodded his agreement. "Okay. I'm sorry. Can I have my twenty dollars?"

"Later. I don't have money in these jeans and you don't need it right now anyway."

The boy gave his father a pleading look and made a whimpering noise like a puppy. Luck didn't want to smile, but he did for a second. Toby was quite a ham when he wanted to be. "Won't work, Toby," Luck said firmly. "Later means later. Have you had breakfast?"

"Cornflakes."

"Would you like some bacon and eggs?"

"Sure," Toby agreed. "I'll help."

While he set the table, Luck put the bacon in the skillet and broke eggs in a bowl to scramble them. Finished with his task, Toby walked over to the stove to watch.

"Dad?" He tipped his head back to look up at his tall father. "Do you want to explain about the brown mouse?"

"The brown mouse?" Luck frowned at him, his expression blank.

"Yeah. Last night when you came home, you said you had talked to a brown mouse," Toby explained. "Was it a hallucination?"

His kid was definitely, most definitely, growing up too fast. "Where did you pick up that word?"

"Vocabulary drill," Toby said importantly. "It means a weird dream you can have with your eyes open."

"That's about right," Luck murmured. "Maybe I was talking to a mouse. I even thought I'd seen her before . . . last Christmas. But I don't really remember. I must have had a few more drinks than I realized. Guess that's why the patrolmen drove me home. Speaking of that, I need to go back and get the car—" He stopped, realizing he had told his son more than the kid needed to know.

"It was because of Mom, wasn't it?" Toby asked quietly.

There was a moment of silence. Then Luck gave him a smiling glance. "What do you want to do today? Do you want to go skating? Hiking in the woods? We can bundle up, bring a thermos of cocoa and sandwiches. You decide. And you can make the sandwiches." He deliberately avoided his son's question, and Toby knew there was no need to repeat it.

"Let's go hiking," Toby said.

"Hiking it is," Luck agreed, and smiled as he rumpled the top of his son's brown hair.

"Can we bring a baseball and my new mitt? Play some catch?"

"In the woods? We might lose the ball if you drop it," Luck pointed out.

"I won't drop it. That mitt is magic, Dad."

"No, it isn't," Luck said.

"Is that a yes?" Toby persisted.

"Only you could turn a no into a yes, kiddo," Luck laughed. "Okay. Stick them both into the backpack and I'll make us a snack."

Two hours later the dishes were washed and the beds were made, and Luck and Toby were hiking a trail partially hidden under the last of the winter snow and ice around the banks of Lake Namekagon. A thick forest crowded the meandering shoreline, with an occasional tree painted with a blue blaze at eye level to mark out the trail.

The last snowfall had left a delicate, featherlike pattern on the rough bark of the trees that still clung to their sheltered sides. Toby patted a trunk now and then, knocking off the snow. He startled an owl out of one tree; it took off into the woods, floating silently away on wide wings.

"Dad, look!"

Luck turned just in time to see the owl strike into a clearing about a hundred yards off. "Wow. Hope he found some breakfast."

"He can't just eat cereal like me, huh?"

"No. And it's slim pickings this time of year for him. Or her."

"How do you tell a boy owl from a girl owl, Dad?"

"I don't know. But they do. Otherwise there wouldn't be any little owls."

They walked on, their booted feet crunching on the icy patches on the trail. Nice to be the first ones on it this morning, Luck thought, even if it was cold. But the early spring landscape had a beauty all its own. The deciduous trees had not leafed out and stood dramatic and stark against the bright white of the snowdrifts beneath them. Conifers, mostly pine and spruce, provided a hint of the green of summer—but that was a long way off. The ice on the lake was breaking up fast, mostly gone in places where the still water reflected the forest.

Luck stopped by a fallen tree and took out a small space blanket from his backpack. "Let's take a rest, look around." He spread the blanket out on the trunk.

"Are we going to see any animals?"

"We might. Some of them have babies in the spring. Bears usually do. We might see one, but you have to be careful around mama bears. They're very protective of their cubs."

Toby leaned back on their improvised seat, half on and half off the blanket, his mittened hands bracing him as he looked around. "I know. I wish I could see something now."

"There might be a rabbit or something like that. But you have to look carefully."

Toby studied the blue-white hollows of the remaining snowdrifts and the muddy ground still covered with last fall's dead leaves, hoping for a glimpse of some wild creature. He gave it up after a while, looking up at the puffy clouds in the blue sky with a frown of concentration.

"Are those cirrus or cumulus? Do you know the difference?" Luck said.

"No. I think those are fluffulus."

Luck laughed. "Good one."

They sat together, equally relaxed, in a long silence that was broken now and then only by a faint cracking sound from a falling branch, or the calling of a distant bird, an early migrant home. His sidelong glance studied his son's intent expression.

"You seem to be doing some pretty heavy thinking, Toby," he observed, and smiled when his son looked at him. "What's on your mind?"

"I've been trying to figure something out." Toby sat up and brushed a trace of wet snow from his mittens. The frowning concentration remained fixed in his expression. "What exactly does a mother do?"

Luck's eyes widened slightly. The question brought to mind the sad fact that their family consisted of the two of them—his son had lost his mother way too early. Toby had grandparents on Lisa's side but they lived far away and so did Luck's father.

Toby had no aunts or uncles. During the school year, the weekends were the times they had to share together. Luck often allowed his son to invite a friend over, sometimes to stay overnight or accompany them on an afternoon outing, but Toby rarely stayed overnight with any of his friends.

All the same, Toby did know what a mother did. Luck got that his son's question was theoretical—and that it was serious. He couldn't avoid answering it. "They do all kinds of things, just like fathers. They have fun with their kids, they cook if they like cooking, clean the house, take care of you when you're sick, do the laundry, stuff like that. And lots of moms work outside the house too."

"I know," Toby said quietly.

Luck sensed that the boy had wanted a different answer. He thought for a moment and then continued. "Moms remember birthdays without being reminded, make special treats for no reason, and think up games to play when you're bored." He knew it was an inadequate answer because he'd left out the motherly devotion that his son had had for the first two years of his life—and didn't have now. Yes, Luck had provided all the love and the caring that he possibly could. But he always worried that it wasn't enough, would never be enough.

When Luck finished, he glanced at his son. Toby was staring at the sky, the frown of concentration replaced with a thoughtful look. "I think we need a mother," he announced after several seconds.

"Oh?" The statement touched off a defensive reaction that made Luck's answer sound a little like a challenge. "Maybe so. But you and I do okay on our own. I thought we had a pretty good system worked out."

"We do, Dad," Toby assured him, then sighed. "I'm just tired of always having to wash dishes and make my bed."

The edges of Luck's mouth deepened in a lazy smile. "You know, women weren't put on earth to pick up after guys. Those are your responsibilities no matter what. Having a mother wouldn't mean you'd get out of doing your share of the daily chores."

Toby made no reply to that unwelcome reminder, just scrambled to his feet and brushed bits of damp bark from the backside of his thick pants. "My butt's cold."

"That's what you get for not sitting on the blanket. Let's move on." Luck got up too and shook out the space blanket, folding it up and putting it into the outer net pocket of his backpack. His son ran ahead and kicked at a half-melted heap of snow, sending it up in soggy chunks and laughing.

Kids, he thought. They take everything to heart and forget about it in a few seconds.

Toby ran back to him. "So how do you go about finding a mother?"

This kid didn't forget anything. "That's my problem." Luck had to make that point very clear. "In order for you to have a mother, I would have to get married again."

"Do you think you'd *like* to get married again?"

"I dunno. Don't you think your questions are getting a little bit personal?" *And a little bit awkward to handle,* Luck thought as he walked on, a tiny crease running across his forehead.

"I'm your son. If you can't talk to me about it, who can you talk to?" Toby reasoned.

"You're much too old for your age." His blue eyes glinted with dry humor when he met the earnest gaze of his son.

"If you got married again, you could have more children," Toby pointed out. "Have you thought about that?"

"Yes, and I don't know if I could handle another one of you," Luck teased.

With a sigh of exasperation, Toby protested, "Dad, will you please be serious? I am trying to discuss this intelligently with you. You wouldn't necessarily have another boy. You could have a little girl."

"Is that what this is about? Do you want brothers and sisters?" There was something at the bottom of all this interest in a mother. Sooner or later, Luck felt he would uncover the reason.

"Da-ad!" Toby declared with irritation. "You never

answer my questions. You just ask me another. How am I ever going to learn anything?"

"All right." Luck crossed his arms in front of him and put on a serious expression, but lost it when Toby laughed at him. "Okay, kid. Show me no mercy. What do you want to know?"

"If you met the right lady, would you get married again?"

"Yes, it's possible," he conceded with a slow nod.

With a satisfied smile, Toby spun around, almost knocking his father down. "I'll help you look."

Luck took a deep breath, started to say something, then decided it was wiser to let the subject drop.

The Rowlands' cottage was built of logs, complete with a front porch that overlooked the lake across the road. Eve's dad had exchanged the porch screens for heat-retaining glass panels and it was almost warm enough to enjoy a cup of coffee or cocoa out there, if you weren't quite ready to go out in the wild woods yet. The rustic cottage was tucked in a forest clearing, a dense stand of pines forming a semicircle around it.

Over the weekend, Eve and her parents had moved in their sports gear and fishing equipment, going back and forth between their house in Cable and here, whenever they'd filled the car with the things they planned to take. There wasn't any way to do it in one trip with one car. Opening up their vacation home again and reawakening happy memories of previous summers was a lot more fun than they'd expected it to be.

Standing on the porch, wearing a thick sweater and a sleeveless down vest, Eve gazed at the waters of Namekagon Lake and the trees around it. Here in the north woods everything grew tall—including the tales of Paul Bunyan and his blue ox, Babe, her favorite stories as a child. According to them, Paul and Babe had stomped around a little in Namekagon, just one of the many lakes in Wisconsin.

Eve could remember first hearing about the mighty duo when she was six. The legendary figure of Paul Bunyan had been as real to her as the Easter Bunny and Santa Claus, even if he didn't pass out presents.

She lifted her head to the clear blue sky and breathed in the clean pine-scented air. With a sigh of contentment, Eve turned and walked into the cottage. It was small, just two bedrooms, the kitchen separated from the living room by a table nook. She let the outer door close behind her and shut the inner one, before she got the standard lecture about the fuel bills.

Her father had the fishing tackle he'd gotten for Christmas spread over the table and was working on one of his reels. He was planning to take up ice fishing come winter, and he and her mother had friendly arguments about whether he really needed more gear. Conceding the point that a long string wound around a stick would be just as good for dropping into a hole in the ice, her dad hadn't gotten around to buying his own little shack on wheels, but was going to share his buddy's. Her mother didn't really object. Like a lot of retired couples, they spent as much time apart as they did together. Mom insisted that after all these years of wedded bliss, she needed the time off.

Another check mark in the why-bother-with-marriage column, Eve thought. Her mother was in the kitchen, fixing hot Swedish-style potato salad with caraway seeds and finely chopped onion and dill.

"Is it all right if I use the car?" Eve asked. "I want to go to the store down the road. I'm out of shampoo and I need sunblock."

"Good idea. Get the moisturizing stuff for skiers." Her mother specified the brand she used to combat winter dryness and keep wrinkles at bay. Eve made a mental note of it as her father reached in his pants pocket and tossed her the car keys.

"Was there anything you needed?" Eve reached to pick up her canvas purse where she'd left it on a sofa cushion.

"Maybe some milk," her mother answered, "but other than that, I can't think of anything."

"Okay. I'll be back later," she called over her shoulder as she pushed open the door to the porch.

Sliding into the driver's seat, Eve felt as bright and sunny as the spring afternoon, although it still wasn't all that warm. She had dressed to match her mood that day. Her sweater was a cheerful canary yellow, trimmed with white. A white fake-fur headband covered her ears and kept her brown hair away from her face, framing its oval shape. She tossed the down vest on the seat beside her, glad she'd decided to do without a heavy coat. The car heated up quickly and she was actually a little too warm.

She flipped down the mirror and looked at her rosy cheeks. Nice. With one swift move, she found the lip gloss in the pocket of her purse and dabbed it on. Even nicer.

It was a short drive to the combination grocery and general store that served the resort community all seasons of the year. The Rowland family shopped there every summer, so Eve was a familiar face to the owners. She chatted with them a few minutes as she paid for her purchases.

When she started to leave, she heard a man's voice ask to speak to the owner. It sounded vaguely familiar, but when she turned to see if it was anyone she knew, the man was hidden from her view by an aisle. Since whoever it was had business with the owner, and since it was possible she didn't even know him, Eve continued out of the store, dismissing the incident from her mind.

The car was in the store's parking area, with the hood facing the wall. She walked toward it, but it was only when she got closer that she began to realize something was wrong. Her steps slowed and her eyes widened in disbelief at the sight of the shattered windshield and the three-inch-diameter hole in the glass.

Stunned, Eve glanced in the side window and saw the baseball lying on the front seat. Reacting mechanically, she opened the door and reached to pick up the ball amid the small, chunky bits of safety glass on the car seat.

"That's my ball." A young boy's voice claimed ownership of the object in her hand.

She turned to look at him. A baseball cap was perched atop a mass of dark brown hair, while a pair of unblinking innocent blue eyes stared back at her. Eve guessed the boy to be about eight, no older than nine. She had the feeling that she had seen him somewhere before, possibly at the local school.

"Did you do this?" She gestured toward the broken windshield, using the same hand that held the baseball.

"Not exactly. You see, my dad just bought me

this new baseball glove." He held up the oversized leather mitt on his left hand. "We were trying it out to see how it worked. I asked Dad to throw me a hard one so I could tell whether there was enough padding to keep my hand from stinging. Only when he did, it was too high and the ball hit the tip of my glove and bounced off, then smashed your windshield. It must have hit it just right," he declared with a rueful grimace. "So it was really my dad who threw the ball. I just didn't catch it."

"A parking lot isn't the place to play catch." She wasn't angry or even upset, but at the moment, that was the only thing Eve could think of to say. It was a helpless kind of protest, since there was no way to change what had happened.

"We know that now," the boy agreed.

He was charming. And polite. What a great kid, she thought. "Where's your father?"

"He went into the store to see if they knew who the car belonged to," he explained. "He told me to stay here in case you came back while he was gone."

The comment jogged her memory of the man who had been in the store asking to speak to the owner. She started to turn when she heard the same voice ask, "Is this your car?"

"It's my dad's." Eve completed the turn to face the boy's father.

Uh-oh. A sense of shock froze her into immobility. It was the stranger she'd met outside the tavern last night. The rumpled darkness of his hair grew in thick waves, a few strands straying onto his forehead. He raised his left hand to push it back and the first thing she thought was *no wedding ring*. But lots of men didn't wear them.

She gazed into his magnetic blue eyes, pleased to realize that he was looking at her with warm interest. The sunlight brought out the rough vitality in his handsome features.

Eve waited, unconsciously holding her breath, for recognition to show in his eyes as she mentally braced herself to watch that mouth form the words "brown mouse." But it didn't happen. He didn't know who she was. Evidently the combination of liquor and the night's shadows had made her image hazy in his mind. Of course, she wasn't bundled up to her ears in a dowdy coat and hat, either. His look at her was definitely appreciative.

Given that he was this adorable little boy's dad, Eve decided to give him the benefit of the doubt. She certainly wasn't going to mention what had happened last night in front of his kid.

He glanced at the baseball in her hand. "We're really sorry. I hope Toby explained what happened." His expression was pleasant, yet serious.

"Yes, he did." She was conscious of how loudly her heart was pounding. "At least he said you threw the ball and he missed it."

"I'm afraid that's what happened," he admitted with a faintly rueful lift of his mouth. "Of course I'll pay the cost of having the windshield replaced—" He patted his pockets. "Oh, no. I brought my wallet but not my checkbook."

"We were walking in the woods. Why would you need a checkbook?" Toby asked.

"Go ahead. Make me feel stupid, son." He grinned down at the boy and held the smile when he looked at Eve again. "If you'd just jot down your name and your address, I'll send a check right away—" He patted his pockets again. "Shoot. I don't have a pen either."

"My name's Eve Rowland. I have a pen. That's because I'm a teacher—I always have a pen." *You're babbling*, she told herself. But between the sack of groceries in one arm and the ball in the other hand, she wasn't able to look for it in her purse. "Wait a minute. I don't know how much a replacement windshield will cost."

"Whatever the amount, just let me know. My name is Luck McClure, and this is my son, Toby." He laid a hand on the boy's shoulder with a trace of parental pride. "Our house is a few miles from here, on the lake."

Odd name, Eve thought. But maybe she hadn't heard him right. "Did you say Luke McClure?"

"No." He smiled, as if it were a common mistake. "It's Luck—as in good luck. It's my real name, but it does derive from Luke or Lucius. I got stuck with it. It's one of those family names that somehow manages to get passed along to future generations."

"I see," she murmured, and glanced at Toby, who had obviously not been named after his father. She wondered if there was another little Luck somewhere at home. At least now she understood why the boy had seemed familiar at first. There was a definite resemblance between him and his father.

"With that windshield smashed, you aren't going to be able to see to drive home," Luck said. "I would appreciate it if you would let us give you a ride."

Under the circumstances, Eve didn't know any other way that she could get back to the cottage if she didn't accept his offer. She nodded. "Yes, thank you."

"Um, can I have my baseball back?" the boy spoke up.

"May I," his father said automatically.

"Of course." She handed it to Toby.

"We're parked over here." Luck McClure reclaimed her attention, directing her toward a late-model Jaguar. "Did you say the car was your father's? He lets you drive it?"

"Yes." She was somewhat taken aback by his question. "I'm, uh, not a teenager."

"Oh. Sorry. You look young. Must be that white fur headband," he said. Yeah, right, he said to himself. Must be the rosy cheeks and glowing eyes and great figure and shiny hair. Ignore those things. Just because your son's baseball hit her windshield doesn't mean you get to hit on her.

Eve was a little annoyed. Did the headband look silly? At least it didn't make her look fat. No headband in the world could do that, and anyway, she wasn't fat.

"My dad's out at the cottage."

"Is that where you'd like me to drive you?" He walked around to open the passenger door for her while his son climbed in the back seat. "Put on your seat belt, Toby. And sit back. No bouncing around."

"Yes, thanks. My parents and I decided to open up early this year. I have a lot of free time and they're retired." Eve waited until he was behind the wheel to give him directions.

"That isn't far from our house," he commented, and Eve wished it was in the opposite direction. What if he recognized her? He could, any minute now, which would make things uncomfortable, if not embarrassing. "Okay. I'll make arrangements with him about paying for the windshield."

Briefly Eve wondered if he thought she couldn't take care of it. She knew perfectly well that she didn't look like a teenager, not that twenty-six was exactly ancient. But around here, where couples often married right after high school, she sometimes felt that way. So it wasn't the worst thing if he thought she looked young. Lately she hadn't exactly been feeling radiantly attractive either and Luck McClure was definitely the kind of man she'd like to attract.

Oh, stop it, Eve, she told herself. He isn't flirting with you. More than likely he'd just said that about her looking young simply because he wanted to deal directly with the owner of the car. And there was the distinct possibility that he was married, even if he didn't wear a wedding ring. Which suited her fine. The less she saw of him, the less chance there would be that he'd remember her.

The rounded bill of a baseball cap entered her side vision as the boy leaned over the seat, holding his pulled-out shoulder belt in one hand. "I really thought you'd be mad when you saw what we did to your car. How come you weren't?"

His father looked in the rearview mirror with a frown. "Toby, sit back. You know how I feel about you breathing down my neck, so don't do it to her. It isn't safe and it's annoying."

"Da-ad!"

"Listen up. You're the kid and I'm the dad. Sit down."

Eve smiled to herself. As someone who taught children, she respected a parent who could lay down the law and be kind at the same time. So many well-meaning adults just seemed to let their kids more or less raise themselves but Luck McClure was obviously on the job.

Toby thumped back against his seat and let the belt mechanism automatically take up the slack in it. Eve turned around to look at him and smiled.

"Hey, things like that happen. But I couldn't believe what I saw at first."

"I couldn't, either," Luck admitted with a low chuckle. "I was trying to impress my son with my fast ball. Usually I can't hit the broad side of a barn with it, but your windshield? Bingo." He seemed to want to share his self-deprecating amusement with her and he winked as he smiled.

Nice wink. Nice smile. With deep, delicious dimples. She smiled back.

With less wariness, Eve let herself forget their first meeting outside the tavern. There was an easy charm about Luck McClure that she found attractive, in addition to his looks. It had a quality of bold friendliness to it.

If she really thought about it, she would have to say that he was flirting. She could even flirt back, given that they were chaperoned by an inquisitive eight-year-old. Nothing, absolutely nothing, was going to happen.

But part of her wished this were their first meeting, because she knew sooner or later he would recognize his "brown mouse." And even though he was being friendly right now, that was probably because he wanted to stay on her good side. And even if he wasn't married, a good-looking, sexy guy like Luck McClure would never be seriously interested in a personality like hers. Shy. Prone to skittering away. A little nervous. Without knowing her at all, he had described her well last night. She had to give him credit for excellent intuition.

His gaze slid from the road long enough to meet her eyes. There was warm male interest in the look that ran over her face, a look that probably had its basis in curiosity just like Eve's. She was briefly excited by it until she reminded herself that she had no reason to let her imagination run away with her. Eve glanced at the road a second before he did.

"Our place is just ahead on the left," she said.

As Luck slowed the car to make the turn into the short driveway, his son announced, "We go by here all the time. I didn't think anybody lived in that house. When did you move in?"

"We just finished up today," she replied, then wondered if that would jog Luck's memory of their accidental meeting at the tavern. A quick glance didn't find any reaction. "We spend the summers here too. This year we winterized the place so we can come here during the holidays to snowmobile or ice fish and do some cross-country skiing."

"Do you like to ski?" Toby's questions continued even after the car stopped.

"With Mount Telemark practically in our backyard, it would be a shame if I didn't." A light smile touched her mouth as she shifted the sack of groceries to open the door. "And I really enjoy it."

"Me, too. Dad took me skiing last Christmas." The boy scrambled out of the back seat to join his father. "Next year I'll be good enough to ski with him." He looked up at Luck for confirmation. "Won't I, Dad? I want to do the cross-country ski event this year."

"Oh, the Barnebirkie. You'll like it. Every kid gets a medal." The world-famous Birkebeiner cross-country race started in Cable. Eve had done it in all divisions, including the children's Barnebirkie event, and she had fond memories of the experience.

"Sure, why not?" Luck said. "And you'll definitely be off the bunny slope by the end of next winter."

He gave his son an affectionate smile, and waited until Eve had walked around the front of the car before starting toward the log cottage.

With this tall, good-looking man beside her, she felt oddly self-conscious—a sensation that had nothing to do with their previous encounter. It was more an awareness of physical attraction than anything else. She didn't notice that Toby wasn't with them until the car door slammed again and the boy came running after them. She and Luck McClure paused to see what had delayed him.

"You left the keys in the ignition again, Dad," the boy declared almost sternly, and handed the car keys to his father. "That's how cars get stolen."

"You're right. Can't argue." Luck grinned and slipped the keys into his pocket. When they started toward the porch again, Toby tagged along.

Her parents recovered quickly from their initial surprise at the strange man and boy accompanying Eve into the house. She introduced them, then Luck took over the explanation of the shattered windshield. Exhibiting his typical understanding, her father was not angered by the accident and seemed more amused than anything.

While they discussed particulars, Eve went into the kitchen to put away the milk and other things. She remained in the alcove, satisfied to just observe the warm way Luck related to her parents. It was a knack few people had. It came naturally to him, part of his relaxed, easygoing style.

Considering how friendly he was, Eve didn't doubt that he could handle authority equally well. There was something about Luck McClure that commanded respect. It was an understated quality, but that didn't lessen its strength.

Her gaze strayed to the boy standing beside

Luck. He was listening attentively to all that was being said, with an oddly grown-up air for a boy of his age. His only motion was tossing the ball into his glove and retrieving it to toss it methodically again.

Eve was running out of reasons to dawdle in the kitchen. Since she didn't want to take part in the conversation between her parents and Luck McClure, she took her skier's sunblock and shampoo and slipped away to her bedroom. She paused in front of the vanity mirror above her dresser and studied her reflection.

She hadn't yet taken off the white fur headband that sleeked her brown hair away from her face, emphasizing features that were a little less serene than usual at the moment. Eve touched her mouth with her fingertips, brushing the curves that looked softer and fuller. There was an added glow of suppressed excitement in the luminous brown of her eyes. The cause of it, of course, was Luck McClure—and that oh-so-interesting question of when he would recognize her.

No wonder they call these things vanity mirrors, Eve thought, and turned away before she became too wrapped up in her appearance.

But she made a silent resolution not to wear brown again. From now on, she'd buy only beautiful colors that looked good on her. And anything shabby or dowdy was going to be set aside. She didn't have to wear things to pieces before she bought new, either. Drab clothing did nothing to improve her looks.

Not that it would really matter to Luck. On further thought, now that she wasn't in his car and sitting so distractingly close to him, Eve decided that he had to be married. Men like him just were.

She dreaded the time when she would meet his wife, but in this small resort community it would be impossible for their paths not to cross sometime during the course of the year. It would be foolish to try to avoid it. But what could she say to a woman whose husband had tried to pick her up?

Thinking about what kind of marriage he had, she cast her mind back to their brief exchange on the sidewalk in front of the tavern. Hadn't he had said he was lonely or that it was lonely at home or something like that? Obviously he'd wanted to talk to someone. He and his wife must have reached the stage of non-communication or were having some other kind of relationship trouble, Eve concluded.

Or maybe he was just the type that had to make a conquest of every woman he saw. No—she shook that thought away. Indulging in an idle flirtation would come naturally to him, but Luck McClure wasn't the type to let it go beyond banter. There was too much depth to him for that.

What did it matter? If he had marital problems, Luck was the type who would solve them with dispatch and fairness, judging by the way he had talked to his son in the car.

Eve yanked off the white headband, running her fingers through her windblown hair and wishing she could straighten out her tangled thoughts just as easily. It was ridiculous to waste her time thinking about a married man, no matter how interesting and compelling he might be.

The closing of the outer door of the porch and the cessation of voices from the front room got Eve's attention. She listened and heard the sound of car doors outside. Her tall stranger—a stranger no more, but something less than a friend—was

leaving with his son. She hadn't said goodbye but
that was just as well.

Now she could come out of hiding—the realiza-
tion stopped her short of the door. She had been
hiding. She thought a little harder about why she
had, and wondered when and how it had become
so automatic to do so that she hadn't given a
thought to saying good-bye to him, only obsessed
over her appearance in secret. Was she hiding because he had looked at her with very masculine interest? One thing for sure, she hadn't wanted him
to remember that she was a plain brown mouse.
But what had she done? Scurried off into a hidey-
hole.

Never again.

Eve straightened up and left to return to the
front room. The only occupant was her mother.
Eve glanced around, noticing the Jaguar was gone
from the driveway.

"Where's Dad?"

"Mr. McClure drove him back to the car. They
called a garage. A man's coming over to tow our
car and see about replacing the broken windshield,"
her mother explained. "He should be back soon."

An hour later her father returned, but it was the
mechanic who brought him back—not Luck
McClure.

Chapter 3

The Rowlands were without transportation for two days. On the morning of the third day, the garage owner delivered the car, complete with a new windshield. The day had started out with gray and threatening skies. By the time the car was returned it began drizzling. And by noon it was raining steadily, a freezing rain that turned to sleet, drilling buckshot-size holes into the very last of the snow and mixing it with the mud underneath. Reluctant to go out in that, Eve was stuck indoors.

Her parents decided to restock their pantry that afternoon, but shopping for groceries just didn't sound exciting to Eve, who they invited to come with them. Since they planned to visit some of their friends while they were out, she declined.

On a miserable day like this, with most of her students' lessons postponed or rescheduled for after spring break, she would usually curl up with a book, but on this occasion she was too restless to read. Since she had the entire afternoon on her hands, she decided to do some baking and went into the kitchen to stir up a batch of chocolate chip cookies, her father's favorite.

Soon the delicious smell of cookies baking in the oven filled the small cottage and chased away the gloom of the cold gray day. Cookies from two sheet trays were cooling on the kitchen counter, on racks set atop an opened newspaper. Eve glanced through the glass door of the oven at the third sheet. Its cookies were just beginning to brown, a mere minute away from being done.

The thud of footsteps on the wooden porch floor made her straighten up from the oven. An instant after they stopped, there was a knock on the door. She cast a glance at the batch, noted that the edges of the cookies were rising slightly and the chocolate chips turning into glorious goo, then went to answer the door. A splash of flour had left a white streak on the burgundy velour of her top. She brushed at it but only succeeded in spreading the white patch across her stomach. Eve was still brushing at it when she opened the door.

She looked up at wide shoulders encased in the slick material of a dark blue windbreaker that glistened with rain. The man outside turned to her at the sound of the opening door and Eve's gaze met a pair of arresting blue eyes.

A tiny electric shock quivered through her nerve ends at the sight of Luck McClure on the other side of the glass-paneled outer door. Dampness gave a black sheen to his dark brown hair. Toby was beside him, his face almost lost under the hooded sweatshirt pulled over his head and tucked under his jacket hood. Both hoods were tied under his chin, and the little boy tugged at the cords, making a dramatic help-me-I'm-choking noise for her benefit. Beyond the shelter of the porch roof, rain and sleet fell in an obscuring gray curtain.

"Hello, Luck," Eve recovered her voice to greet him calmly.

A casual smile brightened his face, wet with rain that he swiped away with an equally wet sleeve. His son at least was protected from the raw weather, Eve thought with an inward smile. As a father, Luck probably took better care of his son than he did of himself. "I stopped to—"

His explanation was interrupted by the oven timer dinging madly. Eve had to get the cookies out of the oven quickly and onto the racks before they burned just from the heat of the pan they were on. "Oh—I have something in the oven." She quickly unlatched the screen door. "Come in, come in." She ran back to the kitchen.

Behind her she heard the door springs groan a little from the cold, and the noise of incoming footsteps. "Don't forget to wipe your feet, Dad," Toby murmured.

Opening the oven door, Eve grabbed a pot holder and lifted the metal cookie sheet up and out. She slid a thin-bladed spatula under each cookie and removed it deftly to the waiting racks, resting this batch on top of the others. Another tray of spooned-out cookie dough was sitting on the counter, ready to be put in to bake. She slipped it on the rack with her free hand, hanging onto the spatula simply because she forgot to put it down, and closed the oven door. The McClures were right in back of her.

"That takes coordination," Luck smiled at her.

"Years of piano playing." She looked at what she held in her hand. "Not with a spatula, of course."

She set the utensil down on the counter. "You know what I mean. My hands can do different things at the same time." Eve blushed. That had sounded sort of suggestive, which she hadn't intended at all.

But Luck didn't seem to notice anything but the smell of cookies in the air, and Toby, who'd slipped off his wet jacket, was sniffing the air like a hungry puppy.

"Are those all for us?" he asked eagerly.

"You can have as many as"—she looked at Luck, who gave her an amiable wink—"your dad gives you."

"What about you?" Toby asked politely, as if he thought she might starve if he ate as many as his little boy's appetite could handle.

"Oh, my parents are gone this afternoon," she said, picking at a cooled one that had broken. "I can have as many as I like."

"You're lucky," the boy said, with no trace of envy. He selected the largest and immediately bit into it.

"I had my eye on that one, you know," his father said. Unrepentant and unwilling to give it up, Toby munched his way into the middle, a straggly melted-chocolate mustache forming on his upper lip.

"That's one almost as big." Eve pointed.

"You sure?" he teased, ruffling his son's messy hair.

"Yeah. So why are you two here? Don't tell me you smelled these cookies miles away."

"No. I told your father he could use my car if he had any errands to run while his was in the shop," he explained. "I stopped to see if he needed it."

"The garage delivered our car this morning."

Eve half turned to answer him and felt the slow inspection of his look.

Her cheeks were flushed from the heat of the oven. The sweep of his glance left behind an odd sensation that heightened her already high color. It was a look she supposed he would give to any semiattractive woman—a man's assessment of her looks—but that didn't alter its effect on her.

Toby appeared at her elbow, offering her a distraction. He peered over the top of the counter to see what she was doing.

"Are you making more?" he said curiously.

"Yup." She smiled briefly at him and moved the cooled cookies off the racks and onto a flat platter.

He breathed in deeply, his blue eyes rounded as if drinking in the sight. "They smell good."

"Would you like another one?" Eve offered. As an afterthought, she glanced at Luck, who had moved closer. "Is it all right if he has a second cookie?"

"Sure." Permission was granted with a faint nod of his head. Luck was unzipping his wet windbreaker and hanging it where it could drip without making puddles on the floor, above the drainage rack for the floor mop. He did the same with his son's jacket.

Toby reached for a cookie that she had just set on the rack. "Careful," she warned, but it came too late. Toby was already jerking his hand away.

"They're hot!" he said, frustration in his surprised look.

"Well, yeah. They just came out of the oven. Try one from the platter." She pointed with the spatula. "They're cool but the chocolate chips are still a little gooey."

The little boy took one of the cookies she'd indicated and bit into it. As he chewed it, he studied the cookie. "They taste as good as they smell," he declared. "Dad, why is that?"

"I don't know. But fresh chocolate chip cookies are irresistible."

Toby munched his second treat a little longer than the first. "Amazing," he said in a muffled voice.

"You'll have to help your mother make some for you." Eve flashed him a smile at the compliment.

"I don't have a mother anymore," Toby replied absently, and took another bite of the cookie.

His statement sent invisible shock waves through her. She darted a troubled glance at Luck, alarmed at how accurate her previous guess had been. Had the problems at home ended in divorce? Except for a brief flicker in his gaze, Luck didn't seem bothered by the topic his son had introduced.

"My wife died when Toby was small," he explained, and regarded his son with a smile. "Toby and I have been baching it for several years now, but I'm afraid our domestic talents don't stretch to baking cookies."

"I see," she murmured because she didn't know what else to say. She wondered why she had been so quick to assume that he was married, and therefore out of circulation. Maybe because she'd felt safer that way, somehow immune to his attractiveness. The discovery that he was a widower caught her off guard, leaving her shaken.

"May I have another cookie?" Toby asked after he'd licked the melted chocolate of a chip from his finger.

She looked to Luck for his okay, which he gave with a nod. "Of course." She'd made a large batch, so there was plenty to spare. Homemade cookies were obviously a special treat for the boy.

As he took his third, Toby glanced at his father. "Why don't you try one, Dad? You don't know what you're missing."

"Go ahead." Eve moved aside as she laid the last cookie down. While Luck took her up on the offer and helped himself, Eve carried the empty sheet to the adjoining counter and began spooning dough onto it from the mixing bowl. The ever-curious Toby followed her.

"What's that?"

"This is the cookie batter. When you bake it in the oven, it turns into a cookie." It was becoming obvious to her that this was all new to him. If he'd seen it before, it had been too long ago for him to remember clearly.

"How do you make it?" He looked up at her with a thoughtful frown.

"There's a recipe on the back of the chocolate chip package." The teaching habit was too firmly ingrained for Eve to overlook the chance to impart knowledge when a kid looked interested. Especially this kid. She paused in her task to pick up the empty chip package and show it to him. "It's right there. It tells you all the ingredients and how to do it."

With the cookie in one hand and the package with its recipe in the other, Toby wandered to the opposite side of the kitchen and studied the fine print with frowning concentration. The kitchen was a small alcove off the front room. When Luck moved to lean against the counter near Eve, she began to realize how limited the space was.

"There's something very comfortable about a

kitchen filled with the smell of fresh baking. It really feels like a home then," Luck remarked.

"Yes, it does," Eve agreed. She knew right then that the casual intimacy between them was unsettling her.

"Have you eaten one of your cookies? They *are* good," Luck said, confirming his son's opinion.

"Only a nibble," she admitted, and turned to tell him there was coffee in the pot if he wanted a cup. But when she opened her mouth to speak, he slipped the rounded edge of a warm cookie inside.

"You need more," he said coaxingly.

If you only knew.

"A cook should sample her wares," he insisted. There was an instant of surprised delay as her eyes met the glinting humor of his. Then her teeth instinctively sank into the sweet morsel to take a bite. Luck held onto the cookie until she did, then surrendered it to the hand that reached for it.

With food in her mouth, good manners dictated that she not speak until it was chewed and swallowed. It wasn't easy under his lazy but watchful gaze, especially when he took due note of the tongue that darted out to lick the melted chocolate from her lips. Her heart began thumping against her ribs like a locomotive climbing a steep incline.

"I'll finish it later with some coffee." Eve set the half-eaten cookie on the counter, unwilling to go through the unnerving experience of Luck watching her eat again. She picked up the spoon and concentrated on replenishing the cookie sheet with dollops of dough.

"And I thought all along that Eve tempted Adam with an apple," Luck drawled softly. "When did you discover a cookie worked better?"

Again her gaze raced to him, taken aback by the implication of his words. No matter how she tried, Eve couldn't react casually to this sexual banter. He was much more adept at the game than she was.

"What does 'tempted' mean?" Toby asked.

Luck turned to look at his son, not upset by the question or by the fact that Toby had been listening. "It's like putting a worm on a hook. The fish can't resist taking a nibble."

"Oh." With his curiosity satisfied, Toby's attention moved on to other things. He set the empty chocolate chip package on the counter where Eve had left it before. "This doesn't look hard to do, Dad. Do you think we could make some cookies sometime?"

"Sure. First rainy day that comes along," he promised, and sent a twinkling look at Eve. "If we have trouble, we can give Eve a call."

"Yeah," Toby said with a wide grin.

Unexpectedly, just when Eve had decided Luck was going to become a fixture in the kitchen for what was left of the afternoon, he straightened from the counter. "Toby and I have taken advantage of your hospitality long enough. We'd better be leaving."

The timer went off. The other sheet of cookies was ready to come out of the oven. Its intrusive sound allowed her to turn away and hide the sudden rush of keen disappointment that he was leaving. It also prodded her to remember the reason for his visit.

"Thanks for stopping by," Eve replied, taking the cookie sheet out.

"No problem," Luck said, and paused in her path to the counter. She was compelled to look into the deep indigo color of his eyes. A half smile slanted his mouth, "I hope you've forgiven me for what happened the other time we met."

She went pale. "Then you do remember. But it wasn't at Christmas—"

Although the smile remained, there was puzzlement in his eyes. "Huh? I was talking about the broken windshield. Was there something else I was supposed to remember?"

She felt the intensity of his gaze probe for an answer, one that she had very nearly given away. "No, of course not." She forced a nervous smile onto her face and stepped around him to the counter, her pulse racing.

For an uneasy moment, Eve thought he was going to question her answer, but he only shrugged and went around the other way to retrieve his windbreaker and his son's jacket. Though still damp, the jackets were no longer dripping.

"Tell your parents I said hello, okay?" He helped his protesting son back into his jacket and slipped his arms into his own, shivering a little when the clammy material touched his skin.

"I will," she promised, and turned when the pair had nearly reached the door. "Stay warm, guys. April in Wisconsin is no day at the beach."

"Good-bye, Eve." Toby waved.

"Bye, honey." She avoided looking at Luck. He was a honey but he wasn't her honey and he never would be. An important distinction.

"Take care," was all he said. Then the door opened and closed behind them.

The cottage seemed terribly quiet and empty after they'd gone. The rain outside the windows seemed to close in, its wet traces on the windows giving the rooms a lonely feeling. Eve poured a cup of coffee and sat at the table to finish the cookie Luck had given her. It had lost some of its flavor.

Time for music. She went over to the sound system and looked through her CDs, selecting a Vivaldi concerto. She pushed the button and the CD drawer slid out, accepting the silver disc that she dropped into it and sliding back. A few seconds later, the sprightly opening melody filled the room. Eve cranked up the volume and even danced around the room a little. Nothing like Vivaldi to chase away rainy-day blues.

A few days later, Eve volunteered to make the short trip to the store to buy bread, milk, and the other essential items that always needed replenishing so her parents could go to the mall fifty miles away, sharing an enormous vintage Cadillac with the old friends who owned it. They planned to make a day of it, doing recreational shopping first and then having dinner at a restaurant together. The other couple had been married for what seemed like forever, just like her mom and dad. Eve almost envied them their contentment.

With spring officially here—okay, just around the corner—it seemed like every living thing in the world had a mate. Sometimes being single felt just plain weird. Of course, it wasn't as if she was alone. Freelance music teaching and a full schedule of private instruction meant she always had her students, although none of them had wanted to participate in an Easter recital this year. She had a few friends she didn't see often enough. And her parents, of course.

When it came to holidays, they preferred a quiet

celebration. The last Christmas had been quieter than most, one in which nothing was stirring, not even a mouse, Eve thought ruefully. And New Year's—she had played board games with them. Monopoly just didn't beat a hot kiss from a special someone, even if she had controlled a block of apartments on Park Place and pocketed most of the pretend money by the time the church bell rang at midnight. Valentine's Day . . . she exchanged nice cards with her parents. The memory depressed her. And the weather wasn't helping. More rain. She frowned. They'd had an interlude of sunshine since Luck and Toby had visited, but today's cold downpour hadn't let up once it started. The usually scenic countryside was mostly mud.

Eve drove carefully, wishing it would snow and cover everything up again, listening to a song on the radio and humming along absently. But when she arrived at the store, she immediately noticed the sleek Jaguar sedan parked in front of it. She wasn't aware of the glow of anticipation that came to her eyes.

Luck and Toby were on their way out of the store with an armful of groceries when she walked in. "Hello." Her bright greeting was a shade breathless.

The wide smile that Luck gave her quickened her pulse. "Hey. You're safe today. Toby left his baseball and glove at the house," he said.

"I should think so, in weather like this." Eve laughed, because she hadn't given the broken windshield incident another thought.

"Look what we bought." Toby reached into the smaller sack he carried and pulled out a package of chocolate chips. "Dad doesn't have time today but we're going to make some the next time it rains. I hope it rains a lot."

"I think you just might be in luck. This has to be the soggiest spring on record. I hope they turn out," she smiled.

"So do I," Luck murmured dryly, and touched the boy's shoulder. "Let's go, Toby. See you around, Eve," he nodded, using that indefinite phrase that committed nothing.

"Bye, Eve."

The smile faded from her expression as she watched them go. Turning away from the door, she went to do her shopping.

Returning to the car with plastic bags full of necessities, she caught a glimpse of her reflection in the side. Her hair was straggly and her baggy sweats did absolutely nothing for her. The car's curved surface made her look enormous, even though she wasn't.

High time she bought a few new things, she thought suddenly. No wonder Luck's greeting had been so uninterested. And maybe she should do something she'd never done before: get highlights in her mouse-brown hair.

She'd have to call her friend Michelle and find out if there was a decent hairdresser within driving distance of Cable. And she could browse through the collection of new catalogs her mother had dragged to the cabin in a cardboard box. Mom read them for fun and she had to be on every mailing list in the universe. Eve had glanced at the ones with clothes, not all that interested at the time. But she was now.

She clicked open the door with the tag on her key and put the bags in the back seat, realizing that what she was feeling was no more and no less than spring fever.

Once everything had been put away in the cottage kitchen and she was safely settled in her favorite chair, Eve took a deep breath and called Michelle's cell number. Five rings later and her girlfriend picked up.

"Hey, Michelle. It's Eve. How are you? Where are you?"

Michelle giggled and Eve could just hear a deeper voice in the background, along with the noise of a bar.

"Florida. It's spring break, dummy. Are you still stuck in Wisconsin with the cheeseheads? You should fly down. I'm having a great time—stop that, you moron!" Eve heard a shriek of glee and sighed inwardly. Michelle loved to party, and the guys she partied with weren't anything to write home about. "He won't let me get off his lap. So whatcha doing?" Michelle asked, after more giggling.

Sitting here watching it rain and feeling fat, Eve wanted to say but didn't. She decided to keep the call as short as possible. "Um, I was wondering if you could give me the name of that hairdresser where you get your highlights done?"

"Eve, I'm wearing a bikini. I don't even know where my address book is."

Eve rolled her eyes. "I asked for her name. I can handle getting the phone number. But I thought your hairdresser was on your speed dial, oh blond one."

Michelle giggled. "Nah. And I can't access the memory functions on this phone—I think I got sand in it or something."

"Just tell me her name and where she lives," Eve said tightly. "That's all I need."

"Whoops!" More laughter, followed by the sound of a cell phone skidding across the floor. Someone picked it up and a deep male voice spoke. "Are you Michelle's girlfriend? Come on over."

"I can't. I'm in Wisconsin," Eve said patiently. "But thanks for the invitation."

"No problemo. Hey, Michelle, here's your phone back."

"Hello-oo," her girlfriend trilled. "The hairdresser's name is Lurleen Caldwell. She lives in—" Michelle named a town about thirty miles away from Cable. "She's really good, Evie. Just tell her what you want."

I want to dazzle Luck McClure, Eve thought unhappily. I want his eyes to light up when he sees me. Come to think of it, he had given her a nice big grin. But his parting words had been on the cool side. She didn't really listen to what Michelle was saying, noticing the conversation was over when all she heard was the noise of the bar again. Eve snapped out of it. "Bye, Michelle. Have fun. Thanks. See you when you get back."

She called information, got Lurleen's number and found out that, owing to a cancellation, she could become a whole new woman before the day was over. The prospect made her stomach constrict. Eve said an automatic yeah, sure, jotted down the name of the shop and the directions to it, then gave in to a sensation of panic.

What if Lurleen gave her wide stripes of platinum blond instead of delicate highlights? She would look really different—too different. What if her hair turned a weird color somewhere between orange and blood red? Things like that did happen. Although Michelle's hair always looked great and her highlights were subtle and natural-looking, that was not to say that Eve's hair would turn out just as well. Maybe mousey people were meant to look like the plain Before and never the fabulous After.

Eve stood up and hitched up her sweats, looking around for her comfortable sneakers. If she was going to get a life-changing makeover, she was going to do it in clothes she could breathe in.

An hour later she was sitting in a salon chair, leafing through a magazine filled with pictures of perfect women with perfect hair.

"See a style you like, hon?" Lurleen inquired. She was putting the final touches on a scrunch-and-go short style that exactly suited the petite brunette in the next chair over.

The other client had come in with long tresses and asked for them to be cut. Eve had watched them being snipped off with fascinated horror, envying her coolness about it all. The hairdresser, a tall, super-curved woman in a red velour track suit that clung to her like a second skin, didn't seem to be afraid to take on a challenge like that. Lurleen's hair was black and chopped into several lengths that showed off her multi-pierced ears and multiple earrings, which jingled as she snipped. The effect was anything but subtle.

You're next. The thought made Eve shiver, even though the salon was warm from the blow-dryers and all the people in it. Not to mention the heat level of the conversations between the stylists and their clients. She was trying not to listen.

Evidently satisfied with her makeover, the brunette tucked twenty bucks under a huge plastic jar of mousse, told Lurleen thanks, and sauntered out.

The hairdresser came over and stood behind Eve's chair, adjusting the cape around her shoulders. "So what'll it be?"

"Oh, just highlights," Eve said offhandedly. She was irrationally afraid that Lurleen would take a pair of scissors to her, and give her a style that was all the rage in a rave club.

"Uh-huh." Lurleen ran her fingers through Eve's hair. "First time?"

"What?" Eve replied, startled. She had no plans to confide any details of her sex life to Lurleen.

"Your hair has never been colored. It's in great condition."

Eve relaxed, soothed by what Lurleen was doing with her hair. "Oh. Thanks. No, I've never done anything with it. Figured it was about time I did."

Lurleen nodded knowingly. "Good thing you came to me. Some stylists just don't have the patience to do them right but I take my time. Tiny streaks of honey blond, some lowlights in a deeper shade—that oughta do it."

"Whatever you say," Eve murmured, and said a silent prayer that all would go well.

"You're Michelle's friend, right? Want highlights like hers?"

"Um, yeah." Actually, if she had her druthers, she wanted to have a body like Michelle's. And the ability to attract men so she could pick and choose like Michelle did. But I'll settle for the highlights, Eve thought.

"Okay." Lurleen summoned an assistant and the two women began to comb and section off Eve's hair. Another assistant rolled over something that looked like a hospital table with small bowls of haircoloring and brushes. Lurleen took a very small section of hair and brushed it lightly to the roots with haircoloring, then wrapped the section expertly in a tiny square of pink foil, an action she repeated several times until one side of Eve's part was completed.

"Those look like candy wrappers," Eve said, peering at the one the assistant was holding to hand to Lurleen.

"That's because they are candy wrappers," Lurleen replied.

"Oh."

The women continued to work and Eve watched, fascinated, in the mirror.

"So how come you're doing this?" Lurleen asked. "Got a new man or kicking a guy to the curb? It's always one or the other," she added philosophically.

Eve looked carefully around the salon, not wanting to move her head very much, considering that she was undergoing a radical transformation and one wrong move might have a drastic effect on the results. Did all the other clients have the same idea? It didn't seem possible. Some leafed through magazines while they waited for their color to take hold, some dozed under bubble-style hair dryers, some talked nonstop with their stylists and each other.

"So?" Lurleen asked again.

Eve had a feeling that she'd better answer if she valued her roots. Probably what Lurleen heard day in and day out beat all the soaps in the universe. Not that Eve had anything particularly exciting to tell. "Um, new guy," she said at last.

"That's great," Lurleen said with sincere enthusiasm. She rotated Eve in the chair a little and began to work on the other side. Eve could no longer see herself but she had a good view of the rest of the clients. "Where did you meet him?"

"At the grocery store. He was shopping with his son." The prickle on the back of her neck told Eve that Lurleen and her assistant were exchanging an uh-oh look. "He's not married or anything like that," she said hastily. "His son broke my car window with a baseball, so he had to talk to me."

"Isn't that nice," Lurleen said in a tone that implied she wasn't too sure that it was.

"But I'm not doing this for him," she said. "I'm doing this for myself. I've been meaning to do it for a long time." *Liar, liar.* "So here I am."

"Ginny, just dip a brush in the lowlighter for me," Lurleen instructed her assistant. Eve shut up as they continued, not really minding the slight tugging on her hair as it was sectioned, painted with dye, and wrapped in foil. She kept still, aware that whatever was on her head was growing in size, until Lurleen turned her to face the mirror once more.

Eve blanched. "Holy cow." The rows of foil squares made her hair stick out in straight wisps all over her head. She looked like a fright. She looked like . . . a Yorkshire terrier that someone had tried to turn into a Christmas ornament. "I'm Frankenyorkie."

Lurleen only laughed. "You have to be a little bit ugly before you turn beautiful, hon. Don't worry."

She set a huge rotating disk into position to heat Eve's hair and set the color, wiped her hands and walked off to see to another client. Eve took another look at her reflection and closed her eyes, praying that the complicated procedure was just how it was done. She hadn't bothered to ask

Michelle exactly what went into making those subtle and expensive highlights. Her girlfriend had been busy, anyway, when she'd picked up Eve's call.

In about twenty minutes Lurleen and Ginny came back, and Eve opened her eyes. Lurleen unwrapped one square of foil and looked critically at the hair. "Good to go." Her assistant took care of the rest of the foil with deft fingers and Eve watched, seeing nothing but dark, dye-smelling hair.

"Follow me," Ginny said.

Eve did, sliding out of her chair onto unsteady legs. It's only haircoloring, she told herself. Take it easy. Even if it comes out bright green, you'll still be you. They didn't cut off your nose or anything. She settled into a shampoo chair and leaned back, letting Ginny swoosh hot water and shampoo into her hair, followed by the salon's special sealer and a conditioning rinse. Eve relaxed, feeling like her brain had been dissolved. And a very nice feeling it was. Much better than worrying about what she looked like or Luck McClure. Anyway, he might never guess who she was now that she'd changed her appearance.

Feeling like a sheep, she let Ginny lead her to a blow-drying station, where the assistant carefully combed her tangles and then began to dry her hair, using a roller brush in tandem with the blow-dryer. The noise of the thing made conversation impossible, for which Eve was grateful. She closed her eyes against the tickling wisps of hair.

Ginny turned off the blow-dryer with a soft click and opened her eyes. Lurleen was standing in back of her, about to do the final comb-out. Looking at her reflection, Eve began to smile a little. Then she smiled a lot.

"Came out nice," Lurleen said. "You happy with it, hon?"

She was more than happy. The highlights were perfect. Natural-looking. Maybe the right term was sun-kissed. Eve Rowland loved the sound of it.

A day or so later . . .

"So when is the rain coming?" Toby searched the blue sky for a glimpse of looming dark clouds, but there wasn't a sign of even a puffy white one. They were slogging over the same trail they'd gone on before, but it was a lot less pretty. There was no snow left and the muddy patches made for slow going.

"It's Wisconsin. It's spring. Wait five minutes," Luck suggested with dry humor at his son's impatience. They were both getting cabin fever and had decided to hike around the lake to combat it.

"Very funny." Toby made a face at him and turned to squint into the sunlight reflected off the lake's surface. "I bet that water is still freezing."

"I'm sure you're right." The damp chill was getting to Luck. He would have been happy to turn back and spend the afternoon with hot nachos, cold beer, and a basketball game, but he knew his son had to work off some of his excess energy. They trudged along, with Toby exclaiming now and then over some natural wonder. The boy picked up a chunk of rippled, strange-smelling fungus from a decaying tree trunk.

"This is gross," he said happily. "Can I keep it?"

"Sure. But not in your bedroom."

A pink cap with a bouncing white pom-pom appeared on the trail ahead but the person wearing it was hidden by a slight rise in the terrain. Then the pom-pom vanished. Luck knew they would meet up with the pink cap's owner soon enough if they kept going and she did too. He assumed it was a she.

He was right.

"Oh, hi," a breathless female voice said. A young blonde in a black ski jumpsuit was clambering over a tree that had fallen smack into the middle of the trail. Another natural wonder, Luck thought wryly. The skintight jumpsuit left absolutely nothing to the imagination and her ski-bunny jacket was unzipped.

"Hi," he said back.

Her smile was wide and totally beguiling. A branch snagged her hat as she straddled the log, and Luck went to the rescue. With one hand he helped her over and with the other, retrieved her hat.

She jammed it back on, not concealing her long, flowing hair very well, which shone like gold in the sunlight. Toby leaned on his father's leg and stared at her. Luck put a reassuring arm around his son's shoulders.

"You okay?" Luck asked.

"Sure," she giggled. "I wasn't really stuck. And my friends aren't far away."

He had been talking to Toby. *Neither is my son,* Luck wanted to reply as his gaze lifted to her face and he caught the knowing sparkle in her eyes. The blonde waited for several seconds, but he didn't say whatever it was she seemed to expect him to say. Disappointment flickered in her expression, which was quickly veiled by a coy smile. She clambered back over the log with no help at all and, Luck figured, ran back to her friends.

"That blonde was really a knockout, huh, Dad?"

"Where'd you learn to talk like that?"

"Um . . ."

Luck hid a smile. One of his son's best friends had an older brother, Luck knew, who no doubt had a stash of interesting magazines under his bed. Every boy in America learned the basics of female anatomy that way or on the Internet, and Luck wasn't going to give Toby the third degree about it.

He cast a glance down at his son, who was still staring after the shapely girl. "Anyway, that's the right word," he agreed blandly, and kept himself busy by tightening the drawstring of Toby's hood to give the knockout time to get farther away.

"She thought you were pretty neat too," Toby observed, a hint of mischief in his smile. "I saw the sexy look she gave you."

"You see too much." Luck gave him a playful push backward, plopping him down into a pile of soggy dead leaves.

Toby just laughed. "Why don't you marry someone like her?"

Luck sighed. He'd thought that subject had been forgotten. He shook his head in mild exasperation. "Looks aren't everything, son." Rolling to his feet, he reached down to pull Toby up. "Let's get back to the house. There's a basketball game on at four and you can get out the Xbox if you don't want to watch it with me."

"Race ya!" Toby challenged, and took off at a dead run, slipping and sliding on the mud and leaves but making amazing progress all the same.

Luck kept the boy in sight but didn't hurry to catch up, lost in a reverie that the wintry day only made more poignant. "What do you think, pretty lady?" Luck murmured. "Have you ruined me for anyone else?"

The image of his wife swirled through the mists of his mind, her face laughing up at him as she pulled him to their bed. Her features were soft, like the fading edge of a dream, her likeness no longer bringing him the sharp stabbing pain. Time had reduced it to a beautiful memory that came back to haunt him at odd times.

Although he still had a man's sexual appetite, emotional desire seemed to have left him. Except for Toby, it seemed that all the good things in life were behind him. Tomorrow seemed empty, without promise.

A squeal of female laughter from the lakeshore's sheltered side make him think of the blonde, who must have found her friends. Her bold bid for his attention had left him cold, even though he had liked her looks. He found the subtle approach much sexier—like the time Eve had licked the chocolate from her lips. Strange that he had thought of her instead of the way Lisa used to run her finger around the rim of a glass.

A handful of mud mixed with leaves hit his jacket with a soft plop. Luck blinked and wiped it off as Toby laughed and ran away again, dashing down the trail. The moment of somber reflection was gone as he took up the challenge of his son.

Thunder crashed and boomed across the sky, a noisy portent of the fast-moving storm that had been predicted for the northwoods area.

"This bulletin just in . . ." droned a news anchor.

Eve usually didn't pay much attention to the weather report but she looked out the window when the forecaster came on and made it sound like an impending natural disaster.

Lightning cracked outside. "My, that looked close," her mother murmured, always a little nervous about that. "Shouldn't we unplug things so the electricity doesn't crawl up the wires or whatever it does during storms?"

"The cable service is going to go down, Teresa. It always does." Her father sighed in disappointment. "Bye, Jim. Bye, Earl. I don't want to start something I can't finish." He switched off the TV and unplugged it.

Eve hid her smile behind the music she was studying. If her father had one passion besides fishing, it was watching fishing shows that seemed to have no beginning, middle, or end. Just what he found so compelling about a couple of amiable rednecks in a bass boat, Eve didn't know, but he glued himself to Jim and Earl and their pursuit of perch every chance he got. "Maybe it'll clear up later this afternoon and—" He was interrupted by the ring of the telephone in the front room. "I'll get it."

"Charles, if it's Miriam and Bunky, tell them to come over," her mother called. "We could play cards. That doesn't require electricity."

"I'm not sure I want to be housebound with Miriam and Bunky," he growled, stopping in his tracks.

"Oh, come on. They're really fun, better than going shopping."

Her father stepped over the boxes and bags from their trip to the mall as her mother continued, "Miriam's a hoot and she's my best friend. They won't stay for dinner just because it's raining hard. Bunky can drive through anything."

Her father just shook his head. On the third ring, he got to the phone and answered it. "It's for you, Eve." He had to raise his voice to be heard above the storm.

Appalachian Spring would have to wait. Eve picked up a folder stuffed with sheet music and put away the Aaron Copland suite she planned to introduce to her students. She got up and walked to the phone. "Hello?"

"Hello, Eve. This is Toby. Toby McClure."

Her surprise widened her eyes. "Hello, Toby." Warm pleasure ran through her voice and expression.

"I'm trying to make chocolate chip cookies," he said. She smiled, feeling positively sun-kissed, when she remembered that his father had promised his son that they would make them on their next rainy day together. "But I can't figure out how to get cream from shortening and sugar."

"What?" A puzzled frown creased her forehead as she tried to fathom his problem.

"The directions say to cream the sugar and shortening," Toby explained patiently.

Eve swallowed the laugh in her throat. No wonder it didn't make sense to him. "That means you should blend them together until they make a thick creamy mixture."

A heavy sigh came over the phone. "I thought this was going to be easy, but it isn't." There was a pause, followed by a reluctant request, "Eve, I don't suppose you could maybe come over and show me how to make them?" There was so much pride in his voice, and a grudging admission of defeat.

"Where's your father? He should be able to help you," she suggested.

"He didn't get home until real late last night, so

he's lying down, taking a nap," Toby explained. "Can you come?"

It was impossible to turn him down, especially when she didn't want to. "Yes, I'll come. Where exactly do you live?" Eve knew it was somewhere close from what Luck had once said. Toby gave her precise directions. After she had promised to be there within a few minutes, she hung up the phone. "Dad, were you or Mom planning to use the car this afternoon?"

"No. We're waiting to call Miriam and Bunky. Let them drive to us." He was already reaching in his pocket for the keys.

"I'm off to the McClures' to give Toby his first lesson in baking cookies," Eve explained with a soft laugh, and told them the boy's problem understanding the directions. Their amusement blended with hers.

"Better get going. That storm could spawn a tornado or two," her mother said. "Button up your coat and bring an umbrella."

"Yes, Mommy. Are you going to make sure my mittens match?"

"If you get caught in a tornado, they're not even going to stay on, honey." Her mother picked up the phone and dialed a number she knew by heart. "Miriam? Hi, it's Teresa . . ."

In her bedroom, Eve brushed her hair and dabbed on a little lip gloss. She didn't allow herself to wonder why she was taking so much trouble with her appearance when she was going to see an eight-year-old. It would have started her thinking about his father, something she was trying to pretend not to do at this point. She hesitated before taking the brown coat out of her closet, but it was the only one she had that was somewhat waterproof. She hated the clamminess of raincoats and never wore them.

The downpour was almost more than the windshield wipers could handle. It obscured her vision so that, despite Toby's excellent directions, she nearly missed the turn into the driveway. The lake house was set back in the trees, out of sight of the road. Eve parked her car behind the Jaguar.

The driving rain got her coat wet, but her hair stayed mostly dry. Even so, it was windblown by the time she walked the short distance from the car to the front door. Toby must have been watching for her, because he opened the door a second before she reached it. He pressed a forefinger to his lips and motioned her inside the warm house. She hurried in, unable to do anything about the water dripping from her and the umbrella.

"Dad's still sleeping," Toby whispered, and explained, "He needs the rest."

The entry hall skirted the living room, paneled in cedar with a heavy beamed ceiling that slanted down over a natural stone fireplace. Toby's glance in that direction indicated it was where Luck was sleeping. Eve looked in when Toby led her past. There, sprawled on a geometric-patterned couch, was Luck, bare-chested, wearing jeans, a muscular arm flung over his head, out cold. It was the first time Eve had ever seen anyone frowning in his sleep.

Dressed, he was handsome. Half-naked, he was absolutely, spectacularly gorgeous, even in a state of post-hot-date exhaustion. Something she didn't know for sure was true but she felt guilty for even thinking it with his young son in the room. She turned and fled.

In the kitchen, Toby led her to the table where

he had all the ingredients set out. "Okay, show me how to make cookies," he said.

"No, I won't show you," Eve said, taking off her wet coat and draping it over a chair back. "I'll tell you how to do it. The best way to learn is by doing."

Step by step, she directed him through the mixing process. When the first sheet came out of the oven, Toby was all eyes. He could hardly wait until the cookies were cool enough to taste and assure himself that they were as good as they looked.

"They taste just like yours," he declared on a triumphant note after he'd taken the first bite.

"Of course," Eve laughed, but kept it low so she wouldn't wake Luck in the next room.

"I couldn't have done it if you hadn't helped me," Toby added, all honesty. "You're a good teacher."

"That's what I am. Really," she emphasized when he failed to understand. "I *am* a teacher."

"Oh. What subject?"

"Music."

"Too bad it isn't English. That's my worst subject," he grimaced. "Dad isn't very good at it, either."

"We all have subjects that we don't do as well in as others," Eve said lightly. "Mine is math."

"Dad is really good at that, and forestry, because he has to use it all the time in his work."

"What does he do?"

"He works for my grandpa." Then realizing that didn't answer her question, Toby elaborated, "My grandpa owns North Lakes Lumber and a bunch of other businesses like that. My dad runs some of them. He has to travel a lot but we have more time together in the summer when I'm out of school.

He had a meeting with Grandpa last night. That's why he was so late coming home."

"I thought he had a date." The words were out before Eve realized she had spoken.

"Sometimes he goes out on dates," Toby admitted, finding nothing wrong with her comment. "We like going places and doing things together, but sometimes Dad goes out. I like to play with kids my own age, and he likes grown-ups. I bet you do too."

"Yes, that's true." She was impressed by his calm understanding of his single dad's life. She got the feeling that Toby didn't know more than he should at his age. Points to Luck for raising him right. Toby was a great kid.

Without being reminded, he checked on the batch of cookies in the oven and concluded they were done. He took the cookie sheet out with a pot holder and rested it on the tabletop while he scooped the cookies off.

"We've been talking about Dad getting married again," he announced, and didn't see the surprised arch of her eyebrow. "Dad gets pretty lonely sometimes. It's been rough on him since my mother died six years ago. A couple of weeks ago it was six years *exactly*," he stressed, and shook his head in a rueful fashion when he looked at her. "Boy, did he ever go on a binge that night!" He rolled his eyes to emphasize the point.

Two weeks ago. Eve did a fast mental calculation, her mind whirling. "Was . . . that on a Thursday?"

"I think so. Why?" Toby eyed her with an unblinking look.

That was the night she'd bumped into him outside the tavern. He had wanted someone to talk to,

Eve remembered. But she had refused, and he had gone back inside the tavern.

"No reason." She shook her head. "It was nothing important." But she couldn't resist going back to the subject. "You said he got drunk that night." She tried not to sound like a nosy social worker but she knew that she did and winced inwardly.

"I guess," Toby agreed emphatically. "He even had hallucinations."

"He did?"

"After I helped him into bed, he claimed that he had talked to a brown mouse." He looked at her, laughter suddenly dancing in his eyes. "Can you imagine that?"

"Yes." Eve swallowed and tried to smile. "Yes, I can." A whole lot of questions had just been answered at once, however inadvertently, and now she wanted off the subject. "I'll help you spoon the cookie dough on the tray," she volunteered, letting action take the place of words.

When the last sheet of cookies came out of the oven, Eve washed the baking dishes while Toby wiped them and put them away. He leaned an elbow on the counter and watched her scrub at the baked-on crumbs on the cookie sheet.

"I don't really mind helping with dishes, or even making my bed," Toby said, and propped his head up with his hand. "But I'm going to like having a mother."

She didn't see the connection between the two statements. "Why is that?"

"Because sometimes my friends tease me when I have to dust furniture or fold clothes," he explained. "Dad told me that mothers clean and cook and do all those kinds of things."

"So do fathers." Eve managed not to smile. It had to be rough to have your manhood questioned by your peers when you were only eight years old. Reading between the lines, she could see where Toby had acquired his air of maturity. He was a happy kid but not as carefree as most children his age.

She rinsed the last cookie sheet and handed it to Toby to dry. Draining the dishwater from the sink, she wiped off the counter, then dried her hands. She glanced at the wall clock and wondered where the afternoon had gone.

"Now that we have everything cleaned up, it's time I was leaving," she declared.

"Can't you stay a little while longer?"

"No, it's late." She removed her brown coat from the chair back and slipped it on.

Toby brought her the umbrella. "Thanks for coming, Eve." He stopped for an instant as a thought occurred to him. "Maybe I should call you Ms. Rowland, since you're a teacher."

"I'd like it better if you called me Eve," she replied, and started toward the entry hall.

"Okay, Eve," he grinned, and walked with her.

As she passed the living room, her gaze was automatically drawn inside. Luck was sitting up, rubbing his hands over his face as though he had just wakened. The movement in front of him attracted his attention. He glanced up and became motionless for an instant when he saw Eve.

The rainstorm had obscured the sunset and there was little light in the entryway. Eve didn't think about that as she started to speak, smiling at the grogginess in his expression.

But Luck spoke before she did. "Don't scurry off into the darkness . . . brown mouse." There was a trancelike quality to his voice. "Is that you? You look different. Even prettier."

Her steps faltered and she touched her hair without thinking. She had escaped recognition for so long that she had stopped dreading it. Now that he remembered her, she felt sick. Tearing her gaze from him, she hurried toward the front door. As she jerked it open, she heard him call her name.

"Eve!"

She didn't stop. She didn't even remember to open the umbrella until the falling rain made her face feel cold. She hurried toward her car.

Chapter 4

A startled cry came from her throat as the hand that caught her arm stopped her and spun her around. Eve hadn't thought Luck would come after her—not out in the rain, even though it had eased up a little. But there he was, standing before her with his naked chest glistening a hard bronze, the sprinkling of chest hairs curling tightly in the wetness. His dark hair was speckled with little drops. Reluctantly, Eve lifted her gaze to the blue of his eyes, drowning in the full recognition of his look.

"You *are* the woman I bumped into outside the tavern that night," Luck stated. The tone of his voice was unquestioning.

"Yes." Her hand, clutching the umbrella handle, wavered, causing Luck to lower his head and duck under the wire spines stretching the material.

His gaze swept her face, hair and eyes. "I thought I'd conjured you out of a whiskey bottle. I don't know why nothing clicked until just now. You don't look the same. You were so pretty that night, wandering down the street."

Eve was tempted to ask if he thought she was pretty now, sun-kissed highlights and all. So much for her subtle transformation keeping him from figuring out who she was.

A frown flickered between his brows, then vanished when he looked down at her coat. "That brown coat . . . that's what you were wearing. It's coming back to me." He held up his hands. "I'm willing to concede that I didn't meet you last Christmas. But why didn't you say anything before?"

"Look, being compared to a rodent is not a big thrill. I recognized you when we met outside the store that day, but I just didn't feel like reminding you who I was." Her low laugh was a little forced.

"What's wrong with being a brown mouse?" The corners of his mouth deepened in an attractive smile. "I recall that I happened to like her. A lot."

"A brown mouse is just a small rat. It's hardly a name that someone wants to be called." This time Eve worked harder to turn the comment into a joke for her pride's sake. She succeeded to a large degree.

"It's all in how you interpret things, Eve," Luck said, giving her a rueful smile. "You really aren't very sure of yourself. I wish we'd had a chance to talk that night. It all might have turned out differently."

How could she say that she'd wished the same thing? And knowing what she knew now—that he was a widower—made her want to go back to that strange, lonely evening and start all over again.

"Dad!" Toby shouted from the opened front door. "You'd better come inside! You'll catch pneumonia!"

"Toby's right." Her gaze fell to the droplets on the muscled contours of his bare chest, all hard sinew and even harder nipples, small and very male. His blatant sexiness made her head spin. In just a few minutes, she was experiencing a whole new set of evocative sensations. "You must be freezing. You should go in the house."

"Come in with me." Luck didn't let go of her arms, holding her as he issued the invitation.

"No. I have to go home." She resisted the temptation to accept, sensing rather than hearing the gentle patter of rain falling on her umbrella, and the deeper rhythm of her pulse.

His mouth quirked. "That's what you said then."

"It's late. I—" The sentence went no further as his cool palm cupped her flaming cheek. Eve completely forgot what she was going to say, her thoughts scattered by the disturbing caress of his touch.

"Da-ad!" Toby sounded impatient and irritated.

It was the diversion Eve needed to collect her senses before she did something foolish. "You'd better go." She turned away, breaking contact with his hand and lifting the umbrella high enough to clear his head. There was no resistance as she slipped out of his grasp to walk the last few steps to the car.

"We'll see you again, Eve." It was a definite statement.

But she wasn't certain what promise it contained. "Yes." She opened the car door and slipped inside, shaking the rain off the umbrella and struggling to close it. Luck just stood there, watching her.

He was indifferent to everything—the rain, his son's worrying, his ice-cold toes—as he watched Eve reverse the car at a right angle to turn around

in the drive. The neon-lit, oddly romantic encounter in the night had not been a figment of an
alcoholic imagination. The woman he'd thought
he had only dreamed about had actually been
under his nose all this time.

A wonderful feeling of sensual closeness—
something he hadn't experienced for six long
years—had happened when he had held her in his
arms, but he hadn't believed it was real. Even now
Luck wasn't sure that part hadn't been imagined.
Comfortable didn't describe the feeling it had
aroused. It was something more basic than that. It
had been right and natural with his arms around
her, feeling the softness of her body against his.

The woman had been Eve. It was strange he
hadn't realized it before. She was quiet and warm,
with an inner resiliency and a gentle humor that
he liked. A smile twitched his mouth as Luck remembered she had a definite will of her own as
well. She wasn't easily intimidated.

"Dad!"

He turned, letting his gaze leave the red taillights of her car, and walked to the house, cold feet
squishing in shoes filled with snow. He barely noticed the disapproving expression on his son's face
when he reached the door.

"Geez," Toby said accusingly. "You wouldn't let
me run out there like that with no coat or anything and catch cold. How come you can do it?"

"Because I'm stupid," Luck replied. He couldn't
argue with the point his son had raised.

"You'd better put on some warm clothes," Toby
advised.

"I intend to." He left a damp trail of footprints
behind him for several steps, then walked to the

private bath off his bedroom where he stripped and put on the thick terry-cloth robe Toby brought him. "Why was Eve here?" he asked, vigorously rubbing his wet hair with a bath towel.

"She came over to help me make cookies. They're good, too." A sharp questioning glance from Luck prompted Toby to explain. "I called and asked her to come over 'cause I was having trouble with the directions and you were asleep." Then it was his turn to tip his head to one side and quiz his father. "How come you called her a brown mouse?"

"Oh . . . I just found out that Eve was the one I talked to that night—that was what I called her then. Don't think she liked it, though." He shrugged, and tossed the towel over a rack.

"Well, you were drunk."

Luck sighed. Somehow hearing your kid say that was hard to take. But it was true enough. "Yeah, Toby. I guess I was. I had a few drinks, more after I met her than before. Which probably explains why I wasn't sure whether it had happened or I had imagined it."

"But I still don't understand why you called her a brown mouse."

"It's a long story," Luck began.

"I know," Toby said with a resigned look. "You'll tell me all about it some other time."

"That's right." He smiled down at his son, turned him around and pushed him gently in front of him out of the bathroom. "Is there any coffee made?"

"Yeah." Toby tilted his head back to frown at him. "I just hope you remember all the things you're going to tell me some other time."

In the kitchen, Luck filled a mug with coffee and helped himself to a handful of the cookies stacked on the table. "What did you and Eve talk about?" Settling onto a chair, he bit into one and eyed Toby skeptically. "Did you really make these?"

"Yeah," was the defensive retort. "Eve told me how. She says you learn best by doing. She's a teacher. Did you know that? I mean a for-real teacher. She teaches music."

"No, I didn't know that," Luck admitted.

"We talked about that some and a bunch of other things." Toby frowned in an attempt to recall the subjects he'd discussed with Eve. "I told her you were thinking about getting married again."

Luck choked on the swig of coffee he'd taken and coughed. "You did what?" He set the mug down to stare at his son, controlling the emotions behind his disbelieving look.

"I mentioned that you were talking about getting married again," he repeated with all the round-eyed innocence of an eight-year-old. "Well, it's true."

"No, *you've* been talking about it." Luck pointed a finger at his son, shaking it slightly in his direction. "Why on earth did you mention it to Eve? I thought it was a private discussion between you and me."

Toby blinked. "I didn't know you wanted to keep it a secret."

"Son, you can't go around discussing personal matters with strangers." He ran his fingers through his damp hair in a gesture of exasperation. "My God, you'll be blabbing it to the whole world next. Why don't you just take an ad out in the paper? Or put it on Craigslist. *Wanted: A wife for a widower with an eight-year-old blabbermouth son.*"

"Do you think anyone would apply?" Behind the boy's thoughtful look, his father saw, was the beginning of a plan.

"No!" Luck slammed his hand on the table. "If I find out that you've put an ad in any paper or on-line, I swear you won't be able to sit down for a week! I don't even want to hear the word marriage spoken in this house!"

"But you said—" Toby started to protest.

"I don't care what I said," Luck interrupted with a slicing wave of his hand to dismiss that argument. "I've played along with this notion of yours, but it's got to stop. I'll decide *when* and *if* I'm getting married again without any prompting from you!"

"But face it, Dad, you should get married," Toby patiently insisted. "You need somebody to keep you company and to look after you. I'm getting too old to be doing all this woman's work around the house."

"Put that in the ad too. *Wanted: unpaid domestic servant for a little boy who doesn't want to make his bed or take out the recycling.* How does that sound?"

"Pretty good," Toby said. "At least to me."

"You don't get married just for companionship and someone to keep house." Luck regretted his earlier, imprecise explanation of a mother's role. It had started this whole mess. "There's a lot more to it than that. A man is supposed to love the woman he marries."

"You're talking about hugging and kissing and that stuff," Toby nodded in understanding.

"That and . . . other things," Luck conceded with marked impatience.

"You mean sex, like in that book you and I read together when you explained to me how babies are made," his son replied quite calmly.

Luck wanted to pull out his hair. He never would have had the nerve to talk to his own father like this at the age of eight, never would have used the word sex within fifty miles of his old man without being ready to run for it.

"Yes, sex is part of love. But it's not all there is to it."

Toby looked at him with interest, obviously hoping for more.

Luck didn't know what the hell to say next. And no matter how romantic his feelings for Eve were, he hardly knew her. He didn't want to do anything impulsive just because he had an unexpected crush on someone and because his son was suddenly obsessed with the idea of finding a new mother.

"Yes, I mean sex and the feelings you have toward the woman you marry."

"Would you consider marrying someone like Eve?" Toby cocked his head at a wondering angle. "You said looks weren't everything."

"Why did you say a thing like that?" he challenged with irritation. "Don't you think Eve is pretty?"

"She is, and I like her, but—"

"No buts!" Luck said sternly. "Eve is very pretty and I don't want you implying otherwise with comments like 'looks aren't everything.' Thoughtless remarks like that hurt people's feelings." He oughta know, Luck thought with regret. He had already wounded Eve when he called her a brown mouse, even though he hadn't meant it to be unkind. "Don't ever say anything to make her feel bad!"

"Gee, Dad, you don't have to get so worked up," Toby said. "Eve just doesn't look anything at all like the blonde we saw in the woods the other day. The one with the pom-pom on her hat. Now she could be a *Playboy* centerfold."

Luck started to ask where Toby had gotten his

hands on a magazine like that, but he decided not to pursue it. Instead he just sighed, "I'm not interested in marrying a woman who has staples in her stomach."

Toby gave him a puzzled look. "Why would she have staples in her stomach?"

"Never mind." He lifted his hands in defeat. "The whole subject of women and marriage is now closed. But remember what I said about Eve," he warned. "I don't want to hear you making any disparaging remarks about her."

"Dad, I wouldn't." Toby looked offended. "She's nice."

"Don't forget it, then," he replied less forcefully, and stood up. "I'm going to get out of this robe and put some clothes on. You'd better find something to stash these cookies in."

"Okay," Toby agreed in a dispirited tone.

Luck hesitated. "I didn't mean to be rough on you, Toby. I know you mean well. It's just that sometimes you make situations very awkward without realizing it."

"How?"

"I can't explain." He shook his head, then reached out to rumple his son's hair in a show of affection. "Don't let it worry you."

The rain had moved on at last and the sky was a fresh clear blue. The green pines stood tall, in sharp contrast to the pure white clouds that drifted high in the air over the lake and the Rowlands' cottage.

Sitting on the seat in front of the upright piano, Eve let her fingers glide over the keys, seeking out the Mozart melody without conscious direction. She played from memory, eyes closed, listening to the individual notes flowing from one to another. The beauty of the song was an indirect therapy for the vague dejection that had haunted her since Luck had recognized her as his brown mouse less than two days ago.

When the last note faded into the emptiness of the room, Eve reluctantly let her fingers slide from the keys to her lap. The applause from a single person sounded behind her. Startled, Eve swung around on the piano seat to discover the identity of her audience of one.

The thick glass of the outer door made the form of the man standing on the porch indistinct, but Eve recognized Luck instantly. Alternating sensations of pleasure and uncertainty ran through her, setting her nerves on edge.

"I didn't hear you come." She rose quickly to cross the room and unhook the door. "Mom and Dad walked over to a friend's house for brunch this morning." As she pushed open the door to let him in, she noticed the only car in the driveway belonged to her parents. "Where's your car?"

"Not far away. I didn't want to block theirs. There's not much room in your driveway." He stepped inside, so tall and so vigorously manly. Eve kept a safe distance between them to elude the raw force of his attraction that seemed to grow stronger with each meeting.

"Oh." The knack of idle conversation deserted her. It was foolish to let that brown-mouse episode tie her tongue, but it had. She should never have allowed herself to become so sensitive about it. Maybe she'd used up all the nerve she had when she'd highlighted her hair, she thought, wondering just why women were supposed to assign so much importance to little things like their appearance.

"Toby and I decided to take the boat out on the lake this morning and thought you might like to come along." That lazy half smile that Eve found so attractive accompanied his invitation.

Her delight was short-lived as she read between the lines. "Oh. Thanks . . . but I don't want you to feel obligated. You don't have to make up for what happened outside the tavern that night." There was a trace of pride in the way she held her head, tipped higher than normal.

His smile grew more pronounced, softening his hard-hewn features. "I'm not going to apologize for anything I said or did then," Luck said. "Maybe I shouldn't have called you a brown mouse, but I meant it in the kindest possible way. I'm asking you to come with us because we'd like your company. If you feel that I need an excuse to ask, then let's say it's my way of thanking you for showing Toby how to make cookies." His blue eyes gently mocked her as he paused. "Will you come with us?"

Eve smiled, feeling a little awkward. "I'd like to, yes," she said at last. "Just give me a couple of minutes to change." She couldn't climb in and out of a boat in the wraparound denim skirt she was wearing.

"Sure." He reached for the screen door to open it. "We'll be stopping for lunch, probably at one of the resorts along the lake."

Eve hesitated, then told herself not to think too much. "If you'll give me another fifteen minutes, I can fix some sandwiches and stuff for a picnic lunch. Toby would like that."

"Toby would love it," Luck agreed. "We'll meet you at the boat in fifteen minutes."

"I'll be there," she promised as he pushed the door open and walked out.

Lingering near the door, Eve watched him descend the steps and strike out across the road toward the lakeshore, a warm feeling of pleasure running swiftly through her. Before he disappeared from view, she retreated to the kitchen to take the picnic basket out of the pantry cupboard and raid the refrigerator. To go with the ham sandwiches she fixed, Eve added a wedge of Wisconsin Cheddar along with some milder Colby cheese, plus crackers and red apples. She filled a thermos with lemonade and packed it in the basket, then laid a bag of potato chips on top.

Most of the allotted time was gone when she entered her bedroom. She quickly changed out of the skirt and blouse into a pair of white shorts and a flame-red halter top. At the last minute, she slipped on a pair of white canvas shoes with rubber soles and grabbed a long-sleeved blouse from the closet, in case she wanted protection from the sun.

With the picnic basket on her arm, Eve crossed the road to the lake. Toby was skipping stones across the flat surface of the water, a picture of intensity. A straw dangled from Luck's mouth; he chewed it absently as he stood in a relaxed stance beside his son. At the sound of Eve's approach, he turned toward her. His gaze swept her in slow appreciation, setting her aglow with pleasure.

"Hi, Eve!" Toby greeted her with an exuberant welcome, letting the handful of stones fall so he could brush the dust from his hands.

"You still have two minutes to go." Luck took the straw out of his mouth, looking a little embarrassed to be caught chewing it like a hayseed, something he obviously wasn't.

"Maybe I should go back to the cottage," Eve laughed, suddenly feeling buoyant.

"Oh, no, you don't," Luck said, a matching liveliness in his look. "Not if there's food in that thing."

She surrendered the picnic basket to his reaching hand. A line tied around a tree moored the pleasure cruiser close to the shore. Luck swung the basket onto the bow, then turned to help Eve aboard. She had only guessed before at the power of the sinewed muscles of his shoulders and arms. But when his hands spanned the bare skin below her halter top and lifted her to swing her up onto the bow as easily as he had the basket, she knew how strong he was.

The imprint of his firm hands stayed with her, warming her flesh and letting her relive the sensation of his touch as she carried the basket to the stern of the boat and stowed it under one of the cushioned seats. Toby was tossed aboard with equal ease and came scrambling back to where Eve was. After untying the mooring line, Luck pushed the boat into deeper water and heaved himself on board.

"All set?" Luck cast them each a glance as his hand paused on the ignition key.

At their nods, he turned the key. The powerful engine sputtered, then roared smoothly to life, the propeller churning up frothy foam. Turning the wheel, Luck maneuvered the boat around to point toward the open water before opening the throttle to send it shooting forward.

The speed generated a wind that lifted Eve's hair, blowing and swirling it behind her. A little

late, she wished she'd brought a scarf or a baseball
cap, but there was nothing to be done about it
now. She turned her face to the wind, letting it
race over her and whip the hair off her shoulders.

Resting her arm on the side of the boat, Eve had
a clear view of all that was in front of her, including
Luck. He stood behind the wheel, his feet braced
apart. The sun-bronzed angles of his profile were
carved against a sky as vividly blue as his eyes. The
wind ruffled the virile thickness of his dark hair
and flattened his shirt against his hard flesh, re-
vealing the play of muscles beneath it. His jeans
outlined his lean hips and the corded muscles of
his thighs, reinforcing an aura of rough sexiness.
Something stirred deep within her.

The instant Eve realized how openly she was
staring, she shifted her gaze to the boy at his side,
a young version of his father. Today Toby was totally eight years old, eager and carefree. She could
imagine Luck at the same age, especially with that
dancing glint in his eyes and easy smile.

The loud throb of the engine made conversation close to impossible, but Eve heard Toby yell at
his father to go faster. She saw the smile Luck
flashed him and knew he laughed, even though
the wind stole the sound from her. He pushed the
throttle wide open until the powerboat was skim-
ming over the surface of the water and bouncing
over the wakes of other boats as the churning
blades sent out their own fantail.

Luck glanced over at her and smiled, and Eve
smiled back. For a brief moment, she allowed herself to consider the intimate picture they made—
man, woman and child. For an even briefer minute,
she let herself pretend that that's the way it was,
until reality caught her up sharply.

After a while, Luck eased the throttle back and turned the wheel over to his son. Toby swelled with importance, his oversized sense of responsibility surfacing to turn his expression serious. Luck stayed beside him the first few minutes until Toby got the feel of operating the boat. Then he moved to the opposite side of the boat to lean a hip against the rail and keep an unobtrusive vigil for traffic that his son might not see. The position put him almost directly in front of Eve.

His sweeping side glance caught her looking at him and Luck shouted, "It's a beautiful day."

"Lovely," Eve shouted back, because it did seem perfect to her. The wind made an unexpected change of direction and blew her hair across her face. Turning her head, she pushed it away. When she looked back, Luck was facing the front.

A quarter of an hour later or more, he straightened and motioned to her. "It's your turn to be skipper!" Luck called.

"Aye, aye, sir!" She grinned, and moved to relieve Toby at the wheel.

She was quick to notice that the small boy was just beginning to show the tension of operating the boat. Wisely Luck had seen it too and had Eve take over before it ceased to be fun for Toby. Out of the corner of her eye, Eve saw Toby dart over to receive praise from his father for a job well done. Then her attention was centered on guiding the boat.

Luck said something to her, but the wind and the engine noise tore it away. She shook her head and frowned to indicate that she didn't hear him. He crossed over to stand in a small space behind her.

"Let's go to the northern side of the lake." He leaned forward to repeat his suggestion.

"I'm not familiar with that area. We don't usually go up that far." Eve half turned her head to answer him and discovered he had bent closer to hear her, which brought his face inches from hers. Her gaze touched briefly on his mouth, then darted swiftly to his eyes, captured by their vivid blueness.

"Neither am I. Let's explore strange waters together," Luck replied, his eyes crinkling at the corners.

"Okay." There was a breathless quality to her voice.

It was some minutes after she turned the boat north before Luck abandoned his post behind her. It was only when he was gone that Eve realized how overly conscious she had been of his closeness, every nerve end tingling, although no contact had been made.

Moving even faster, they ventured into unknown waters. When a cluster of islands appeared, Eve reduced the boat's speed to find the channel through them. She hesitated, hoping to make the right choice.

"Want me to take over?" Luck asked.

"Yes." She relinquished the wheel to him with a quick smile. "That way if you run into a submerged log, it will be your fault instead of mine."

"Good thinking," he grinned.

"Look!" Toby shouted, and pointed toward the waters ahead of them. "It's a deer swimming across the lake."

In the lake off their port side was the antlered head of a young buck swimming across the span of water between two islands. Luck throttled the engine to a slow idle so they could watch him. When the deer reached the opposite island, he scrambled onto shore and disappeared within seconds in the thick stand of trees and underbrush.

"Boy, that was really something, huh, Dad?"

"It sure was."

With a child's ability to change the subject lightning-fast, Toby asked, "When are we going to have our picnic?"

"When we get hungry," Luck replied.

"I'm hungry."

Luck glanced at his watch. "I guess we can start looking for a place to go ashore. Or would you rather drop anchor and eat on the boat?" He included Eve in the question.

She shrugged. "It doesn't matter to me."

"Maybe we can land on one of the islands," Toby suggested.

"I don't know why not." Luck smiled down at the boy, then began surveying the cluster of islands for a likely picnic spot.

"Who knows? Maybe we'll find Chief Namekagon's lost silver mine," Eve remarked.

Toby turned to her. "What lost silver mine?"

"The one that belonged to the Indian chief the lake was named after. Legend has it that it's on one of the islands on the lake," she explained.

The little boy frowned. "Is that true?"

"No one knows for sure," she said. "But he paid for all his purchases at the trading post in Ashland with pure silver ore. Supposedly the old chief was going to show the location of his mine to a friend, but he saw a bad omen and postponed the trip. Then he died without ever telling anyone where it was."

"Wow!" Toby declared with round-eyed excitement. "Wouldn't it be something if we found it?"

"A lot of people have looked over the years," Eve cautioned him. "No one has found it yet."

"How about having our picnic there?" Luck pointed to an island with a wide crescent of sand stretching in front of its pine trees.

"It looks perfect." Eve approved the choice with a nod, and Luck nosed the boat toward the spot.

Chapter 5

The three of them sat cross-legged on a blanket Luck had brought from the boat while Eve unpacked the picnic basket. "Cheese, fruit, crackers," Luck said, observing the items she removed. "All that's missing is a bottle of wine. You should have said something."

There were too many romantic overtones in that remark. Eve wasn't sure how to interpret it, so she tried the casual approach and reached in the basket for the cold thermos.

"I guess we'll have to make do with lemonade," she said brightly.

"I like lemonade," Toby insisted as she set the thermos aside to arrange a sandwich and a portion of chips on a paper plate and handed it to him. "This looks good, Eve."

"I hope you like it." She fixed a plate for Luck, then one for herself, leaving the cheese, fruit, and crackers on top of the basket for dessert.

"Have you ever looked for the lost mine, Eve?"

Toby munched thoughtfully on his sandwich while he studied her.

"Not really. Just a few times when I was your age."

The subject continued to fascinate him. Throughout the meal, he pumped her for information, dredging up tidbits of knowledge Eve had forgotten she knew. Toby refused the slice of cheese she offered him when his sandwich was gone but took the shiny apple.

Luck ate his. When it was gone, he used the knife to slice off another chunk. "This is good cheese."

"From Wisconsin, of course." She smiled.

"Did Chief Namekagon really have seven wives?" Toby returned to his favorite subject.

"Yes, but I guess he must have kept the location of the mine a secret from them too," Eve replied.

"Seven wives." Toby sighed and glanced at his father. "Gee, Dad, all you need is one."

"Or none," Luck murmured softly, and sent a look of silencing sharpness at his son. "More lemonade, Toby?"

"No, thanks." He tossed his apple core into the small sack Eve had brought along for garbage. Rising, Toby dusted the sandwich crumbs from his legs. "Is it okay if I do a little exploring?"

At Luck's nod of permission, Toby took off. Within minutes, he had disappeared along a faint animal path that led into the island's thick forest. For the first few minutes, they could hear him rustling through the underbrush. When that stopped, Eve became conscious of the silence—and that she was alone with Luck. Her gaze strayed to him, drawn by an irrepressible compulsion, only to have her heart knock against her ribs when she found him watching her.

"More cheese?" The question sounded ridiculously mouselike to her but at least it served to cover the feelings inside her. In the far distance, there was the sound of a boat traversing the lake, reminding her they weren't the only ones in the vicinity, no matter how isolated they seemed.

"No. I'm full." Luck shook his dark head.

Inactivity didn't suit her at the moment because she knew it would take her thoughts in a direction that wasn't wise. "I'd better pack all this away before it attracts all the insects on the island."

Eve tightly wrapped the cheese that was left and stowed it in the basket with the thermos of lemonade and the few remaining potato chips. As she added the paper sack with their litter to the basket, she was conscious that Luck had risen. When he crouched beside her, balanced on one bent knee, she found it difficult to breathe normally. His warm scent was all around her, heightened by the heat of the sun. She was kneeling on the blanket, sitting on her heels, aware of him with a fine-tuned radar.

"The food was very good. Thanks for the picnic, Eve." His hand reached out to cup the back of her head and pull her forward.

Lifting her gaze, she watched the sensual line of his mouth coming closer. She couldn't have resisted him if she wanted to, which she didn't. Her eyes closed an instant before his mouth touched her lips, then moved onto them to linger briefly. The kiss started her trembling all the way to her toes. Much too soon he was lifting his head, leaving her lips aching for the warm pressure of his mouth.

The very brevity of the kiss reminded her that it was a gesture of gratitude. It had meant no more than a peck on the cheek. She would be foolish to read more into it than that. Lowering her head, she struggled to appear unmoved by the experience, as casual about it as he seemed to be. Her fingers fastened on the wicker handle of the picnic basket.

"Do you want to put this in the boat now?" She picked it up to hand it to him, her gaze slanting upward.

For an instant Eve was subjected to a probing look from his narrowed eyes. Then his smooth smile erased the sensation as he took the picnic basket from her.

"Might as well," Luck said idly, and pushed to his feet.

Standing up, Eve resisted the impulse to watch him walk to the boat. Instead she shook the crumbs and sand off the blanket and folded it into a square. Feeling the isolation again, she turned her gaze to the trees that edged the beach. The blanket was clutched in front of her, pressed protectively to her fluttering stomach. Behind her Eve heard the infinitely soft sound of Luck's footsteps in the sand.

"Where do you suppose Toby has gone?" she wondered.

"He's a good kid. He knows not to go too far."

"But even so . . ."

"Leave the blanket here. We'll see if we can find him," Luck suggested, and took her hand after she'd laid the blanket down.

His easy possession sent a warm thrill over her skin. Eve liked the sensation of her slender hand being lost in the largeness of his. Together they walked to the narrow trail Toby had taken, where they would have to proceed single file.

"I'll go first, in case we run into some briars. I wouldn't want your legs to be scratched up." The downward sweep of his gaze took note of the bareness of her legs below the white shorts.

Instead of releasing her hand to start up the path, as Eve had expected he would, Luck curved his arm behind his back and shifted his grip to lead her. The forest shadows swallowed them up, the ground spongy beneath the faintly marked earth, the smell of pine resin heavy in the air.

Out of sight of their picnic spot, a fallen timber blocked the trail, its huge trunk denoting the forest giant it had once been. Luck released her hand to climb over it and waited on the other side to help her. The rubber sole of her shoe found a foothold on the broken nub of a limb, providing her with a step to the top of the trunk. All around them was dense foliage, with only a vague glitter of the lake's surface shining through the leaves.

"I'm glad this is a small island," Eve remarked. "A person could get lost in this."

"It's practically a jungle," Luck agreed.

His hands gripped the curves of her waist to help her down. Eve steadied herself by placing her hands on his shoulders while he lifted her off the trunk to the ground. When it was solidly beneath her, she discovered the toes of her shoes were almost touching his.

Beneath her hands she felt his flexed muscles go taut, his hands retaining their hold on her waist. Looking up, Eve saw his keen gaze taking her in. She became conscious of her lack of lipstick and her wind-ratted hair. Her tension forced her to speak to break it.

"I should have brought a comb. My hair is a mess."

Luck's gaze wandered slowly over it and back to her face, the color of his eyes changing, deepening. "It looks like a man did it. While he was making love to you."

His hand reached to smooth the hair away from her face. The idle caress parted Eve's lips in a silent breath, fastening his attention on them. While his mouth began moving inexorably closer, his other hand shifted to her lower back and drew her to him.

The tension she'd felt flowed out of her with a piercing sweetness as his mouth finally reached its destination. It rocked slowly over her lips, tasting and testing first one curve, then another. The triphammer beat of her heart revealed the havoc he was raising with her senses.

His intimate investigation didn't stop there. His hard warm lips continued their foray, grazing over her cheek to the sensitive area around her ear. Growing weaker, her hands inched to his shoulders, clinging to him for support and balance in this dizzying embrace.

"Do you have any idea how good this feels, Eve?" he murmured huskily.

She felt the shuddering breath he took and moaned softly in an aching reply. He turned his head, bringing it to a different angle as he took firm possession of her lips, the territory already familiar to him from the last exploration. Now Luck staked his claim to her tender mouth.

Eve curved her arms around his neck, seeking the springy thickness of his hair. His hands began roaming restlessly over her shoulders and back, left bare by the red halter top she wore. The softness of her curves were pressed and shaped to his hard body and taut muscles. The kiss deepened until Eve was raw with the hot ache that burned within her.

Gradually she felt the passion withdrawing from his kiss. It ended before his mouth reluctantly ended the contact. Breathless and dazed, she slowly lowered her chin. She was conscious that Luck was forcing himself to breathe normally. She tried to get hold of her own emotions, but without his success. His head continued to be bent toward her, his chin and mouth at a level with her eyes.

"We'll never find Toby this way," he said finally.

"No, we won't," Eve agreed, and self-consciously brought her hands down from around his neck.

He loosened his hold, stepping back to create room between them. She slid a glance at him, trying to obtain a clue as to how she was expected to treat this kiss. Luck was looking down the trail. Something was troubling him but his expression smoothed into a smile when he glanced at her. Yet Eve saw a faint look of puzzlement in his eyes.

"Toby can't be far. The island is too small," he said, and reached for her hand again before starting up the trail.

Twenty yards farther, they reached the opposite shore of the island and found Toby sitting on a waterlogged stump at the lake's edge. He hopped down when he saw them.

"Are we ready to go?" he asked with an unconcern that didn't match the bright curiosity of his eyes.

"If you are," Luck replied.

Toby's presence brought back the friendly mood between them that had marked the beginning of the excursion. Not once did Eve feel uncomfortable, yet an uncertainty stayed with her. She couldn't tell whether Luck regarded her as a

woman or a friend. He glanced at her only occasionally during the journey back, paying attention
mostly to Toby.

Which was how it should be, she told herself.
Somehow just being with him and his son in this
easy way made her feel more confident in general,
even if she couldn't know exactly how Luck felt
about everything minute to minute.

He beached the boat on the shore in front of
her parents' cottage and gave her a hand to dry
land. Considering he had to travel home on water,
she didn't think he would accept an invitation to
come to the house for a drink, so Eve didn't issue
one.

"I enjoyed myself," she said instead. "Thanks for
asking me to come along."

"It was our pleasure. Maybe we'll do it again
sometime." Once again, he gave her a noncommit-
tal reply that promised nothing.

Eve tried not to let her disappointment show as
she clutched the picnic basket and the blouse she
hadn't worn. After waving good-bye to Toby aboard
the boat, she struck out for the road and the log
cottage opposite it.

Since he'd left Eve, the frown around his forehead and eyes had deepened. As he walked the
path from the lake to his house, Luck tried to recall the last time he'd felt as alive as he had those
few brief moments when he'd held Eve and kissed
her. The deadness inside him had gone. He worried at it, searching for it in some hidden corner
of his mind, barely conscious of Toby ambling
along behind him.

"Dad?" Toby tried to get his attention and received an abstracted glance. "Why do people kiss?"

That brought Luck out of his reverie. He shortened his strides to let Toby catch up with him and raised a suspicious eyebrow. "Because they like each other." That was general enough, he hoped.

Toby turned his head to eye him thoughtfully. "Have you ever kissed anybody you didn't like?"

Luck knew it was a loaded question, but he answered it anyway. "No."

"If you only kiss people you like, then you must like Eve," Toby concluded. His father's sharply questioning look couldn't be ignored, and the boy said at last, "I saw you and Eve. I was coming back to see if you were ready to leave, but you were so busy kissing her that you didn't hear me."

"No, I guess I didn't," Luck admitted. The hot rush of emotion had deafened him to everything but the soft sounds of submission she'd made. He was bothered by a vague sense of infidelity. "And, yes, I like Eve."

"Why don't you marry her?"

"Liking isn't loving." Luck cast an irritated glance at his son. "And I thought it was understood that that subject was closed."

Toby gave a long sigh but made no comment.

Later that night Toby was sprawled on the floor of the living room, arms crossed on a throw pillow, his chin resting in the hollow of his fists while he watched television. At a commercial, he turned to glance at his father in the easy chair—only he wasn't there.

Frowning, Toby pushed up on his hands to peer

into the kitchen, but there was no sign of him. His father hadn't been acting right since the boat ride. That fact prompted Toby to go in search of him.

He found him in a darkened bedroom. The hallway light spilled in to show him sitting on the bed, elbows on his knees and his chin resting on clasped hands. Toby paused in the doorway for a minute, confused until he saw that his father was staring at the framed photograph of his mother on the dresser.

Toby walked up to him and laid a comforting hand on his shoulder. "What's wrong, Dad?"

Bringing his hands down, Luck turned his head, paused, then sighed heavily. A smile broke half-heartedly. "Nothing, sport."

But Toby glanced at the picture. "Were you thinking about Mom?"

There was a wry twist to his father's mouth. "No, I wasn't." Pushing to his feet, he rested a hand on Toby's shoulder. Together they left the room. As they walked out the door, Toby stole a peek over his shoulder at the picture of the smiling blonde. He slipped his hand into his father's, but he knew it was small comfort.

Halfway through the next day Toby's stomach insisted it was lunchtime. Entering the house through the back door, he walked into the kitchen. His arrival coincided with his father saying a final good-bye to someone on the kitchen phone.

"I'll tell him. Right . . . I'll be there," Luck said, and hung up.

The little boy's curiosity overflowed, as it usually did. "Who was that? Tell me what? Where will you be?" The questions tumbled out with barely a breath in between.

"Your granddad said hello," Luck replied, answering two questions.

"Why didn't you let me talk to him?" Toby frowned in disappointment.

"Because he was busy. Next time, okay?" his father promised, and glanced at the wall clock. "I suppose you want lunch. What'll it be? Hamburgers? Grilled cheese? How about some soup?"

"Hamburgers," Toby said without much interest or enthusiasm. Hooking an arm around a chair back, he watched his father take the meat from the refrigerator and carry it to the stove, where he shaped portions into patties to put in the skillet. "You said you'd be there. Be where? When?"

"I have to drive to Duluth this Friday to meet with your grandfather," Luck replied. "Put the ketchup and mustard on the table."

"I suppose you're going to ask Wanda Jackson to come over to stay with me," Toby grumbled as he went about setting the table and putting on the condiments.

"You are absolutely wrong. I'm calling a new sitter that a friend recommended, after we have lunch."

"Oh, Dad, do you have to?" Toby groaned. "Having a babysitter is a real pain."

"Has it ever occurred to you that they might think you are a real pain?" his father countered.

"Sometimes they think I'm making up stories. Wanda believed me, though."

"Wanda would believe anyone who was willing to give her twenty dollars," Luck murmured dryly.

Toby let the silverware clatter to the table as a

thought occurred to him. "Why couldn't you ask Eve to come over? If I have to have somebody sit with me, I'd rather it was Eve."

Luck hesitated, and Toby studied that momentary indecision with interest. "I'll ask her," his father said finally.

"So you'll call her after lunch?" Toby persisted.

"Yes."

Eve was halfway out the door with her arms full of sunblock lotion, a blanket, and a paperback for an afternoon in the sun—her last for a while, because spring break was winding down—when the telephone rang. She ended up dropping everything but the lotion onto the couch cushions before she got the receiver to her ear.

"Rowlands," she answered.

"Hello, Eve?" Luck's voice responded on the other end of the line.

She tossed the tube of sunblock on top of the blanket and hugged her free arm around her middle, holding tight to the pleasure of his voice. "Yes, this is Eve."

"Luck McClure." Not as if he needed to identify himself. "Are you busy this Friday?"

"No." She and her mother had tentatively talked about a shopping expedition into Cable, but that could be postponed.

"I have a big favor to ask. I have business to take care of on Friday, which means I'll be gone most of the day and late into the evening. Toby asked if you would stay with him while I'm gone. We had some problems with his usual sitter—"

"What kind of problems?"

"Ah, she wasn't all that responsible." The last thing Luck wanted to tell her was that he had come home drunk to find Wanda Jackson gone. "Anyway, I'm not too sure Toby would be comfortable with someone new just yet."

Swallowing her disappointment that he wasn't calling to ask her out, Eve answered, "Sure. Toby's a great kid. We had a lot of fun that time I came over and made cookies. What time do you need me to be there?"

"I'd like to get an early start. Is eight A.M. possible?" Luck asked.

"Yup." Holy cow. She would have to be up by at least seven to look presentable. Even her gloriously subtle new highlights would not distract from sleep-puffed eyes and a pillow mark on one cheek. Welcome to womanhood, she told herself. Where no matter what you look like, you think you never look good enough.

"Thanks. Toby will be glad to know you're coming," he said. "We'll see you on Friday."

"On Friday," Eve repeated, and echoed his good-bye.

Toby would be glad she was coming, he'd said. Did that mean that Luck wouldn't? Eve sighed wearily because she simply didn't know.

On Friday morning her father dropped her off at the McClures' lake house a few minutes before eight. As she got out of the car, he leaned over to remind her, "If you need anything, you be sure to call us. Your mother or I can be over in a matter of minutes."

"Thanks, Dad. I'm twenty-six years old. But if

there's a dire emergency, like a missing can opener, I'll call you." She waved to him and hurried toward the house.

Toby had obviously been watching for her because the front door opened before she reached it. He stood in the opening, a broad smile of welcome on his face.

"Hi, Eve."

"Hello, Toby." Her gaze went past him to the tall figure approaching the door as she entered.

The fluttering of her pulse signaled the heightening of her senses. Eve had never seen Luck in business clothes, and the dark suit and tie altered his appearance in a way that intensified the aura of male authority, dominating and powerful.

"Right on time." He smiled in an absent fashion. "I left my cell-phone number by the telephone so you can reach me if there's an emergency."

Why did everyone seem to treat her like she was only a few years older than Toby? "Thanks. Will do," she replied, trying to respond with her usual naturalness and feeling a little guilty for smart-mouthing her father for a similar remark. "But nothing's going to happen."

After a nod of agreement, he laid a hand on Toby's head. "Behave yourself. Otherwise Eve will make you stand in a corner."

"No, she won't." Toby dipped his head to avoid his father's caress.

When Luck turned to Eve, his smile held a trace of affection and indulgence toward his son. "I shouldn't be too late getting back tonight."

"Don't worry about it," she assured him. "Toby and I will be all right."

"You know how to reach me if you need me," Luck reminded her, and she tried not to be disappointed because the remark held no underlying meaning. It was a straightforward statement from a father to a sitter. "I have to be going," he addressed both of them and smiled at his son. "See you later."

"Tell Granddad 'hi' for me," Toby instructed.

"I will," Luck promised.

To get out the door, Luck had to walk past Eve. His arm inadvertently brushed against hers, sending a little quiver through her limbs. When she breathed in, she caught the musky scent of his aftershave, as potently stimulating as the man who wore it. The essence of him seemed to linger even afer he'd walked out the door.

With Toby standing beside her on the threshold, Eve watched Luck walk to the car. She returned his wave when he reversed out of the driveway onto the road and felt a definite sensation of being part of the family—standing at the doorway with her "son" and waving goodbye to her "husband."

Eve shook the thought away. That was dangerous thinking, the kind that led to heartbreak. It was definitely not wise. She was a babysitter—that was all.

Fixing a cheerful smile on her face, she looked down at Toby. "What's on the agenda this morning?"

He shrugged and tipped his head back to give her a bright-eyed look that reminded her a lot of his father. "I don't know. Do you want to play catch?"

"Do you think we'll break a window?" Eve teased.

"I hope not," Toby declared with a grim look. "I had to spend half the money I was saving for a mountain bike to pay my share of the damage to your windshield. Dad paid for most of it 'cause it was mostly his fault for throwing the ball too high, but he wouldn't have been playing if it hadn't been for me. We share things."

"Yes, I can see that." The two McClures seemed to have a remarkable relationship, unique compared to anything she'd come across in her meetings with parents at school.

"So do you want to play catch?"

"Sure," Eve said. The idea of being active appealed to her. "Go get your ball and glove."

"I'll bring Dad's for you," he offered. "Sometimes I throw it pretty hard—" Toby warned "—and it stings your hand when you catch it."

The driveway seemed the safest place to play catch since there weren't any windows in the line of fire. When Toby tired of that, they walked down by the lake, where he gave her lessons in the fine art of skipping stones on the water's surface.

At noon they returned to the lake cabin. "What would you like for lunch?" Eve asked as they entered through the kitchen door.

"A peanut butter sandwich and a glass of milk is okay." He didn't sound enthused by his own suggestion.

"Is that what you usually have?"

Toby shrugged. "It's easy. Dad and I don't do much cooking."

"How about if I check the refrigerator and see if there's anything else to eat?" Eve asked, certain that Toby would like something more imaginative if she offered to fix it.

"Go ahead," he agreed, then warned, "There's not much in there except some dinners in the freezer."

When she opened the refrigerator door, she discovered Toby was right. The shelves were nearly bare except for milk, eggs, bacon, and a couple of jars of jam.

Toby watched her expression. "I told you," he reminded her. "Dad fixes breakfast and sometimes cooks steaks on the grill. Otherwise we eat out or have frozen dinners. They're pretty good, though."

Eve found a package of cheese in the dairy drawer of the refrigerator. "Do you like grilled cheese sandwiches?" she asked.

He nodded. "Yeah."

While the skillet was heating to grill them, Eve searched through the cupboards and found a lone can of condensed tomato soup. She diluted it with milk and added a dab of butter. When she set the lunch on the table, Toby consumed it with all the gusto of the growing boy that he was.

"Boy, that was delicious!" he declared, and leaned back in his chair to rub his full stomach. "You sure are a good cook."

"Grilling a sandwich and opening a can of soup isn't exactly cooking," she smiled. "I was thinking that I might call my father and see if he would drive us to the store this afternoon and pick up some groceries. I'll cook you a *real* dinner tonight. Would you like that?"

"You bet!"

Eve wondered where all this domesticity was going to get her, but she couldn't come up with an answer. If it made Toby happy, that was good enough. Not as if she had anything else to do, and he really was a great kid.

Chapter 6

After a few inquiries, Eve was able to discover some of Toby's favorite dishes. Being a young boy, he had simple tastes. Dinner that evening consisted of fried chicken, mashed potatoes and gravy, and some early sweet corn on the cob. For dessert she fixed fresh strawberry shortcake with lots of whipped cream.

"I can't ever remember eating food that good," Toby insisted. "It was really delicious, Eve."

"Why, thank you, sir." With her hands full of dirty dishes to be carried to the sink, she gave him a mock curtsy.

"I'll help wash the dishes," he volunteered, and pushed away from the table. "Dad usually dries them."

"You don't need to help." She had already learned while she was preparing the meal that Toby was accustomed to doing household chores. His sense of duty was commendable, but he was still very young and needed a break from it once in a while. "You can have the night off and I'll do them."

"Really?" He seemed stunned by her offer.

"Yes, really," she laughed.

"I'll stay and keep you company." He dragged a chair over to the kitchen counter by the sink.

"I'd like that," Eve said, and let the sink fill with water, squirting liquid dish detergent into it.

Kneeling on the chair seat, Toby rested his arms on the counter and propped his chin on an upraised hand to watch her. "You know, it'd really be great to have a mother. It's getting to be a hassle cleaning the house, washing dishes and all that stuff."

"I can imagine." She smiled faintly as she began washing the dishes and rinsing them under the running faucet, then setting them on the draining board to dry.

"I'd sure like to figure out how to find someone for Dad to marry." Toby sighed his frustration. "I thought about putting an ad in the paper or online, but Dad really got upset when I mentioned it to him."

Her initial pang of envy came from an odd feeling that she wouldn't mind the role of Toby's mother—and Luck's wife. It wouldn't take much encouragement to fall head over heels in love with Luck. Without her knowing quite how it had happened, she was already more than halfway there now.

But then she felt nothing but amusement and sympathy for Luck's plight. The idea of advertising for a wife had to have come as a shock to him.

"It would have been a little embarrassing for your father, Toby," Eve murmured, the corners of her mouth deepening with the smile she tried to contain.

"Dad seemed to think that too." He frowned

with childish disapproval. "I told Dad that you'd make a good mother and he should marry you."

"Toby, you didn't!" She nearly dropped the dish in her hand, a warm pink flooding her cheeks.

"Yes, I did," he assured her innocently. "What's wrong with that? He likes you. I know he does. I saw him kiss you."

Eve became very busy with the dishes, trying to hide her agitation and embarrassment with her work. "Just because you kiss someone doesn't necessarily mean you want to marry them, Toby."

"Yeah, that's what Dad said," he admitted.

She hated the curiosity that made her ask, "What else did your dad say when you suggested he should marry me?"

"Nothing. He told me the subject was closed and I wasn't supposed to discuss it anymore, but we need someone around here to take care of us." The comment revealed he hadn't let go of the idea. "There's too much work for a boy like me to do, and Dad's busy. There has to be someone that Dad will marry. I just gotta find her."

"Toby McClure, I think you should leave that to your father."

"Yeah, but he isn't *trying* to find anybody," Toby protested. "I thought I'd have better luck." Then he laughed. "I made a joke, didn't I? Better luck for Luck."

"Yes, you did." Her smile widened into a grin.

"That's my name, too, you know," he declared, and settled his chin on his hand once more.

"No, I didn't know that." Her brown eyes widened in surprise. "I thought it was Toby—Tobias." She corrected it from the shortened version.

"That's my middle name," Toby explained. "My real first name is Luck, like my dad's. My mom insisted on naming me after him when I was born, but Dad said it was too hard growing up with a name like that. He said I'd wind up getting called Little Luck, and he didn't like the idea of being Big Luck. So they called me Toby instead."

"I think that was probably best."

In Eve's experience at the school, she'd seen how cruel children could be sometimes when one had an unusual name. Sometimes a kid would be teased unmercifully. As a rule children didn't like being different. It wasn't until later, when their sense of individuality surfaced, that they actually wanted unique names.

Yet she couldn't help remembering when she had first been introduced to the father and son, and Luck had explained the family tradition of his name. At the time she had wondered if there was a "little" Luck at home to carry it on. It was funny to discover it had been Toby all along.

After the dishes were done, she and Toby went into the front room and watched television for a while. At nine o'clock she suggested that it was time he took a bath and got ready for bed. He didn't argue or try to persuade her to let him stay up until Luck came home.

Squeaky clean from his bath, Toby trotted barefoot into the living room in his pajamas. He flopped himself across the armrest of the chair where Eve was sitting.

"Are you going to tuck me into bed?" he asked.

"I sure am." Eve smiled at the irresistible appeal of his look. Toby was just as capable of twisting her around his finger as his father was.

Toby led the way to his room while Eve followed. He made a running leap at the bed, dived under the covers and was settled comfortably by the time Eve arrived at his bedside. A white pillow-case framed his dark brown hair and his bright blue eyes looked back at her.

She made a show of tucking the covers close to his sides while he kept his arms on top of them. Then she sat sideways on the edge of the mattress.

"You don't have to read me a story or anything," Toby said. "I'm too old for that."

"Okay. Would you like me to leave the light on for a while?" Eve asked, referring to the small lamp on the bedside table. She already suspected he was too old for that too.

"No."

Her gaze had already been drawn to the night table, where it was caught by the framed photo-graph of a beautiful blond woman with sparkling green eyes. A feeling of pain splintered through Eve as she guessed the identity of the smiling face in the photograph.

"Is this a picture of your mother?" she asked Toby.

"Yes. Her name was Lisa." Toby blithely passed on the information.

"She's very beautiful," Eve admitted, aware that Luck would never have called this woman a brown mouse. She was golden—all sunshine and spring-time—and not because a hairdresser had made it happen. Eve despised herself for the jealousy that was twisting inside her. But she didn't have a prayer of ever competing with someone as beauti-ful as Luck's first wife—not even with her memory. It was utterly hopeless to think Luck would ever love her.

"Dad has a picture just like that in his room," Toby informed her. "He talks to it a lot . . . although he hasn't lately," he added as an afterthought.

"I'm sure he loves her very much." She tried to

smile and conceal the aching inside. "It's time you were going to sleep."

"Will you kiss me good night?" he asked with an unblinking look.

"Of course." There was a tightness in her throat as Eve bent toward him and brushed his forehead with a kiss. She longed for the right to do that every night. She straightened, murmuring, "Sleep well, Toby."

"G'night, Eve." With a contented look on his face, he snuggled deeper under the covers.

Her hand faltered as she reached past the framed photograph to turn out the light. Standing up, she moved silently out of the room. Unwanted tears burned the back of her eyes. All of a sudden she regretted being born plain. Obsessing over improving her looks was a waste of time. And her daydreaming about motherhood and marriage wasn't going to get her anywhere. She wondered why it had seemed so appealing in the first place.

In the living room Eve turned down the volume on the television set and picked up a business magazine lying on the coffee table. Curling up in the large armchair, she forced herself to read an article in it on the giant strides women had made in the corporate world.

Hooray for them, she thought wistfully. But that wasn't going to happen to her in a small Wisconsin town. What she should do was go back to college, get a graduate degree in music, and move somewhere else. Reverend Johnson had told her a thousand times that she should reach for the stars—he was a great one for corny inspirational speeches but she secretly took his encouragement to heart.

Somehow, since Luck McClure and his son had

come into her life, she'd pretty much forgotten about what she wanted to do. But that wasn't right. Even if he was genuinely interested, which was by no means a sure thing, she had to get back on track. Eve stopped reading the magazine but left it open in her lap. She thought the situation over as the clock on the fireplace mantel ticked away the time.

It was after midnight when Luck pulled into the driveway, much later than he had anticipated. Switching off the engine, he grabbed his briefcase and his suit jacket from the rear seat. The briefcase, which held his laptop and a bulging folder of documents, was heavy in his hand as he climbed out of the car. He swung his jacket over his shoulder, held by the hook of a finger. His tie was draped loosely around his neck, the top buttons of his shirt unfastened.

The tension of a long drive and the mental fatigue from a full day of business discussions cramped the muscles in his shoulders and neck. Weariness drew tired lines in his handsome face.

As Luck walked to the front door of the cabin, he noticed the light burning in the window and smiled at the welcoming sight. When he opened the door, he heard the muted sound of the television set. There was a warm run of pleasure as he realized Eve must have waited up for him to come home.

Setting his briefcase down just inside the door, he walked into the living room and paused. Eve had fallen asleep in the big armchair, with a magazine in her lap. His smile widened at the sight of her curled up like a velvety brown mouse. Luck tossed his suit jacket onto the sofa along with his tie and walked over to turn off the television set.

Silence swirled through the room as he approached the chair where she was sleeping. He intended to wake her, but when he looked down at her, the tiredness seemed to fall away from him. In repose, her serene features reminded him of the gentle beauty of a madonna—or a sleeping beauty waiting to be wakened with a kiss. The latter was a tantalizing thought.

Leaning down, Luck placed his hands on the chair's armrests. He felt alive and whole, renewed by her presence. He lowered his mouth onto her lips, stimulated by their sweet softness. At the initial contact, they were unresponsive to the mobile pressure of his kiss. Then Luck felt her lips move against his. Raw emotions surged through him, an aching pressure building inside him.

Eve stirred with the beginnings of wakefulness and he pulled back, not straightening but continuing to lean over her. The desire was strong to pick her up and carry her into his bedroom where he could give in to those feelings that swept him— and persuade her to explore them too.

Her lashes slowly drifted open and he watched the light of recognition flare in her dark brown eyes. His blood was warmed by the pleasure at seeing him that ran wild in her look.

"You're home," she murmured in soft joy.

"Yes," Luck answered huskily, because it seemed he had come home. It was a sensation he couldn't quite explain, not even to himself.

One minute he could see the welcome in her eyes and in the next it was gone, as a sudden rush of self-consciousness hid it from him. Eve seemed somewhat nervous.

"I must have fallen asleep." She brushed a hand across her eyes, then reached for the magazine in her lap.

A little annoyed by her sudden remoteness, Luck pushed himself erect, withdrawing physically from her as she had withdrawn from him. He saw the flicker of her hurt in the velvet darkness of her eyes. Luck rued the day he'd ever called her a brown mouse. Her sensitive nature had taken it the wrong way, and now, when she was a little sleepy and vulnerable, he could see that she still didn't really trust him.

He wanted her to. But that wasn't likely to happen and he wasn't even sure he could explain what was going on inside him.

All Eve knew about that was the displeasure written on his features. She touched a finger to her mouth, wondering why her lips felt tender, as if he had kissed her. In her dreams.

"What time is it?" There was a crick in her neck from sleeping in the chair. She rubbed her stiff muscles as she uncurled her legs.

"It's nearly one." His answer was abrupt. "Sorry I got back so late."

"It's all right." Eve smiled in his direction without actually meeting his gaze.

"You didn't have to wait up for me." It almost sounded like a criticism. "You should have napped on the couch."

"I didn't plan to fall asleep. I was reading and . . . I guess I dozed off," she explained, feeling a little awkward.

"Let me check on Toby, then I'll drive you home," he said.

Luck disappeared into the darkened hallway leading to the bedrooms as Eve forced her cramped body out of the chair. She noticed his suit jacket and tie on the sofa when she retrieved her purse from the coffee table. She remembered how incredibly handsome he'd looked when she'd opened her eyes and seen him standing there, bent over her to wake her.

He must have seen her admiration in her eyes. And all those other pointless emotions that Luck McClure seemed to evoke in her so easily. Including the scariest of all, love. There didn't seem to be any other explanation for the way he'd withdrawn from her—his sudden curtness. He probably thought she was going to start fawning all over him and didn't want the embarrassment of her unwanted attentions. She resolved not to let him see the way she felt toward him, not again.

When he returned to the living room, Eve managed to appear calm and controlled—and very casual. Yet there wasn't any approval in his inspecting glance.

"Ready?" he asked.

"Yes." She had to look away from him. The open collar of his shirt had a hi-honey-I'm-home sexiness that made her want to jump him. "Is Toby all right?"

"He's sound asleep," Luck replied. "He'll be okay alone until I get back."

She gave him a doubtful glance, then decided not to worry about it if he wasn't worried. Her parents' cottage was really close and there wasn't any traffic at this time of night. "Up to you," she murmured, and moved toward the front door.

Outside, a full moon bathed the night with its silvery light and the sky was atwinkle with stars. A breeze whispered through the pines, scenting the air with their freshness. Eve paused beside the passenger side of the car while Luck opened the door for her.

Nervousness made her say, "It's a lovely evening, isn't it?" The ambience seemed too romantic for her peace of mind.

"Yes, it is," Luck agreed, and waited until she was inside before closing the door.

Her gaze followed him as he walked around the car and slid behind the wheel. When he started the motor, Eve faced the front. Her nerve ends quivered with his nearness, making the silence intolerable.

"So, how was your business trip?" she asked, to make conversation.

"Fine." It was an uninformative answer, but Luck made it easier by asking, "Did Toby give you any trouble today?"

"None," Eve assured him. As she'd thought, they had the road all to themselves, not another car in sight. "We played catch—and didn't break a single window," she added with feigned lightness.

"You're luckier than I am." He slid her a brief glance, one side of his mouth lifting in a half smile, his voice dry with amusement.

"We were careful about the area we picked," she explained, relaxing a little.

It was a short drive to the cottage. Part of her wished the trip home hadn't been so quick, and another part of her was relieved. When they drove in, Eve noticed her parents had left the porch light on.

"I hope they weren't worried about you," Luck commented as he stopped the car.

"I doubt it," she replied. "They sort of accept that I'm a big girl now. My hours are my own."

Letting the engine idle, he shifted the gear into park and half turned in the seat to face her. "How much do I owe you for staying with Toby?"

She stiffened at the offer of payment for her services. "Nothing," Eve insisted.

"Hey, I didn't ask you to stay with Toby with the intention of getting a free babysitter. If you hadn't come, I would have had to pay someone else," Luck reasoned.

"Please don't ask me to take money for this," she appealed to him, not wanting to be paid for something she had done gladly. "Just consider it a favor from a neighbor."

"All right." He gave in reluctantly. "I won't argue with you."

"Thank you." Eve looked away to reach for the door handle, but she was kept from opening it by the staying hand that touched her arm.

Almost against her will, she looked back at him. The sheen of the moonlight bronzed the masculine angles and planes of his face, giving them a rugged look. A hunger rose within her that she couldn't deny.

"Thank you for staying with Toby." His voice was pitched disturbingly low, vibrant in its rich tone.

"You're welcome," Eve whispered the reply, too affected by his touch and his nearness to speak normally.

Nor could she draw away when his head bent toward hers. She trembled under the possession of his hard lips, her resolve shattering into a thousand pieces. His hand reached out, brushing just under her uplifted breasts, and silently urged her closer.

Eve arched nearer, trying to satisfy the hunger she tasted in his kiss as she let him part her lips to savor her response. A soft moan came from her throat at the ache Luck aroused in her.

He was everything. Her senses were dominated by him. The feel of his rock-hard muscles excited her hesitant hands, which rested lightly on his chest; she was warmed by the heat and aroused by the scent of his male body. And the taste of him was in her mouth.

The world was spinning crazily, but Eve didn't care—as long as she had him to cling to. Kissing him was so delicious she wasn't about to consider the consequences.

Luck dragged his mouth from her lips and lightly kissed her cheek several times, trailing fire. Her breath was so shallow, it was practically nonexistent. He combed his fingers into her hair as if to hold her head still.

"And thanks for waiting up for me, Eve," he murmured thickly against her sensitive skin. "Even though you fell asleep—but it's been a long time since anyone has done that. I can't explain how good it made me feel."

"Luck, I . . ." But she was afraid to say the words. Then he kissed her again and she didn't need to say anything.

But this time it was brief, although she had the consolation of sensing his reluctance when it ended and he drew away.

"I've got to get back. Toby's alone," Luck said, as if he needed to explain.

"Yes." This time he made no move to stop her when she opened the door. "Good night," she murmured as she stepped out of the car.

"Good night, Eve," he responded.

She seemed to glide on air to the lighted porch, conscious that Luck was waiting to make sure she got safely inside. Opening the door, she turned and waved to him. She watched the red taillights of his car until they disappeared onto the road.

It would be so easy to read something significant into his kisses. Eve tried desperately to guard against raising false hopes. Thinking about the photograph of his beautiful late wife helped. That—and the memory of the time when he had hinted he was lonely.

God, she was good at making herself miserable, Eve thought. She was almost surprised that she had allowed herself to enjoy his kisses.

As she undressed for bed, Eve berated herself for being a fool for love. He hadn't said he loved her. A couple of smooches didn't make a relationship and they shouldn't rock her world. But it was very difficult to listen to her inner critic when she felt so good.

The light he'd left on in case Toby awakened in his absence didn't seem welcoming. The magic of Eve's presence in his house had vanished with her. Luck entered the cabin, not bothering to put away his briefcase or hang up his suit jacket before he made his way down the hallway.

"Dad?" Toby's sleepy voice called out to him.

"Yes, son, it's me." He paused by the doorway to Toby's room.

"Did you take Eve home?"

"Uh-huh. I just got back," he explained. "Are you okay?"

"Yeah." There was the rustle of bedcovers shifting. "How was Granddad?"

"He's fine," Luck assured him. "It's very late. You go back to sleep, Toby. We'll talk in the morning."

"Okay, Dad," he replied in the middle of a yawn. "Good night."

"Good night, Toby." Luck waited until he heard silence from the room, then entered his own.

The moonlight shining in through the window illuminated the room, allowing him to undress without turning on the bedside lamp. Unbuttoning his shirt, he pulled it from his pants and shrugged out of it to toss it into the clothes hamper.

He sat down on the edge of the bed to take off his shoes. The moonlight fell on the framed photograph sitting on his dresser. Luck stopped to gaze at it.

"We had a good thing, Lisa," he murmured. "But it was a long time ago." There was an amused lift to his mouth, a little on the wry side. "Why do I have the feeling that you don't mind if I fall in love with someone else?"

But she didn't answer him . . . it had been quite a while since she had. Luck wasn't haunted anymore by images from the past, and he didn't feel any guilt that it was so.

Chapter 7

The long, wet spring had seemed to drag on forever, but summer had come on strong. Eve shifted her position in the reclining lounge chair. She had earned her time in the sun and she was enjoying every minute of it. Her intensive tutoring sessions for a seventeen-year-old boy in the next town whose doting mom and dad considered him a musical prodigy had paid off. She'd done what she could for him and his parents had paid her double. All the same, she doubted he was headed to Juilliard, although he did have talent. At least she got to take the summer off as a result.

She had liked the intensive tutoring, though, and wanted to do more of it. All part of her master plan to get back to college and have a fabulous life. With or without Luck McClure. She couldn't deny that she was more attracted to him than ever. But he hadn't called for a while, which was causing her to stupidly waste a lot of time and energy wondering why.

She had used some of the extra money to order

new clothes from the better catalogs, not mousey ones. The hot-pink swimsuit she had on was just plain sexy.

When she reached for her glass of iced tea sitting under the chair in the shade, Eve held the top of her swimsuit in position with her hand so that the top wouldn't fall down when she bent over. She was going for just a little bit of a tan and didn't want the lighter marks that straps would leave. The sip of tea momentarily cooled and refreshed her. She'd promised herself to walk down to the lake for a swim, but so far she hadn't found the energy.

The front screen door creaked on its hinges and Eve turned her head toward the cottage as her mother stepped onto the porch. She saw Eve and smiled.

"There you are," she declared. "I was ready to hike down to the lake. You're wanted on the phone."

"Me?" She almost forgot about the untied straps of her swimsuit as she sat up abruptly. A quicksilver run of excitement sped through her nerves. "Who is it?"

"Luck McClure."

"Tell him I'll be right there!"

Her fingers turned into thumbs as she tried hurriedly to knot the straps behind her neck. While she struggled with that, her flip-flops refused to cooperate with her attempts to slip her bare feet into them. She heard the screen door swing shut behind her mother.

The message was being passed to Luck that she was on her way, but Eve was afraid he'd get tired of waiting and hang up if she took too long. When she finally had the straps tied and the flip-flops on, she ran to the cottage.

The telephone receiver was off the hook, lying

beside the phone on the table. Eve grabbed it up, ignoring the amused glances her parents exchanged.

"Hello?" She was winded from her panicked rush to the phone and the breathless excitement she couldn't control—and annoyed at herself for acting like a teenage girl.

"Eve? You sound out of breath," Luck said, and she closed her eyes in silent relief that he hadn't hung up.

"I was outside." She swallowed in an attempt to steady her breathing.

"Your mother told me that she thought you were down by the lake."

"Actually, I wasn't," Eve explained. "I was out front, sunbathing."

"Wearing a skimpy little bikini, I hope," Luck murmured.

"No." She half smiled, wondering if she should describe what she was wearing. Not with her parents within earshot. "I have on a semi-respectable one-piece bathing suit."

"I should have guessed." His voice was dry.

His reply stung. She knew exactly what he was thinking. A one-piece suit was precisely what a brown mouse would wear. After all, they weren't very daring creatures.

"Why are you calling, Luck?" Feeling resentful, she mentally answered her own question: maybe all he wanted was for her to stay with Toby again. It was really quite a bargain when babysitters could be paid with a kiss. Two months later, she still hadn't forgotten that kiss. And maybe, she thought, neither had he. Eve wanted to kick herself for even thinking about it, but it was awfully hard to do in flip-flops.

"Well, we haven't seen you for a while," he began.

We? Not a great start. If only Luck had said something datelike. Such as *I* haven't seen you for a while.

That would have demonstrated actual interest. In her.

"So I—"

Better.

"I mean, Toby and I—"

Worse.

"We were wondering if you'd like to go strawberry picking."

A date couldn't get any more wholesome than that. Still, to her surprise, Eve heard herself say yes.

Luck rattled off the details as if he was afraid she would change her mind. She agreed, hung up, and sauntered back outside to her lounge chair to bask some more.

Eve moved down a long row of strawberry plants laden with juicy berries. The day was hot and her shorts were hitching up. Every time Luck was looking the other way, she tugged them down.

Her basket was almost full, although Toby's was empty. He'd picked plenty and eaten them all, despite his father's warnings about bellyaches. The little boy was far down the row, looking for creepy-crawlies to collect instead.

Luck tugged a particularly succulent berry from under a leaf and dangled it by its stem under her nose.

"Can I tempt you?"

"Not with your kid around," she said pleasantly. "He's having a great time."

"Yeah, he loves to do things like this. He said something about that strawberry shortcake you made—he wants to make one, of course. I figured I could get those spongy things they sell in the supermarket and a spray can of whipped cream, and have that."

Eve shook her head. "No way. Not with fresh berries. Strawberry shortcake isn't hard to make. Just roll out sweet dough, bake it, top it with sliced strawberries in sugar, and whip heavy cream for the topping."

Luck gave her a look. "Just hearing you say that is sexy. Say it again."

She smiled primly. "No." She hunkered down to get some hard-to-reach berries and Luck tried not to stare.

"Have mercy. Do you know what you're doing to me?"

Pleased that her shorts and tank top were having the desired effect, Eve concentrated on filling her basket. "Must be my muddy knees. Drives men wild every time. Or maybe it's the bug bites." She stopped to scratch a welt on her upper arm and sat back on her haunches. "There. I'm done."

She looked up at Luck, a little startled by the hungry look in his eyes. Then Toby ran up, waving his basket. "I got some caterpillars! Wanna see?"

Luck nodded and took the basket his son handed up to him, looking at the wiggly critters inside. Eve took the opportunity to get to her feet unassisted, and looked inside as well.

Toby had captured an assortment of caterpillars and some healthy-looking pink worms too. He picked up the biggest one and waved it at his father. "This is Squirmy. Can I keep him, Dad? Huh? Can I?"

"May I keep him."

"Da-ad!"

"I think Squirmy would be happier right here," Luck said seriously. "Where he can see his family and friends."

Toby sighed and put the worm back under a strawberry plant. "How about the caterpillars? Can I keep them?"

"You know, son, the farmer probably appreciates your picking them off his plants but bringing them home is not a good idea."

"Oh. Well, if I can't let them go and I can't bring them home, what should I do?"

Luck looked around and gave the basket back to his son, pointing to a windbreak of low trees not far away. "Catch and release. You can put them right over there."

Toby scampered off.

"Considering how hot it is, he has an amazing amount of energy," Eve said.

Luck nodded. "Good thing he's going to camp this year. He's wearing me out."

"Sleepaway camp?"

"Yup."

"Big step. You sure he's ready for that?" Eve asked.

"It was his idea," Luck sighed. "Toby's grown-up for his age."

She laughed softly. "Maybe you're the one who's not ready."

"There's some truth to that." Luck smiled at her. "But I was hoping that you and I would be

able to spend more time together. You know . . .
alone time."

Eve drew in a breath, not able to come up with a
reply that sounded calm and collected. Fortunately
for her, Toby was racing back, swinging the empty
basket in huge circles.

"So . . . we were wondering if you wanted to
have dinner with us."

"Yeah!" Toby shouted. "Steaks and strawberries!"

Luck ruffled his son's sweaty hair. "I think we
can do a little better than that. What do you say,
Eve? The rest of the menu is up to you. That strawberry shortcake you described sure sounded
tempting."

"You have a lot of nerve, Luck McClure." But
she couldn't help laughing. "Okay, you're on. But
I have to go home and change."

"Deal," Luck said warmly, and Toby tore off in
another direction, zigzagging down the rows of
strawberries. He watched the little boy go and
turned to Eve. "Pick you up at six?"

"Sure."

As part of her campaign to rid herself of the
brown-mouse label, Eve wore a crop top of eyelet
lace that buttoned down the front, and artfully
faded jeans with cornflower-blue embroidery on
the back pockets. She looked herself over in the
mirror, realizing that the mosquitoes were going
to feast on her bare tummy.

A little insect repellent would take care of that,
she decided. She rummaged through her dresser
drawer for the bottle, squeezed a dab into her
palm, and smoothed it on over her exposed skin.

144 *Janet Dailey*

It didn't exactly smell like fine cologne, but Wisconsin skeeters were hungry monsters and she preferred not to be eaten alive.

Promptly at six o'clock, Luck drove up to the cottage, accompanied by Toby. Ready and waiting, Eve bolted from the cabin before her father had a chance to comment on her clothes.

When Luck rolled the windows down, Toby tried out a wobbly wolf whistle that made his dad laugh. Eve flushed a little. She hadn't thought an eight-year-old would notice.

Toby hopped into the rear seat so Eve could sit in front beside Luck. She was immediately subjected to an admiring rake of his blue eyes. Her cheeks grew even warmer as she pulled out the seat belt over her chest, blushing when it slid between her breasts. Talk about lift and separate, she thought.

"Safety first," Luck murmured wickedly.

Eve looked straight ahead. "Oh, shut up."

"Sorry. You look great."

A compliment from him was something she couldn't handle, so she tried to turn it aside with a self-effacing remark. "You mean, great for a brown mouse," Eve corrected.

"No, not a brown mouse anymore. A blue one," he declared with a glance at her jeans. "Buckle up back there." After his son complied, Luck reversed onto the road, checking for oncoming traffic.

"We got the steaks," Toby said importantly. She heard him thump the cooler in the back seat. "Right here."

"That's great."

"How do you like yours cooked?" Luck asked.

"Medium rare." Her sensitive nerves felt just

about that raw at the moment, ultraconscious of the man behind the wheel.

"I guessed you were the red-blooded kind." He looked away from the road long enough to send a mocking glance at her, which only served to heighten her awareness of him.

"That's the way we like ours too, isn't it, Dad?" Toby said, unconscious of any hidden meaning in the talk.

"It sure is," Luck agreed, a smile playing at the edges of his mouth.

"You have to watch him, though," Toby told Eve. "Or he winds up burning them."

"Now wait a minute," Luck said in protest. "Who's the cook around here?"

"Eve," his son was quick to answer.

A low chuckle came from Luck's throat. "That's a point well taken. Anything we need to pick up so you can make that strawberry shortcake, Eve?"

She was grateful for the distraction. "Yeah. And the QuikMart is right up ahead."

He pulled into the parking lot and she dashed inside to get what she needed, taking the opportunity to calm down a little. She felt better once she was back in the car but her nerves started acting up again as they approached the drive to the cabin.

Preparations for the evening meal became a family affair. With Toby's help, she made another fresh shortcake that was a towering, delicious mess of strawberries, sweet biscuit dough, and whipped cream. They put it in the refrigerator to chill for dessert.

Luck started the grill in the backyard and cooked the steaks, while Toby took care of setting the table and helping Eve. She fixed a fresh spinach salad and wild rice to go along with the steaks.

When they sat down at the table, the meal seemed flawless. Eve wasn't sure whether it was the food or the company that made it all taste so good, but all three of them ate every bite of food on their plates.

"Didn't I tell you Eve was a good cook?" Toby stayed at the table while they lingered over their coffee. Like his father, he had devoured a huge piece of shortcake. And he was probably going to be just as tall as Luck, Eve thought fondly, which gave him the usual unfair advantage in metabolism. She contented herself with a small piece.

"You certainly did," Luck agreed. "And you were right too."

"Your father deserves some of the credit," Eve insisted. "I don't know about yours, but my steak was perfect."

"Thank you." Luck inclined his dark head and accepted the compliment. Thick strands of rich brown hair fell across his forehead, adding to his rakish air.

"Mine was good too," Toby assured him, then took away the compliment. "But all you had to do was watch them so they wouldn't burn. Eve really did the cooking."

"And an excellent job too." He didn't argue with his son's opinion. The magnetic blue of his eyes centered on her, lazy and disturbing. "You really know the way to a man's heart."

All her senses went haywire at that remark, throwing her into a state of heady confusion. She struggled to conceal it, quickly dropping her gaze and busying her hands with the dessert dishes still on the table.

"Don't bother with the dishes," Luck instructed. "We'll just stack them in the sink for now."

"Nonsense." There was an agitated edge to her voice that betrayed her inner disturbance. "It'll only take a few minutes to do them and they'll be out of the way."

"In that case, we'll all help." He pushed out of his chair. "You can clear the table and stack the dishes by the sink, and Toby can wash them while I dry."

They seemed to get them done in record time. Eve finished wiping the stove, table, and countertops a little before Toby and Luck were through.

As the trio entered the living room, Toby turned to walk backward and face them. "Why don't we start a fire in the fireplace, Dad?"

"It's summer, Toby," Luck reminded him with an indulgent look.

"I know, but it would be fun," he shrugged. "We could toast marshmallows."

"You can't still be hungry," Eve laughed.

"No, but I'll eat them anyway," he replied, and she understood that most of the pleasure came from toasting them, rather than eating them. "Please, Dad. Just a little fire."

"Okay," Luck gave in. "Just a small one."

While Toby dashed back to the kitchen for the bag of marshmallows and a long-handled toasting fork, Luck built a small fire in the stone fireplace. When it was burning nicely, the three of them sat on the floor in a semicircle around the hearth.

Toby did the actual toasting of the marshmallows, passing around the finished product in turns. Half a bag was consumed—mostly by the fire—before he finally tired of the task. All of them had to wash the gooey residue from their hands. Once that was done, the flickering flames of a fading fire drew them back to their former positions.

A contented silence settled over the room, broken only by the soft crackle of the burning wood. Outside, darkness had descended and the soft glow of the fire provided the only light in the front room. Sitting cross-legged between them, Toby yawned loudly.

"Gosh, I'm tired," he declared. "I think I'll go to bed."

Luck seemed surprised that his son was actually volunteering to go to bed. A little thread of self-consciousness laced its way through Eve's nerve ends at the prospect of being alone with Luck.

"I guess it is your bedtime," Luck remarked as his son got to his feet and kicked off his grubby sneakers.

"Yeah." Toby paused to look at Eve. "Thanks for cooking dinner tonight. It was really good."

"You're welcome." Her smile trembled a little.

"Good night," he wished her.

"Good night."

"I'll be in shortly," Luck promised.

"You don't need to. You can stay with Eve," Toby said, then turned to hide the frowning look of reproval he gave his father. She heard him whisper, "I'm big enough to go to bed by myself. Don't embarrass me in front of her."

A slow smile broke over Luck's features at his son's admonition. "Get to bed." He affectionately slapped Toby on the butt to send him on his way.

When he'd gone, Luck smiled in Eve's direction, encompassing her with casual, intimate warmth. There had been an ease between them. Eve had definitely felt it, yet without Toby's presence to serve as a buffer, it started to dissipate. She became conscious of there being only the two of them in the room. The silence that had been so pleasant and comfortable began to grow heavy. She'd never had the knack for making idle conversation, but the situation seemed to demand it.

"He's a good-natured kid," Eve remarked. "Always seems so happy."

"I hope he is." His smile was not as assured as it had been before and Eve looked at him curiously.

"You've done a great job raising him," she said at last.

"I guess so." Luck stared at the fire and seemed to lose himself in the tiny yellow flames darting their tongues over the glowing log.

Eve couldn't think of a response, and the silence lengthened. She supposed that he was thinking about his late wife, probably remembering past moments shared.

No more sounds came from the direction of Toby's bedroom, and the tension ran through her system. Her legs were becoming cramped by her curled sitting position, but Eve was reluctant to move and draw attention to herself. She didn't want Luck to look at her and mentally compare her to the beautiful blonde in the photograph.

At that moment he seemed to rouse himself and become aware that he wasn't alone. "That fire is becoming hypnotic," he said, explaining away his preoccupation.

"Yes." Eve pretended she had been fascinated by it too, when the only fascination that existed within her was for him.

Luck made a move as if to stand, then paused. "Was there any coffee left?"

"Yes." She rose quickly to her feet. "I'll heat it up for you. It will only take a minute."

"I can get it." But Luck didn't protest too much, willing to be persuaded to remain where he was.

"No, you stay here," Eve insisted. "I've been sitting so long I'm starting to get stiff. I need to move around a bit." Which was the truth, although the greater truth was a need to be alone and get herself together. Her feelings for him were confusing her.

"Okay." Luck didn't argue the point further, remaining by the fire. "If you insist."

Activity helped. She busied herself in the kitchen, pouring coffee into two cups and reheating them in the microwave. Yet she couldn't forget that another woman had once brought him coffee and kissed his son good night as she had done the previous evening. The latter thought prompted Eve to check on Toby while she waited for the second cup of coffee to heat.

When she entered the hallway, it was at the precise moment that Luck entered it from the living room. Eve stopped, a little guiltily.

"I thought I'd see if Toby was all right," she explained.

The slight curve to his mouth captivated her with its male charm. "That's where I was headed too," Luck replied. "Shall we go together and both be satisfied?"

He took her agreement for granted, linking an arm around her waist to guide her down the darkened hallway. The sensation was much too enjoyable for Eve to resist—something she had believed her pride would never let her do.

The doorway to Toby's room stood open and they paused there, standing side by side. In the semidarkness they could see his shining face, all youthful innocence in sleep. His dark hair waved across his forehead. Deep affection for the sleeping child tugged at her heartstrings.

"That's about the only time he's quiet," Luck murmured softly.

A faint smile touched her mouth as Eve turned her head to look up at him in silent understanding. Toby was always doing, saying, or up to something. Luck's comment held a wry truth.

When she met his downward glance, something warm and wonderful shone in his blue eyes. There was a caressing quality in the way they wandered over her upturned face. It started her heart pounding at a rapid speed.

He bent slightly toward her, brushing her lips in a light kiss that stirred her senses and left her wanting more. That desire trembled within her, but Eve lacked the strength to resist it.

"Do you suppose the coffee's hot yet?" Luck murmured, not lifting his head very far from hers.

"It should be," she whispered, and doubted if her voice had the strength to speak louder.

As they turned to leave the doorway, neither of them noticed the little boy in bed cautiously open one eye, or the satisfied smile on his face.

Luck accompanied her to the kitchen and carried his own cup of hot coffee into the living room. He walked past the sofa and chairs to the fireplace, lowering himself to sit on the floor in front of the dying fire. Reaching out, he pulled a couple of throw pillows from the sofa closer to his position and patted them to invite Eve to join him. She sat on one, bending her legs to the side and holding her cup in both hands.

"Toby likes you a lot, Eve," Luck remarked, eyeing her with a sidelong glance.

"I like him a lot too," she admitted. "So I guess it's mutual."

"Toby and I have led a bachelor's life for a long time," he said, continuing to regard her steadily. "I always thought we managed very well." He paused for a brief second. "Tonight I realized there were a lot of things we've been missing. I'm glad you came to dinner."

"I'm glad you asked me," Eve replied, and guessed at his loneliness.

She knew he liked her, knew she should be happy about that, but there was a part of her that wished he could be insanely in love with her, wanting her above all other women. She told herself that she was silly to wish for the moon. Here she was with Luck, who looked unbelievably sexy by the glow of the firelight—and any other woman would be thrilled to trade places with her.

"What I'm trying to say is that meeting you was one of the best things that has happened to us in a long while." Luck appeared determined to convince her of something, but Eve wasn't sure what it was.

Again, she couldn't help but notice the way it was always "we" or "us," never "I" or "me." He was linking himself with Toby. It was her effect on "them"—not "him." She lowered her gaze to the cup in her hands.

"I'm handling this badly, aren't I?" His voice held a sigh.

"I can't answer that because I don't know what you're trying to handle," Eve said, attempting to speak lightly but unable to look at him.

"It's really very simple." He curved a hand under her chin and turned it toward him. "I want to kiss you. I've been wanting to do it all evening, but I never found the opening. So I was trying to make one."

Her heart fluttered at the hint of desire in his blue eyes. Luck had finally said "I," and her senses were on a rampage, wild with the promise that the word held. With a total lack of concern for the deliberateness of his actions, he took the coffee cup from her hands and set it on the stone hearth beside his.

Her composure was so rattled that she wondered how Luck could go about this all so calmly. Anticipation had her trembling on the brink of raw longing for his embrace. The sensation was becoming so strong that she didn't think she could hide it.

When his hands closed on her arms to draw her to him, Eve abandoned herself to the moment, ready to go for it. The fire in the hearth was dying, but the one inside her was kindled to a full blaze by the sure possession of his lips.

His hand caressed her hair, holding her head as his driving kiss forced it backward. Her arms went around his middle, her sense of touch excited by the solidness of his muscled body, so hard and virile.

A mist of sensuality swirled itself around her consciousness and made any thought of caution a hazy, ill-defined one. His hand roamed along her spine, alternately caressing and urging her closer. Eve strained to comply and arched nearer. The unyielding wall of his body flattened her breasts, but it wasn't enough.

Her breathing was so shallow she was almost panting. Then Luck took his mouth from her lips to nibble at her throat and kiss the pulsing vein he found there, right up to the sensitive hollow below her ear. Eve quivered with the intensity of the passions he was arousing.

"I've needed this for so long, Eve," he declared in a voice thick with desire, the heat of his breath inflaming her skin. "I've been so empty. Fill me up, Eve. Fill me up."

But she didn't need to be urged. Her hunger and emptiness had been as great as his. Her eagerly parted lips were already seeking his when his mouth came back to claim them. The whole weight of him was behind the kiss, bending her backward farther and farther until she slipped off the pillow onto the carpeted floor.

Within seconds they were lying together, and the hard pressure of his male body was making itself felt on every inch of hers. No longer needing to hold her, his hands were free to explore the soft curves that had been against him.

He stroked her bare belly, arousing a sensual fire deep inside her that was hotter than anything she'd ever felt.

When Luck shifted his position to make a more thorough exploration, a shirt button caught in the eyelet lace of her cropped blouse. He swore under his breath, as impatient with the obstacle as Eve was. There was a reluctant delay as Luck paused to free the button. When his knuckles rubbed against a breast, Eve couldn't help breathing in sharply at the inadvertent contact, a white-hot rush of desire searing through her.

Her reaction didn't go unnoticed. The instant he had dealt with the button, his hand covered her breast and a soft moan of satisfaction trembled from her throat. He kissed the source of the sound and unerringly found the pleasure point at the base of her neck that sent excited shivers over her skin.

With her eyes closed to lock the delirious sensations in her memory, Eve caressed the taut muscles of his shoulders. His deft fingers unfastened the front of her lace top and pushed the material aside. When his hand slipped inside her bra and freed a breast from its confining cup, she arched to him instinctively, wanting more.

"Uh, Dad . . ."

Oh, no. With a gasp, Eve clutched her unbuttoned top together, even though her back was to the door that led into the living room—Toby couldn't have seen anything.

Chapter 8

Toby's voice shattered the erotic moment into a thousand pieces. Both of them froze at the sound of it. Luck reacted swiftly, pulling her even closer to him. Eve had a glimpse of the anger that took over his hard features before he turned his head to glare at Toby.

"What the hell are you doing out of bed?" he demanded harshly.

"I woke up 'cause I was thirsty, so I came out to the kitchen to get a drink," his son explained, unabashed by the intimate scene he had interrupted and apparently oblivious to the awkward situation he was causing.

"You've got two seconds to get into your bed," Luck warned. "Or, so help me, you won't be able to sit down for a month!"

"But I was only wondering—" Toby began to protest, frowning in bewilderment.

"Now!" Luck snapped the word and brought a knee up as if to rise and carry out his threat.

Toby kept his distance and started toward the

hallway, grumbling to himself. "I don't know why you're yelling at me."

"Go to your room and stay there." The line of Luck's jaw was iron hard.

The response from Toby was a loud sigh that signaled compliance. The instant he was out of sight, Luck sat up and combed a hand through his hair before casting a grimly apologetic look at Eve's reddened face. She sat up quickly, half turning from him to button her blouse, mortified by the incident.

"I'm sorry, Eve," Luck sighed heavily.

"It wasn't your fault," she murmured self-consciously, and tried to smooth her rumpled clothes.

She wasn't sure which embarrassed her more—what Toby had seen or what he might have seen if he'd come a few minutes later. She had been ready to go all the way in front of the fire, when they should have been in a room with a door that locked.

"I'm going to have a talk with that boy." Irritation vibrated through his taut declaration.

"You shouldn't be angry with him." Despite the momentary uproar Toby had caused, Eve defended his innocent role in the scene. She scrambled to her feet the minute she was decent, and Luck followed to stand beside her. She was too disconcerted by the incident to meet his eyes squarely, so her sidelong glance fell somewhere short of his face. "Toby didn't mean to do anything wrong."

"I wouldn't be too sure about that," Luck muttered, more to himself, as he sent a hard stare toward the hallway to the bedrooms.

Then he was bringing all of his attention back to her. She stiffened at the touch of his hand on her shoulder. There were still yearnings within her that hadn't been fully suppressed and she didn't want things to get out of hand twice.

"Eve—" he began in a low tone that seemed to echo the emotions she was feeling.

She knew she didn't dare listen to what he wanted to say. "I think you'd better take me home, Luck," she interrupted him stiffly.

Even without looking at him, she sensed his hesitation and trembled inwardly at the thought of trying to resist him if he decided to persuade her to change her mind. She didn't think she had the willpower for a long struggle.

"All right, I will." He gave in grudgingly and removed his hand from her shoulder.

"I think it's best," Eve insisted faintly.

"Of course." There was a clipped edge to his voice. "Give me a minute to tell Toby where I'm going."

"Yes," she murmured.

He moved reluctantly away from her and Eve shuddered uncontrollably when he was out of the room. She had known she wanted him, had even considered the possibility that she was in love with him, but she hadn't guessed at the intensity of those feelings. It was sobering to realize she would probably go that far again, given the opportunity.

When Luck entered the bedroom, Toby looked at him with affronted dignity. Subjecting the kid to a four-star lecture about why it was wrong to spy on people was probably a waste of time. It was all Luck could do to hold on to his temper and not let it rage.

"I'm taking Eve home." The anger was there in his abrupt tone of voice. "When I get back, you and I are going to have a talk."

"Okay," Toby agreed with equal curtness. "But I don't see what you're so uptight about."

"Don't say another word," Luck warned, "or we'll have that talk now."

Toby pressed his lips together in a thin straight line that showed his resentment. Pivoting, Luck walked from the room.

When he rejoined Eve in the living room, Luck noticed with aching regret how withdrawn she seemed. His senses remembered the way she had responded to him without inhibition. He craved it again, but after the way his own son had embarrassed her, he couldn't bring himself to impose his desires on her just to experience that wild feeling she had aroused one more time.

Without a word she turned and walked to the door, avoiding his look.

A raw tension dominated the drive to her parents' lake cottage. Eve sat rigidly in the passenger seat, staring straight ahead. Luck made a couple of attempts at conversation, but her short one-word answers ended them. She felt that she didn't dare relax her guard for a second.

She'd thought fast during the brief time since they'd left his cabin, suddenly realizing that Luck could want to make love to her without being in love with her. Her embarrassment would have been doubled otherwise.

Luck stopped his car behind her father's sedan. This time he switched off the engine and got out to walk around the hood and open her door. He silently accompanied her to the front porch.

"Good night, Luck." Eve wanted to escape in-

Zebra Contemporary

To start your membership, simply complete and return the Free Book Certificate. You'll receive your Introductory Shipment of FREE Zebra Contemporary Romances, you only pay $1.99 for shipping and handling. Then, each month you will receive the 4 newest Zebra Contemporary Romances. Each shipment will be yours to examine FREE for 10 days. If you decide to keep the books, you'll pay the preferred subscriber price (a savings of up to 30% off the cover price), plus shipping and handling. If you want us to stop sending books, just say the word... it's that simple.

FREE BOOK CERTIFICATE

Yes! Please send me FREE Zebra Contemporary romance novels. I only pay $1.99 for shipping and handling. I understand that each month thereafter I will be able to preview 4 brand-new Contemporary Romances FREE for 10 days. Then, if I should decide to keep them, I will pay the money-saving preferred subscriber's price (that's a savings of up to 30% off the retail price), plus shipping and handling. I understand I am under no obligation to purchase any books, as explained on this card.

NAME _____

ADDRESS _____ APT. _____

CITY _____ STATE _____ ZIP _____

TELEPHONE (____) _____

E-MAIL _____

SIGNATURE _____
(If under 18, parent or guardian must sign)

Offer limited to one per household and not to current subscribers. Terms, offer and prices subject to change. Orders subject to acceptance by Zebra Contemporary Book Club. Offer Valid in the U.S. only.

Thank You!

CN026A

Be sure to visit our website at www.kensingtonbooks.com.

Zebra Contemporary Romance Book Club
Zebra Home Subscription Service, Inc.
P.O. Box 5214
Clifton NJ 07015-5214

PLACE
STAMP
HERE

side the cabin without further ado, but he wasn't of the same mind.

His hand caught her arm near the elbow. "I'm not letting you go inside feeling the way you do," he said.

"I'm all right," she lied.

His other hand cupped the side of her face, a grimness in his expression. "I don't want Toby's interference spoiling those moments for us."

"It doesn't matter." Eve tried to evade the issue.

"It does matter," Luck insisted. "It matters a great deal to me."

"Please." She just did not want to discuss the subject.

His hand wouldn't let her move away from its touch. "I'm not ashamed of wanting to make love to you, Eve," he declared. "And I don't want you to be, either."

His bluntness seemed to weaken her knees. After avoiding his gaze for so long, she finally looked at him. His steady regard captured her glance and held it. "Okay?"

"Okay." Her voice was no more than a whisper.

He kissed her warmly as if to seal the agreement, then lifted his head. "You and I will talk about this tomorrow," he said. "In the meantime, I've got to go back and have a father-son talk with Toby."

"All right." Eve wasn't sure what he wanted to talk about, and that uncertainty was in her voice.

Luck heard it and seemed to hesitate before letting her go. "Good night, Eve."

"Good night," she called softly after him as he descended the porch steps to his car.

* * *

Returning to the cabin, Luck went directly to his son's bedroom. He switched on the light as he entered the room. Toby sat up and made a project out of arranging his pillows to lean against them. When Luck walked to the bed, Toby crossed his arms in a gesture that implied determined tolerance.

"Sit down, Dad," he said. "I think it's time we talked this out."

Luck didn't find the usual amusement in his son's pseudoadult attitude and had to smother a rush of irritation. "I'll sit down," he stated. "But I'm going to do the talking and you're going to listen."

"Whatever you say."

Luck counted to ten. "Do you have any idea how much you embarrassed Eve?" he demanded, taking a position on the edge of the bed.

"You kinda lost your cool, too, Dad."

"I said I was going to do the talking," Luck reminded him sternly. "It wasn't so bad that you walked in when you did, Toby. But you shouldn't have stuck around for one more second."

"I wanted to find out what was going on," he explained with wide-eyed innocence.

"It was none of your business," Luck countered. "Grown-ups are entitled to some privacy."

"But you're my dad." *Argue with that*, Toby's expression seemed to say.

"That is beside the point." Luck's gaze narrowed on his son. "Right now, I want you to understand that what you did was wrong and you owe Eve an apology."

"Was what you and Eve were doing wrong?" Toby inquired.

"Toby." His voice held a warning: don't sidetrack the conversation. Toby seemed to get it.

"Okay," he sighed with mock exaggeration. "I'll apologize to Eve," Toby promised. "But since you like Eve that much, you oughta marry her. Why not? Did you find out if she has staples in her stomach?"

"Staples?" Luck frowned, ignoring his son's mention of marriage.

"Don't you remember when we met that real sexy blonde on the trail and you said you didn't want to marry anyone with staples in her stomach?" Toby reminded him.

It took Luck a minute to recall his reference to the centerfold type. "No, Eve isn't the kind with staples," he replied.

"Then why don't you ask her to marry you?" Toby argued. "I'd really like it if she became my mother."

"You would?" He tilted his head to one side. "After what you pulled tonight, she might not be interested in becoming your mother even if I asked her."

A look of guilty regret entered Toby's expression. "She was really upset, huh?" He was worried by the question.

"Yes, she was. Thanks to you." Luck didn't lessen the blame.

"If I told her I was sorry, maybe then she'd say yes if you asked her," Toby suggested.

"I've already told you that you're going to apologize to her in the morning."

"Are you going to ask her to marry you after that?" Toby wanted to know.

"I don't recall even suggesting that I wanted to marry Eve," Luck replied.

"But you do, don't you?" Toby persisted.

"We'll talk about that another time." He avoided a direct answer. "Tonight you just think about what you're going to say to Eve tomorrow."

"Will you think about marrying her?" His son refused to let go of the subject as Luck straightened from the bed. Toby slid under the covers to lie down once again while Luck tucked him in.

"I'll think about it," he conceded.

"Good night, Dad." There was a satisfied note in Toby's voice.

"Good night."

Luck was shaking his head as he walked from the room. After checking to make sure the fire in the fireplace was out, he went to his own room and walked to the dresser where Lisa's photograph stood. He picked it up and studied it for a minute.

"You taught me so much," he murmured to the picture. "What we had, I'll never lose. But I love Eve now. I never thought that would happen again."

He held the photograph for a minute longer, saying a kind of farewell to the past and its beautiful memories. With deep affection he placed the picture carefully inside one of the dresser drawers. He had not believed it possible to fall in love twice in a lifetime, but he had. Once as a young man— and now as a mature adult. By closing the drawer, he turned a page in his life.

A round beverage tray was precariously balanced on Toby's small hand as he quietly turned the knob to open his father's door. The orange juice sloshed over the rim of its glass, but he miraculously managed not to spill the hot coffee. With both hands holding the tray once more, he walked to the bed where his father was soundly sleeping.

When he set the tray on the nightstand, Toby noticed something was missing. His mother's photograph was gone from the dresser. He turned a curious look on his father.

"It's time to get up, Dad." He shook Luck's shoulder to add action to his summons.

His father stirred reluctantly and opened a bleary eye. He closed it again when he saw Toby.

"Come on, Dad." Toby nudged him again. "Wake up. It's seven-thirty. I brought you some orange juice and coffee."

This time both sleepy blue eyes opened and Luck pushed himself into a half-sitting position in the bed. Toby handed him the glass of orange juice and crawled onto the bed to sit cross-legged.

After downing the juice, Luck set the glass on the tray and winked at his son. "You sure are bright-eyed this morning." There was a trace of envy in his sleep-thickened voice.

Toby shrugged. "I've been up awhile. Long enough to make the coffee and have some cereal."

Luck picked up the coffee cup and took a sip from it. "After last night, I think it would be a good idea if you started knocking before walking into somebody's room."

"You mean, so I won't embarrass Eve when she starts sleeping in here after you're married," Toby guessed.

"Yes—" The affirmative reply was out before he realized what he'd admitted. The second Luck realized what he'd said, he came instantly awake.

Toby laughed with glee. "You did decide to marry her!"

"Now, you wait just a minute," Luck ordered, but there wasn't any way he could retract his previous admission. "That doesn't mean Eve is willing to marry me."

"I know." Toby grinned. "You haven't asked her yet. When are you going to propose to her?"

"You will have to apologize for last night," Luck reminded him. "You aren't getting out of that."

"We can go over there this morning, just like we planned." Toby began laying out the strategy. "I'll apologize to her, then you can ask her to marry you."

"No, Toby." His father shook his head. "That isn't the way it's going to happen. We'll go over there and you'll apologize. That's it."

"Ahh, Dad," Toby protested. "You're going to ask her anyway. Why not this morning?"

"Because you don't ask a woman to be your wife while there's an eight-year-old kid standing around listening," his father replied with mild exasperation.

"When are you going to ask her, then?" Toby demanded impatiently.

"I'm going to invite Eve to have dinner with me tonight," he said. "You're going to stay home and I'll have Mrs. Kornfeld come over to sit with you."

"Mrs. Kornfeld?" Toby cried with a grimace of dislike. "She's mean. Why does she have to come over?"

"We've been through this before," Luck reminded him. "You aren't going to stay here by yourself."

"Well, why do you have to go out to dinner with Eve?" he argued. "Why can't she come over here like she did last night? I'll leave you two alone and promise not to listen."

His father sighed heavily and glanced toward

the ceiling. "How can I make you understand?" he wondered aloud. "When a woman receives a marriage proposal, she has a right to expect a few romantic touches along with it—a little wine and candlelight. You don't have her come over, cook dinner, wash dishes, then propose. It just isn't done like that."

"Sure sounds like a lot of trouble," Toby grumbled. "Eve wouldn't mind if you just asked her without going through all that."

"I don't care whether she doesn't mind. I do," Luck stated, and finished the coffee. "Off the bed," he ordered. "I want to get dressed."

"Are we going to Eve's now?" Toby hopped to the floor.

"Not this early in the morning," Luck told him. "We'll wait until later."

"But it's Sunday. She might go to church," he protested.

"Then we'll drive over there the first thing this afternoon."

"Aw, Dad." Toby sighed his disappointment and left the bedroom dragging his feet.

It was noon when Eve and her parents returned to the lake cottage from Sunday church services. Reverend Johnson had preached a sermon on respecting one another, and she had smiled inwardly, wondering if Toby had heard something similar from his father. Luck had been pretty steamed about his young son's intrusion, but once Eve got over her initial shock, she just didn't see any reason to worry about it.

She checked the dinner in the oven, glad that they were able to sit down to the table without making much of a fuss. By one o'clock the dishes were done and Eve went to her room to change out of her good dress.

"Eve?" The questioning call from her mother was accompanied by a knock on the door. "Your father and I are going for a boat ride on the lake. Would you like to come with us?"

Zipping her jeans, Eve went to the door and opened it. "No, thanks, Mom. I think I'll just stay here and finish that book I was reading."

She didn't mention that Luck had indicated he would see her today. No definite arrangement had been made. Eve preferred that her parents didn't know that she was staying on the off chance he might come by or call.

"Is Eve coming with us?" her father asked from the front room.

"No," her mother answered him. "She's going to stay here."

"I'll bet she's expecting Luck McClure," he declared on a teasing note, and Eve felt a faint blush warming her cheeks.

"Don't mind your father," her mother declared with an understanding smile. "He's remembering the way I sat around the house waiting to hear from him when we were dating." She made a move to leave. "We probably won't be back until later this afternoon."

"Have a good time," Eve said.

"You too," her mother called back with a wink.

Chapter 9

Toby was slumped in the passenger seat of the car, a dejected expression on his face. "Boy, I wish Mrs. Kornfeld had been busy tonight." He grumbled the complaint for the sixth time since Luck had phoned her to sit with him.

"She's coming and there's nothing you can do to change that," Luck stated, looking briefly away from the road at his son. "I don't want you pulling any of your shenanigans, either."

Toby was silent for a minute. "Have you thought about how expensive this is going to be, Dad?" He tried another tactic. "You not only have to pay Mrs. Kornfeld to stay with me, but you've also got to pay for Eve's dinner and yours. With the money you're spending tonight, I'd have enough to buy my mountain bike. It sure would be a lot cheaper if you just asked her this afternoon."

"I don't want to hear any more about it." They had hardly been off the subject since this morning, and his patience was wearing thin.

"But don't I have some say in this?" Toby argued. "After all, she is going to be my mother."

"I wouldn't bring that up if I were you," Luck warned. "You haven't squared yourself with Eve about last night. She might not want to be the mother to a boy who doesn't respect other people's privacy." Okay, that was manipulative. What in hell had gotten into him, Luck wondered. Was his relationship with Eve going to affect his relationship with his son? He looked over at Toby, who seemed not to have heard his father's last remark.

"Yes, but I'm going to apologize for that," Toby reasoned. "Eve will understand. I'm just a little kid."

"Sometimes I wonder about that," Luck muttered.

Taking the ice-cube tray out of the freezer, Eve carried it to the sink and popped out a handful of cubes to put in the glass of tea sitting on the counter. The rest she dumped into a plastic container and set it in the freezer for later use. She turned on the cold water faucet to fill the ice-cube tray. The noise made by the running water drowned out the sound of the car pulling into the drive.

As she carried the tray full of water to the refrigerator, she heard car doors slamming outside. Her heart seemed to leap at the sound. In her excitement, Eve forgot about the tray in her hands and started to turn. Water spilled over the sides and onto the floor.

"Damn," she swore softly at her carelessness, and set the tray on the counter. Hurriedly she tore some paper towels off the roll and bent down to sop up the mess. Her pulse raced with the sound of footsteps approaching the cottage. Her haste just seemed to make it take longer to wipe up the spilled water.

A knock rattled the screen door in its frame. She carried the water-soaked wad of paper towels to the sink, a hand cupped under them to catch any drips.

"I'm coming!" Eve called anxiously, and dropped the mess in the sink.

Her glance darted to the screen door and the familiar outline of Luck's build darkened by the wire mesh. She paused long enough to dry her hands on a terry towel and run smoothing fingers over her gleaming brown hair.

There was a wild run of pleasure through her veins as she hurried toward the door. But, not wanting to look like she was trying too hard, she tugged the V neckline of her top up a little. Damn and double damn—the hem popped out of her snug-fitting jeans.

Eve didn't notice the shorter person standing next to Luck until she was nearly at the door, and realized he'd brought Toby with him. Not that she minded; it was just that Luck had indicated he wanted to talk to her privately. After last night's scene, the kid might be feeling awkward around her.

"Hello." She greeted them through the screen and unlatched the door to open it. There was a nervous edge to her smile until she met the dancing warmth of Luck's blue eyes. It eased almost immediately as a little glow started to build strength. "Sorry it took so long, but I had to mop up some water I spilled."

"That's all right. We heard you inside," Luck assured her. The admiring run of his gaze over her face and figure seemed to give her confidence. She could tell he liked what he saw, even if she wasn't the type to turn heads—although she was working on that.

"Hello, Toby." Eve smiled at the young boy as he entered the cottage at his father's side.

"Hi." His response seemed a little more subdued than normal, but his bright eyes were just as alert as always.

"Come in," Eve said. "I just fixed myself a glass of iced tea. Would you two like some?"

Luck seemed about to refuse, but Toby was quick to accept. "Yeah, I'd like a glass."

"And some cookies too?" Eve guessed.

"Chocolate chip?" he asked hopefully, and she nodded. "I sure would."

"What do you say?" Luck prompted his son to show some manners.

"Thank you." Toby frowned. "Or was it supposed to be 'please'?"

"It doesn't matter," Eve assured him with a faint smile. "You've got the idea." Her glance lifted to the boy's father. "Did you want a glass of tea and some cookies?"

"I'll settle for the tea," he replied, changing his mind, probably just to be polite.

The pair followed her into the small kitchen. Toby crowded close to the counter to watch her while Luck stayed out of her way, leaning against the countertop like he owned the place. Eve never lost her awareness of his lean masculinity, even though he wasn't in her line of vision. Her body's finely tuned radar was aware of his presence.

She fixed two more glasses of tea without any mishap and even managed to put the ice-cube tray filled with water in the refrigerator's freezer section without spilling any. Lifting the lid of the cookie jar, Eve took out three chocolate chip cookies and placed them on a paper napkin for Toby.

"Here you go, Toby." She turned to give them to him.

"Wait a minute," Luck stated, and laid a hand on his son's shoulder to stop him from taking them. "Before the refreshments are passed around, there's something Toby wants to say to you, Eve. Isn't there, Toby?" There was a prodding tone in his voice when he addressed his son.

A big sigh came from Toby as he lowered the hand that had reached for the cookies. "Yes," he admitted, and turned his round blue gaze on Eve. "I'm sorry for embarrassing you last night. I didn't mean to."

"I know you didn't." She colored slightly all the same.

"Dad explained about respecting other people's privacy," he said slowly.

Just as she'd thought, he'd gotten a lecture. Eve smiled at him encouragingly. She appreciated Luck insisting that his son apologize and she knew it was never easy for a kid to do that to an adult.

"I was wrong to come into the room without you knowing I was there. I'm really and truly sorry, Eve. All I wanted to do was find out what was going on. I never meant to embarrass you."

Toby was as curious as any other kid—and given the circumstances, she and Luck had avoided the worst-case scenario. They'd kept their clothes on and her back had been to the boy. She'd known all along that Toby hadn't meant any harm. It was obvious he wasn't shocked by what little he'd seen, which really was the most important concern.

"It's all right, Toby," Eve promised him. "You're forgiven, so we can all forget about it."

His blue eyes widened in a hopeful look. "Then you aren't mad or upset?"

"No, not at all," she replied with a shake of her head.

Tipping his head back, Toby turned it to look up at his father. "See?" he said. "I told you she wouldn't be."

"I know you did," Luck admitted. "But she deserved an apology just the same."

"Now will you ask her to marry you instead of—" Toby didn't get the question finished before Luck clamped a hand over his mouth to muffle the rest of it.

An electric shock went through Eve as her gaze flew to Luck's face. Her own complexion had gone pale at Toby's suggestion. There was displeasure in his expression, and Eve knew she had been right to doubt that Toby knew what he was talking about. It seemed she had been catapulted from one awkward situation into another.

"Toby, I oughta ground you," Luck muttered angrily, and took his hand from the boy's mouth. "Don't you dare say another word."

"But—" Toby scowled, not understanding.

"I mean it," Luck interrupted him sternly. "Get your cookies and iced tea and go outside," he ordered. "I don't want to hear so much as a peep out of you."

"Okay," Toby grumbled, and moved to the counter to take the napkin of cookies and a glass of iced tea. Eve was too frozen to help him.

"You stay outside and don't come walking back in," Luck warned. "Remember what you promised me about that."

"Yes, Dad," he nodded, and trudged toward the screen door.

Eve continued to stare at Luck as he rested a hand on the counter, tracing its tilework in a preoccupied way. There was regret in the hard line of his mouth when he finally looked at her. She heard the door bang shut behind the departing Toby.

"I'm afraid my son has a big mouth," Luck said.

A sudden, constricting pain wrenched at Eve's heart. She turned away to hide it, wondering why it hurt to hear what she instinctively knew: Luck wasn't ready to get serious. Maybe because she hadn't imagined that word—marriage—would come up soon . . . if ever. She summoned up a little composure.

"Don't worry about it," she declared with forced lightness. "I was just kind of startled by what Toby said, that's all. I know he wasn't speaking for you."

Her pulse raced as Luck moved to stand behind her. His hands settled lightly on her shoulders. At the moment she wasn't up to resisting his touch. A tremor of longing quivered through her senses.

"Maybe he read my mind," he murmured, very close to her.

She pretended not to understand. "Wh-what do you mean?" Her voice wavered.

"Since Toby has already let the cat out of the bag, I might as well ask you to marry me now, instead of waiting," Luck replied.

She half turned to look at him over her shoulder. He couldn't be serious, but his steady gaze seemed to imply that he was. It didn't seem possible that a sweet dream like that was going to come true. Not that easily.

"Luck, you don't have to do this." That lazy half smile went right through her.

"I know I don't," he agreed.

"Then . . ." Eve continued to hesitate.

"I want you to be my wife," Luck said in an effort to make it clear to her that he *was* serious. It wasn't a joke. "And Toby wants you to be his mother—although I wouldn't blame you if you have second thoughts about taking on that role. He talks when he shouldn't—he sees things he shouldn't—and he knows me too well. It isn't going to be any bed of roses."

"I don't mind." She breathed the reply because she was beginning to believe that he meant all this.

"You'd better be sure about that." He turned her around to face him and let his hands slide down her back to gather her closer to him. "We haven't known each other long. I don't want to rush you into something. If you want to think it over, I'll wait for your answer."

Spreading her hands across the front of his shirt, Eve could feel his body warmth through the material. The steady beat of his heart assured her that this was all real. It wasn't a dream.

"It isn't that." Eve hadn't realized that she hadn't got around to accepting his proposal until that minute. "I'd like to marry you." That sounded so unreal that she hesitated again.

Luck gave her a wary look. "Did I hear a 'but' at the end of that?"

"No." She hadn't said it, not in so many words; yet it was there—silently. "It's just so sudden. I can't think why you'd want to marry me," she admitted at last.

"Will the usual reason do?" A warm dryness rustled his voice. "I love you, Eve."

The breath she drew in became lodged in her throat. She hadn't realized what joyful, beautiful words they were until Luck uttered them. She just looked at him, her eyes misty.

"I love you too," she declared in a voice choked with emotion.

His mouth closed on hers and there was no more need for words. Her hands slid around his neck and into the thickness of his dark hair as his molding arms crushed her to his length. Eve reeled under the hard possession of his kiss, still dazed that he actually wanted her. But he seemed determined to prove it with action as well as words.

When her parted lips were at last convinced, Luck touched her face with light kisses. Her eyes, her brows, her cheeks—he was thorough and infinitely gentle. It left her so weak she could hardly breathe. Her racing heart threatened to burst from the sudden sensation of awakened love.

A sweet yearning throbbed through her limbs. His hands stroked her shoulders, back, and hips to caress and arouse her flesh to a fever pitch of delight. For Eve there was no holding back. She gave him her heart and soul in return—she wanted to be all his.

A faint tremor went through Luck when he lifted his head an inch or so from hers to study her with a heavy-lidded look of desire. "I thought it would take more convincing than this to persuade you to marry me," he said huskily.

"Hardly." Eve smiled at that, knowing she had been his for the taking for a while now.

He withdrew a hand from her back to cup her upturned face. She pressed a kiss in its palm. His fingers traced the curve of her cheekbone to the outline of her lips.

"That night I bumped into you outside the tavern, I knew I didn't want to let you go," Luck murmured. "But I didn't dream that I'd eventually marry you."

Even though the first meeting was a special and vivid memory, Eve wished he hadn't mentioned it. She didn't want to remember that he had regarded her as a brown mouse. She closed her eyes to shut it out.

"I thought you were a figment of my imagination," he went on, and slid his hand to her neck, where his thumb stroked the curve of her throat. "Until I finally recognized you that rainy afternoon you came to help Toby bake cookies. And there you were, right in my own home."

"I remember," Eve said softly, wishing he would talk about something else. She hardly trusted her response to him. Had she been so lonely for so long that she was surrendering unthinkingly now?

Luck drank in a deep breath and let it out slowly. "Before I met you, I was beginning to think I wasn't capable of caring for another woman."

There was an instantaneous image in her mind of the photograph of his first wife. A painful sweep of jealousy washed over her because she would never be first in his life. Eve wasn't sure if she was willing to settle for being second. There was a nagging feeling at the back of her mind that she would be compared to someone else—and never measure up—if she let herself get too close to Luck.

"Toby has been wanting me to get married for some time," Luck told her. "He even chose you before I did. I have to admit my son has very good taste."

Eve managed to smile. "He's still outside—and probably dying of curiosity."

"Let him." His arm tightened fractionally around

her waist. "It's what he deserves." Then Luck sighed reluctantly. "I suppose we should let him in on the news, although he was positive you'd agree to marry me."

"He was right." For a glorious few seconds, she allowed herself to bask in the blue light of his unswerving gaze. So this was adoration—it felt pretty good. Even if it wasn't necessarily going to last.

"He's never going to let us hear the end of it. You know that, don't you?" he said lightly.

"Probably not," Eve agreed ruefully.

"We might as well go tell him."

As he turned to guide her out of the kitchen, he kept his arm curved tightly around her and her body pressed close to his side. It was a very possessive gesture and it thrilled Eve.

When they walked outside, they found Toby sitting on the porch steps waiting patiently—or perhaps impatiently, judging by how quickly he bounded to his feet to greet them. His bright glance darted eagerly from one to the other.

"Did she say yes?" he asked.

"What makes you think I asked her?"

The boy cast an anxious look at Eve, who was trying not to smile. "You did, didn't you?" Again the question was addressed to his father.

"I did." Luck didn't keep him in the dark any longer. "And Eve agreed to be my wife."

"Whoopee!" Toby shouted with glee and practically jumped in the air. "I knew she would!" He had to rub it in. "I told you that you didn't have to wait until tonight, didn't I?"

Luck glanced at Eve to explain. "I was going to do it up right. I had it all planned—to take you out to dinner, ply you with champagne, sway you with candlelight and flowers. Then I was going to propose. Unfortunately, blabbermouth jumped the gun."

"Now you don't have to do that," Toby said. "And I don't have to stay with Mrs. Kornfeld. Eve can come over to our place tonight and we'll all have dinner together."

Luck shook his head. "No, she can't."

"Why can't she come?" Toby crossed his arms over his puny chest and frowned.

"Because I'm taking her out to dinner just the way I planned," he said. "And Mrs. Kornfeld is coming over to stay with you just as we arranged it."

"Da-ad," came the inevitable protest.

"I'm going to have to share her with you a lot of evenings in the future, but on the first night of our engagement, I'm going to have her all to myself," Luck declared.

"I'd stay in my room," Toby promised.

"That isn't the same," he insisted, and looked again at Eve. "You will have dinner with me tonight if I promise you you won't have to cook it?"

"Yes." Even if she had to cook it, she would have agreed.

"I'll come over early, around seven, so I can talk to your parents." Luck smiled as he realized, "I haven't asked you—how soon would you like the wedding to be?"

"Uh—*what?*" His phrasing of the question—not "when" but "how soon"—nearly took her breath away. For a second she could only look at him, confused love shining in her eyes.

"The sooner the better, don't you think?" she suggested, wondering if she had lost her mind. Had she, Eve, mouse extraordinaire, just hinted that she expected him to marry her right away? As if there were a few other handsome princes who just weren't going to wait indefinitely for their answer?

"Absolutely." His agreement was very definite as he bent his head to claim her lips once more.

What started out as a brief kiss lingered. Eve leaned more heavily against him, letting his strength support her. Before passion could flare, they were reminded that they weren't alone.

"I have a question," Toby said, interrupting their embrace.

"What is it?" But Luck was more than a little preoccupied with his study of her soft lips.

"Am I supposed to leave you two alone every time you start kissing?" he asked.

"Not necessarily every time. Why?" Luck dragged his gaze from her face to glance at his son.

"If I did, it just seems to me that I might be spending an awful lot of time by myself," Toby sighed. "And I'd really kinda hoped the three of us could be together like a family."

"Believe me," Eve assured him. "You won't be spending much time alone." She didn't want to speak to his natural need for a family. Considering how unreal all this seemed, the last thing she wanted to do was see Toby get too attached just yet—in case this beautiful, crazy feeling didn't last in the real world.

"Eve's right." Luck reached out to put an arm around his son's shoulders and draw him into their circle. "Part of the plan was for you to have a mother, wasn't it?"

"Yep." Toby smiled widely.

"But don't tell anyone yet, son."

The little boy put his hand over his heart. "I promise. I don't want to jinx this."

Chapter 10

The three of them spent the afternoon together, just talking and hanging out. Eve knew she was just imagining it, but the sun seemed to shine brighter and the air smelled fresher than it ever had before.

Her parents hadn't returned from their boat ride by the time Luck and Toby left to go home. Eve had some time alone to think over the unexpected proposal and all that had been said. She finally came out of the wonderful daze that had numbed her and pondered a few home truths.

Luck had asked her to marry him for many reasons. He had said that he loved her, and she didn't doubt that in his own way he did. But a previously married man with a child came with emotional baggage, no matter how good and loving his intentions were. Was she ready for all that? Eve had to admit that she really didn't know—and she told herself that the answer to that compelling question wasn't a nice, neat yes or no.

Another factor was Toby: he had needed and

wanted a mother, and he really liked her. Doing things with him and his dad was one thing, and as easy as pie, but was she ready to be a mother? That Toby assumed as much undoubtedly had a lot of influence on Luck's decision. Only natural. It must have been incredibly difficult for him to be both father and mother to his son and work through his own grief and sense of loss.

And Eve had understood at once he was a lonely man. He wanted the company of a woman and not just in a sexual way. But she was sure he could find that easily enough. That night in front of the tavern, Luck had said he wanted to talk to her—that she was the kind he could talk to. He needed that in a woman, just as she needed to be able to talk to him. But part of his reason for proposing had to be the desire for companionship.

There was nothing wrong with any of his reasons. None of them were bad. As a matter of fact there were a lot of couples starting out their wedded life with less solid foundations than theirs. But the realizations brought Eve down out of her dreamworld to face the reality of their future. Luck wanted to marry a comfortable, practical Eve, not a starry-eyed romantic. Meaning that he really did want the brown mouse.

And just when she was getting up to speed on her magical transformation. Eve sighed.

Well, it didn't alter the special significance of the evening to come. It was still their engagement dinner. And being engaged, if they were going to call it that, meant they were giving themselves time to think things through before rushing into marriage.

She was glad that she'd found a man who wasn't deathly afraid of commitment, come to think of it.

Maybe being married once meant that it didn't seem so scary the second time around. His second. Her first.

Eve took extra care in choosing a dress to wear and fixing her hair and makeup. The results weren't too bad, even to her critical eye. The rose color of the dress was a little drab, but its lines flattered her slender curves. Her soft chestnut hair was almost back to its natural state, sans expensive highlights. Not that he had ever specifically noticed them—or the other subtle changes in her appearance.

True to his word, Luck arrived promptly at seven, with a bouquet of scarlet roses for Eve. She hadn't mentioned anything to her parents about his proposal, waiting until he came so they could tell them together.

They were overjoyed at the news, especially her mother, who had remarked once too often that Eve would never find a man to satisfy her. Her father seemed to take pride in Luck's old-fashioned gesture of asking his permission to marry his daughter. It was granted with a lordly wave of the paternal hand—and a wink at his wife.

By half-past seven the congratulations were over and they were driving to the restaurant. Eve realized how difficult it was to stay rational when she was with Luck. Her hand rested on the car seat, held in the warm clasp of his.

"Are you happy?" he asked.

"Yes." She could say that without any doubt, even with the facts before her concerning his reasons for wanting to marry her.

"I thought we could drive to Duluth sometime soon," he said. "I need to buy you a ring, unless you want to wait."

"I-I'm not sure," she said hesitantly.

"Then we can hold off on that. Whatever you want."

Eve nodded.

"I want you to meet my father eventually." It was his turn to hesitate. She didn't know why.

"That would be good," she agreed. "I'd like to get to know him."

"You'll like him." He sent her a brief smile. "And I have no doubt that he'll like you."

"I hope so." Would his father compare her with Luck's first wife and wonder what his son saw in plain old her? Eve fretted inwardly. His friends who had known Lisa would probably wonder about that, also. She wouldn't blame them if they did.

"Would you mind if Toby came with us when we visit my father?" Luck asked as he slowed the car to turn into the restaurant parking lot.

"Of course I don't mind," Eve assured him. "If we don't include him, he'll probably become convinced he's being neglected."

"That's what I thought, too." He parked the car between two others.

After climbing out of the car, Luck walked around it to open her door and help her out. He lingered on the spot, holding her hand and smiling at her.

"Have I told you that you're beautiful tonight?" he asked.

"No, but thank you." Eve smiled, but she wondered if he was just being kind. Perhaps it was a nice way of saying she looked as good as she could look.

Bending his head, he let his mouth move warmly over hers. The firm kiss didn't last long, but it reassured her of his affection. Eve doubted if that brief kiss disturbed him as much as it disturbed her, though.

When it was over, he escorted her to the restaurant entrance, his hand pressed against the back of her waist. Inside they were shown to a small table for two in a quiet corner of the establishment.

"Didn't I promise you candlelight?" Luck gestured to the candle burning in an amber glass when they were both seated in their chairs across from each other.

"Yes, you did." The memory made her smile. "You neglected to mention the soft music playing in the background. Easy listening for that special someone." Eve referred to the muted strains of romantic mood music coming over the restaurant's audio system.

"I saved that for the finishing touch." The corners of his mouth curved in amusement.

A young and very attractive waitress approached their table. With her blond hair and blue eyes, she seemed the epitome of everything sexy, without being trashy in any way. She smiled at both of them, yet Eve jealously thought she noticed something other than professional interest in the girl's eyes when she looked at Luck.

"Would you care for a drink before dinner?" she inquired.

"Yes, we'd like a bottle of champagne," Luck said with a responding smile.

Eve would probably have checked his pulse to see if he was sick if he hadn't noticed the blonde's obvious beauty. Yet when he did she was hurt. It made no sense at all. Somehow she managed to keep the conflicting emotions out of her expression.

The waitress left and came back with the bottle of champagne. After she had opened it, she poured some in a glass for Luck to sample. He nodded his approval and she filled a glass for each of them.

When she'd gone, Luck raised his glass to make a toast. "To the love of my life, who is soon to be my wife."

It was a very touching sentiment, but Eve knew it was an exaggeration. He had promised her a romantic evening and he was trying to give it to her. But minute by minute, she was getting more skittish. And she wanted their relationship to be honest.

"That was very beautiful, Luck," she admitted. "But it wasn't necessary."

"Oh?" His eyebrow arched at her comment. "Why isn't it necessary?"

"Because"—she shrugged a shoulder a little nervously —"I don't expect you to pretend that you are wildly and romantically in love with me. You don't have to make flowery speeches."

"I see." The line of his jaw became hard, even though he smiled. "And it doesn't bother you if I'm not wildly and romantically in love with you?" There was a trace of challenge in his question.

"I've accepted it." Eve didn't want him to act the part of a romantic lover unless that was what he truly felt.

"I'm glad you have," he murmured dryly, and motioned for the waitress to bring them menus. "I understand the prime rib is very good here."

The dinner conversation was dominated by mundane topics. The meal was enjoyable, yet Eve sensed some underlying tension. Luck was pleasant and friendly, but sometimes when he looked at her she felt even more uneasy. He'd always been able to get to her physically, yet this was different—almost as if he were angry, though he didn't appear to be.

The dinner had stretched to a second cup of coffee after dessert before Luck suggested it was time to leave. Eve accepted his decision, still unable to put her finger on the source of the troubling sensation.

In silence they crossed the parking lot to the car. Luck assisted her into the passenger seat, then walked behind the car to slide into the driver's seat. He made no attempt to start the car.

Eve folded her hands in her lap and looked down at them. "Is something wrong?"

"There seems to be," he said with a nod, and turned in the seat to face her.

"What is it?" She wasn't sure if he meant something was wrong with the car or something else.

"You," Luck answered simply.

"What have I done?" She drew back in surprise.

"Where did you get this ridiculous notion that I'm not wildly in love with you?" he demanded.

"Well, you're not," Eve said defensively, then faltered under his piercing gaze. "I believe you when you say you love me, but—"

"That's good of you, Eve. If I'm not madly in love with you, maybe you should explain why I want to marry you. I'm sure it has something to do with Toby."

"Why are you asking me?" Eve countered. "You know the reasons as well as I do."

"Sure do, since they happen to be mine." Luck stretched an arm along the seat back and appeared to relax. "But I'd like to hear you tell me what they are."

"I can provide some of the things that are missing in your life," she said uneasily, not sure why he wanted her to explain, unless it was to make sure she understood.

"Such as?"

"You need a mother for your son, someone to take care of your house and do the cooking, someone to care about you and be there when you want company . . ." Eve hesitated.

"You left out bed partner," he reminded her coolly.

"That too," she conceded.

"I'm glad. For a minute I thought I was hiring a full-time housekeeper instead of acquiring a wife." This time some of his anger crept into his voice.

"I . . . .don't understand," Eve stammered.

"Listen up. There is only one reason why I'm marrying you. I love you and I don't want to live without you!" Luck snapped.

"But Toby—"

"I haven't done too bad a job raising him alone. If he's managed without a mother this long, then he can make it the rest of the way," he retorted. "I mean, I'm glad the two of you like each other, but I wouldn't give a damn if he hated you as long as I loved you."

"But I thought—" Eve tried again to voice her impressions, and again Luck interrupted her.

"As for the cooking and cleaning, I can hire someone to do that. Believe me, I can afford it, especially if that was what you wanted."

"You admitted you were lonely," she said quickly before he could cut her off again. "You said it was lonely at home that night outside the tavern."

"So I did," Luck admitted. "Eve, a man can have a hundred women living in his house and still be lonely if none of those women is the right one."

"Please." She turned her head away, afraid of being convinced by him. "I know how much you loved your first wife."

"Yes, I *loved* Lisa"—he stressed the verb—"but it's in the past tense, Eve. I *did* love her, but I love *you* now. It's completely different."

"I know that," she murmured with a little ache.

"Do you?" Luck sighed behind her, then his hands were turning her toward him. "I loved her as a young man. I'm not the same person anymore. I've changed. I've grown up a lot—I had to. Eve, I want you and I want to love you as only a man can—wildly, deeply, and romantically."

"Luck." Eve held her breath, finally beginning to believe it could be true.

"Come here." He smiled and began to gather her into his arms. "I want to prove it to you."

She could hardly argue when his mouth was covering hers with such hungry force. And she didn't want to anymore. But they still had a long way to go and a lot of things to talk about . . . .not that they were going to do much talking tonight.

Chapter 11

Two weeks later . . .

"I can't put Squirmy on a hook. I feel like I know him." Toby looked at the big worm that wriggled between his finger and thumb, then circled his grubby fingers around it and tucked it into the pocket of his polo shirt.

Luck sighed. "Toby, is that the worm from the strawberry farm? Did you bring him home?"

The little boy nodded. "I let the caterpillars go. But I kept him in a can of dirt."

"Aha. That would be the can I just found in the picnic basket. Stupid me. I assumed you'd brought along a little extra bait."

Eve wanted to laugh but seeing the stern look on Luck's face, she managed not to.

"I wanted a pet."

"I told you to let him go. That wasn't nice to the worm," Luck said.

"Well, putting him on a hook isn't very nice either, Dad."

They had been drifting on the lake, trailing lines in the water in the hopes of catching something. They'd started out with frozen bait: chunked-up small fish that smelled terrible. But something swimming down there thought they were tasty and had eaten all the chunks off the hooks in no time.

Something big, according to Toby. He'd been talking a blue streak from the minute his father stopped the motor: the muskie was going to be a record-breaker, he was going to have it mounted for his bedroom wall, his grandfather would be impressed.

But when it came to the moment of truth, he couldn't bring himself to put a worm on a hook. Eve hoped Luck wasn't going to give his son a be-a-man speech.

Instead, he looked down at Toby and said, "Fish gotta swim. Worms gotta wriggle."

Toby nodded. He didn't look at Eve, who hadn't known that he'd sneaked his pet worm into the picnic basket.

"All right. Put Squirmy back in the can. Maybe we can catch a muskie with cheese balls." He kneeled down to rummage around in the tackle box, and pulled out a jar of small, bright orange spheres, rubbing a fingertip over the peeling label. "Hm. These are kinda old. But that's all we have left." He shot a look at his son. "Now if I catch a fish, you understand it's not a pet, right?"

"Yeah. The difference is that I don't know the fish. But I know Squirmy."

Luck grinned at Eve. "Sounds like a song, doesn't it?"

"Yes, it kinda does." She watched Toby cross the deck and lift the lid of the picnic basket, then take out an old bread bag. That's why she hadn't noticed the stowaway. He took Squirmy out of his shirt pocket and put him in the can inside the bread bag. He shoved the basket back into the shade to keep the food and his worm cool.

Luck unscrewed the jar and took out a cheese ball, sticking it carefully on the empty hook on the line that his son had just reeled in. "Yummy yummy. A delicious hundred-year-old cheese ball. Let's see if that works."

Toby held his pole over the gunnels of the boat, unreeling the line, then settling back into the small chair that was his. He squinted under his baseball cap, watching the surface of the water for a telltale bubble.

Eve stifled a yawn. The only thing more boring than fishing was watching fishing. Her hook had been picked clean right away and she hadn't bothered to put anything else on it.

Luck had kept rebaiting his with the frozen fish chunks. He reeled in his line to check it. The hook was empty. With a wink at Eve, he added a cheese ball from the jar and set his rod down without putting the hook and line back in the water. "Having fun yet?"

"Huh—oh, yes. Definitely."

Toby turned around and flashed her a proud smile. "Got a nibble. Maybe this time—" His rod bent over in a tense arc and he pulled back. "Dad!"

"Set the hook! Then reel him slow!" Luck put his hands over Toby's to show him how. Whatever had taken the hook was heavy and pulling hard. She stayed on her side of the boat with the two of them on the other, envisioning it tipping over if she went to see.

She heard a splash. Then Luck and Toby laughed as their catch swung free of the water. It was a waterlogged tennis shoe full of mud—and one cheese ball.

"Shoot!" Toby declared. "After all this time, one old shoe!"

Luck reached out to catch it as it swung in midair, while Toby hung onto his rod and reel. "Sorry about that, kiddo." He got it, drained the mud, and cut the line to the hook, then threw the shoe back into the water. "Better luck next time."

Toby looked disgusted. "Huh. The heck with it." He set down his rod and went over to the picnic basket. "I'm tired of feeding fish."

"Help yourself," Eve said. She was content to sit in the sun, enjoying the slight rocking of the boat and the lapping of the water at its sides, and she knew Toby would pick out the sandwich and drink he wanted. Luck crossed to stand beside him, ready to do the same thing.

"You ready to eat, Eve?"

"No, thanks. You two go ahead."

It was nice to know that she didn't have to wait on them. In their own way, Luck and his son really were used to taking care of themselves. They set out their lunch on paper plates and began to eat but not before giving her, the provider of the feast, smiles of pure affection.

Eve smiled back. It was a perfect summer day, with the timeless feeling she remembered from her childhood, as if summer had only just begun and was going to last forever. Then a brief memory of last winter came back to her—the same vista but shrouded in white and achingly cold—and she shivered a little. The loneliness of that time had vanished since Luck had come into her life. She hoped it would stay gone forever. Imagining spending the seasons, and the holidays that marked their passing, with Luck and his son, was something that warmed her more than the sun beating down from above.

The intense green of the surrounding woods was reflected in the lake waters, and she could hear the distant shouts of swimmers and other boaters. An occasional flash of metal deep in the forest caught her eye—there were miles of mountain bike trails throughout the area and probably a lot of bikers out on them.

Toby went back to the picnic basket and found the cookies that she made, holding one in his mouth while he took three more. Unable to talk, he shot her a guilty look for taking so many, as if he'd forgotten that she was right there watching him.

"Wash those down with a little milk, pal," she said with a smile. He nodded and took a small plastic bottle of milk with his free hand, then went to sit by his dad again. Luck finished off his sandwich, and held out a hand for his share of the dessert. With a sigh and a put-upon look, his son surrendered two of the cookies, then went back for two replacements.

If she had to make a list of the really good things in life, homemade chocolate chip cookies would be near the top. Watching two hungry McClures devour them was a very satisfying feeling.

And the loving look in Luck's eyes was another good thing. Eve felt herself blush under his gaze. She got up from her chair and walked around, tugging her shorts down so he didn't get too much of a show from where he was sitting.

Luck turned to look at Toby, whose mouth was filled with cookies.

"You look like a hamster," Luck said to him, uncapping the plastic bottle of milk for his son.

The boy chewed and swallowed, then took a long swig. "Mmm. That's Eve's fault."

"Don't forget to thank her."

Toby held up the bottle of milk in an impromptu salute. "Thanks, Eve!"

"You're welcome."

He patted his stomach. "Full up. Okay if I take a nap, Dad?"

Luck tried not to look too pleased. "Sure. Want to stretch out on the cabin bench?"

Toby nodded. "Then we can do more fishing later."

"You bet." He got up to make his son comfortable inside the small cabin, and Eve waited outside, hearing the padded bench top lift, then close, as Luck took out a blanket and pillow from the storage area under it.

He came out carrying two lightweight mats, and unrolled one with a flourish, handing it to her.

"Might as well do the same, right?"

Eve set her mat in the sun and stretched out on it as Luck eyed her appreciatively. Feeling a little uncomfortable under his gaze, she flung an arm over her eyes to block out the bright light, which made her T-shirt rise up. The sun felt pleasantly warm on her bare skin. She heard him sigh, then put a mat down next to hers and stretch out as well.

"Not like we can fool around," he said with amusement. "So let's talk."

"Mmm . . . okay." She wasn't sure she wanted to.

"You're a good sport, you know that? Getting up early to go fishing without a word of complaint."

"Wouldn't be the first time, Luck. My dad has spent half his life in pursuit of the mighty muskellunge, like almost every guy in Wisconsin."

"Mine too."

She raised her arm and turned her head to look at him. "Tell me about him. You've never said much about your parents."

Luck hesitated. "Well, my mom passed away when I was a teenager. They had an old-fashioned kind of marriage. He was in charge of everything, and she pretty much went along with that." He was silent for a minute. "Not what I want out of a relationship, believe me. People should be able to grow."

"Glad to hear it," she said wryly. "Especially since I'm not done growing up."

He reached out and stroked the section of bare tummy between the waistband of her shorts and the bottom of her T-shirt. "You're not? You look nice and grown up to me."

Eve didn't push his hand away. "I moved back in with my parents after I got out of college. I've never been on my own."

"Oh."

She wasn't sure whether he was listening to her or plotting further exploration under her T-shirt.

"Do you want to be, Eve?"

She didn't exactly know how to answer that. "We got engaged in such a hurry. It makes me wonder if I—if we—ought to think about it more. And I could find a place to be, um, alone." Uh-oh, she thought. That means no announcement. No ring.

Luck gave her tummy a pat and withdrew his hand. She missed it immediately. His touch was soothing and sensual—and very distracting. But she had been thinking off and on about what she might lose if she went from being the Rowlands' daughter to Luck's wife without ever having tried to live by herself.

Her parents were probably eager to have their house and the summer cottage all to themselves. Sure, her mom would make the obligatory honey-you-don't-have-to speech and her dad would be typically overprotective, but when it came down to it, they would have to agree. In any case, the decision would be hers alone to make.

"I think you should give it a go."

Eve sat up and stared at him. "Are you kidding?"

Luck shook his head. "No. I have to be really sure that marrying me is what you want. Toby thinks we're all going to be a happy family just like that, but he's eight years old. Marriage is a big commitment and a lot of responsibility, especially if someone else's kid is involved. If you feel like you need to be on your own for a while before that happens, then go for it. We haven't told anyone but Toby, and I made sure he would keep it a secret."

His expression was completely serious. But not angry, not at all. He genuinely understood a need she hadn't even been aware of until very recently, and hadn't been able to express in so many words.

And she couldn't come up with any now. Instead, Eve bent down and touched her lips to his in a grateful kiss.

He must have been expecting that, because he wrapped his arms around her and made her stay where she was. Eve struggled to stretch out again, half-laughing, half-kissing him.

Once she was by his side, he took the liberty of running a strong hand over the swell of her hip—

and her backside too. They were as close as two people with clothes on could get, a little too warm in the brilliant sunshine but neither of them cared. His mouth sought hers, opening her lips with his tongue, which ventured inside until Eve was breathless.

She pulled her head back, gasping a little, and he seized the opportunity to nibble the side of her neck, bestowing sensual kisses on her skin and reaching up to cup her breasts.

Eve ached for him, wanted him to do more. Being held in Luck's arms, even if it meant getting hot and sticky in the summer sun, was bliss. But she was well aware of the boy napping in the boat cabin. Toby might be lulled for the moment by the slight motion of the boat and the lunch he'd devoured but he wouldn't be indefinitely.

They both heard small, sneakered feet hit the floor of the cabin, and they rolled apart, looking up into the cloudless blue sky and laughing.

"What's so funny?" Toby came out on deck, rubbing his sleepy eyes.

"Oh, nothing," Luck said. "Eve and I were just wondering how, uh—how Squirmy liked being on the water."

Toby looked worried. "I shouldn't have brung him. A fishing trip is like death row for worms."

"Yeah, but he got a last-minute reprieve," Luck pointed out. "Must be his lucky day."

The boy nodded. "Are there any more cookies?"

"Look in the basket," Eve said with a smile. "And say hello to Squirmy for me."

Toby complied, and Luck scrambled to his feet, reaching out a hand to pull Eve to hers.

"Let's head in, crew. We're out of bait and I think the fish in this lake are smarter than we are."

Eve rolled up their mats and Luck took his son with him into the cabin. She sat in the back, refreshed by the breeze and feeling lighthearted.

"So where do you want to live?" Luck asked. He'd bought a county map of the land within a fifty-mile radius and laid it out on her parents' dining room table. They were out for the evening, visiting Bunky and Miriam again for a killer game of penny poker. As Eve had suspected, they seemed to think that living on her own for a while was a good idea, although her dad hadn't been certain she'd be able to afford it.

But her plan to rent seemed sensible to him—a small house in a small town in Wisconsin was still within the budget of a freelance music teacher. The biggest obstacle was finding the right place. So far, nothing. Her mother thought that she'd have better luck by early September, which seemed to be when everyone moved.

But she'd already looked at a few just outside of Cable with a local real estate agent. One, a charming Victorian with gingerbread trim, had an ancient furnace and turn-of-the-century storm windows. Her father had pointed out bluntly that neither would serve to keep her warm, and she didn't want to pay more for heating than she did in rent.

Another she'd seen on her own had been a definite no. She'd stood in the sunny upstairs bedroom and listened to the unmistakable sound of squirrels scampering in the attic. Eve remembered the countless stratagems her parents had employed to rid their own house of squirrels without hurting them—and the way the ungrateful critters had repaid their kindness by chewing through the phone wires.

It was nice of Luck to help her. He'd taken most of the summer off, one of the privileges of working in his father's company, and he didn't see any reason not to take advantage of it. With Toby at sleepaway camp, they were enjoying the time to themselves.

Luck tapped on the map. "I took a detour down this road yesterday. There was a house for rent near where it forks. Nice little place, about five acres. Kitchen garden, flower garden. Most of it's in pasture. Looked like they had a few cows."

"I'm a music teacher," she reminded him, "I don't have time to take care of cows."

"Well, they might not come with the deal," he said with a grin. "But maybe they do. Rent-A-Cow. I like that idea."

"Why?" Eve hadn't belonged to 4-H or anything like that. Music had interested her much more, although she'd gone to plenty of county fairs and admired the prizewinning goats and sheep and pigs and calves—it was a Wisconsin tradition. But she'd preferred to admire the animals from a safe distance when she was a kid, keeping the cotton candy she loved away from their curious lips ever since the summer when a billy goat snatched the treat out of her hand and ate it, spun sugar, paper stem, and all.

"Because it tickles me. Do I have to have a better reason than that?"

"No." She smiled and came over to look at the map. "So where is this place?"

Luck put an arm around her waist and pulled her onto his lap. "Right here."

Eve settled in, enjoying the feel of his muscular

thighs under her butt. She wriggled, trying to turn him on . . . .and succeeded.

"Stop that," he growled. "It's almost six."

"So?"

"We could drive out and look, but not if you want to fool around. The real estate office closes at six-thirty."

"Okay, okay," Eve sighed. She got up and adjusted her clothes, smiling at him. Clearly, it was all he could do to restrain himself. But she did appreciate his help with her decision to live on her own—and his willingness to wait.

Just as Luck had said, the farmhouse was a nice place. Its owner, Hannah Gunderson, was proud of the improvements her late husband had made, pointing out the new furnace the way some people would point out a new grand piano. Her grown sons had put in raised beds for her, making it easy for her to tend her kitchen garden well into old age.

Something Eve could see herself doing, soaking up the sun while she was at it. It would be a cheaper way to keep highlights in her hair, not that she would mind going back to Lurleen one of these days.

But living in a small farmhouse didn't require her to be a glamour-puss. She could just be . . . herself. On her own at last. She could do all right with a little luck, she thought absently, then smiled, remembering when and how that phrase had been explained to her. She thought it over, admiring the round melons ripening on their stems and the last of the beefsteak tomatoes, streaky red and green.

Everything looked perfect, not a bruised spot or nibble in sight. Her boys, as Mrs. Gunderson called them, had also built fences that kept out marauding critters, so her efforts were not in vain.

They cared for the house too, which boasted its original wooden clapboard siding, scraped and painted annually, and in excellent condition, considering the harshness of Wisconsin winters. Set on a slight rise, it was sheltered by a windbreak of massive old trees. A hammock hung motionless between two of them, set exactly where the best view of the surrounding countryside was to be had.

Eve took a deep breath of the fragrant, late-summer air and looked out at the patchwork of neat fields. They were dotted with other farmhouses and the red barns and small silos typical of a rural landscape.

She glanced at the cows, which were clustered at one side of the paddock and mooing to each other. Mrs. Gunderson had explained that her neighbor saw to their care and feeding, got them in and out of the barn each day, and had been doing it since her first visit to her ailing sister in Milwaukee. The visit Mrs. Gunderson planned this time would be much longer, at least nine months' duration.

Eve guessed—correctly, as it turned out—that Mrs. Gunderson's sister was undergoing chemotherapy for cancer. She was eager to find someone reliable who would care for her house in her absence, and it was clear that she thought Eve would be ideal.

Mrs. Gunderson had been pleased when Eve played a few chords on her fine old upright, praising its mellow tone and how well it had been kept

in tune. She showed them all over the house and
the outside more than once, then went inside,
telling Luck and Eve to stroll around before a decision was made. Mrs. Gunderson had seemed to
understand that they wouldn't be living together—
Eve had made that plain, although the words came
awkwardly.

"What do you think, Eve?"

"It's so homey—and so pretty. It's not a great big
commitment in terms of money. And I wouldn't
be too far from my parents or my students." Her
dad had promised her a good used car, so that was
taken care of. "Or the church or the school."

"Or me," Luck pointed out. Though his year-
round house was outside of Cable, the driving distance on well-maintained county roads wasn't
anything to worry about. "I can come out whenever. Me and Toby," he amended. "We could get
you set up here before school starts."

"Right," she said softly. "Toby would love the barn.
Did you see that big orange cat with the white
belly? I think she's about to have kittens."

Luck gave her hand a squeeze. "And the cows
are taken care of, so long as you don't mind Joe
Farmer coming by a couple of times a day."

"I don't mind a bit."

They stood together near the hammock, and
Eve wished she could just jump in it with him and
swing the afternoon away.

She turned when she heard Mrs. Gunderson
open an upstairs window. "Yoo-hoo! Go ahead and
test drive it!"

They couldn't very well say no to an offer like
that. The shrewd old lady undoubtedly knew that
it was likely to clinch the deal.

"That hammock is my favorite place in the

summertime. Once my chores are done, I settle into it with a murder mystery and I don't get out until I find out who done it."

She shut the window with a smile and drew the curtain, leaving the young people alone to enjoy the hammock however they saw fit.

Chapter 12

The last days of summer . . .

With Mrs. Gunderson's help, Eve had settled in quickly. She was glad not to have to decorate, and the older woman's homespun taste in décor suited her just fine. Every one of the antique quilts on the beds came with an explanation, of course, and so did the sepia-colored photographs of previous generations of Gundersons and Thorvalds, looking down benignly from the walls.

The bedroom Eve had chosen for her own was done in white wainscoting, with a matching head-board that the late Mr. Gunderson had built out of the leftovers. The two square pillars at either side framed a heap of rose-pink pillows atop a quilt that the older woman's grandmother had made. Faded but still pretty after all the years, the quilt was a sweet touch of tradition in a room that was otherwise the most modern in the house.

Being on her own was a novel sensation. At first the unfamiliar noises of the old place had spooked her, but she'd come to realize that it had been lived in for so long by a happy family that had rushed up its stairs and flung open its doors and bounced on its beds that the house had its own voice.

She thought about composing something that would capture it, something she had been wanting to do. Trying out bits and pieces of melody this way and that, over and over, was apt to drive her dad crazy, but there wasn't any other way to write music. It would be a challenge and one she was looking forward to.

As old as the house was, its owners had put a lot of thought into making it a pleasant place to live. And every time she turned around, some useful contrivance hammered or built by the late Mr. Gunderson caught her eye. With a farm wife's efficiency, Mrs. Gunderson had insisted that Eve use up the meat in the freezer and the preserves and pickles in the pantry, saying something about not being able to take it all to Milwaukee with her. Eve had smiled her acceptance. Luck and Toby would have to pitch in and chow down. She couldn't eat twenty jars of blue-ribbon piccalilli, not in a mere nine months, without a couple of hungry McClures to help her.

The first jar was going to be opened for dinner tonight, at Toby's insistence. He had visited the pantry right after he'd come back from sleepaway camp, impressed by the tall jars full of fruit and vegetables and jellies and jam on the shelves. According to Luck, the boy hadn't stopped talking about it since and had been begging for a dinner invitation. That morning, Eve had gone out to the freezer on the enclosed back porch and selected a small brisket to defrost, admiring Mrs. Gunderson's neat handwriting. Wrapped, labeled, and dated, there was enough beef for a year.

She couldn't bring herself to even think about eating any of the chickens that patrolled the garden when they got into it, joyfully pecking at bugs and giving wild squawks of indignation when she shooed them out. Her neighbor, Joe Farmer, whose real name was Arvid Bergen, had offered to do the honors in case she wanted to roast one for Sunday dinner. Eve had politely declined.

A car pulled into the driveway and she looked out the window. Luck and Toby were early, but that was good. The little boy still loved to help her cook, and as for Luck, he got to do the dishes. A traditionalist when it came to keeping house, Mrs. Gunderson had never installed a dishwasher.

Eve went out the side door to greet them. Toby was already on his way to say hello to the cows. Luck waved to her but followed his son. The biggest cow sidled over to the fence, chewing its cud and studying the boy to determine if he was friend or foe.

Eve walked after them, bringing up the rear of the parade. She took note of the calm expression on the cow's face as it finished chewing—at least she thought it was calm. Reading the minds of cows was not something she was very good at. She had come to the conclusion that they just were not very intelligent, although she had read somewhere that they appreciated music. Maybe Arvid got out his fiddle and played to them sometimes, but he probably wouldn't tell her if he did.

Toby reached the fence first and clambered up. The cow swung its heavy head in his direction, then stuck its long tongue up one nostril, and then the other. "That's disgusting," the boy said, a note of awe in his voice.

Luck laughed, putting his arm around Eve's shoulders as she caught up to him. "Don't even think about trying it, son," he called.

"Da-ad!"

Luck waited until the boy turned around to watch the other cows cross the field just to make sure they hadn't missed out on some treat, taking slow, squelching steps through the cowpies amid the scrubby grass.

"Gross," Eve heard Toby say. But Luck was kissing her quickly while he had a chance and her eyes closed. She wasn't aware of much more than how good it felt to be circled by his strong arms, hugged and loved up.

Their relationship had changed since she'd moved into the Gunderson place, and for the better. The initial, heady excitement Luck's very first kiss had sparked in her all those months ago still got to them, though, and having a place where they could be alone was an unexpected thrill. But the time the three of them spent together, "like a real family," as Toby said, meant just as much.

They heard him jump down from the fence and they moved apart. The boy ran over to Eve and took her hand. "Can I see the new kittens now?"

"Just so long as you don't touch them. Mama cats will move their babies if you bother them," his father chided him gently.

Eve smiled down at the boy. "She's a nice cat and this isn't her first litter. I don't think she'll mind." They walked to the barn and Toby ran to the stack of squared-off hay bales where China— named by Mrs. Gunderson after an orange-and-

white china cat she kept on the windowsill—hid
her kittens under a cloth that stretched between a
gap in the bales.

The cat looked up and mewed softly when she
saw Eve and Toby gazing down at her. Her furry
body was curved around five kittens, their eyes still
closed, lined up for milk and pressing their paws
rhythmically in and out to keep it flowing. One,
the smallest, let go of the nipple and peeped mis-
erably until Eve picked it up and got it in the right
place. The kitten latched on again, sucking hard.

"You're a good mom, Eve," Toby said.

"Oh, I think China knows what to do. But she
has a lot of kittens to look after. I'm just lending a
hand." She ruffled the boy's hair and looked up to
see Luck smiling at both of them, a wealth of tenderness in his eyes.

"When they're older, can I have one?" Toby
asked.

"Sure."

They put the cloth back where it was, and then
Toby went over to the rope swing that Arvid Bergen
had rigged from the beam at the top of the barn
door, wrapping his bare legs around the scratchy,
thick rope without a care in the world and kicking
off from the dusty barn floor to get going.

Luck and Eve moved a little way off, staying inside, and talked in low voices so he couldn't hear
them.

"I can't stay the night," Luck said.

Eve felt a flash of disappointment. "Oh. Is Mrs.
Kornfeld busy?"

"No, I promised my dad I'd drive to Duluth to
see him early tomorrow. We've got some business
to take care of and I—"

"On Saturday?"

"Hey, when my dad says jump, I jump. That's how it's always been."

Hearing that made Eve more than a little nervous. She had yet to meet Luck's father and had no idea how the older McClure would feel about her when that day came. No matter how often Luck told her he loved her—and proved it to her, with his lovemaking, his tenderness, and his plans for their future—it still didn't mean that his father was going to like her.

And if his wife had died, like Lisa, too soon, Grant McClure might be stuck in the same time warp that his son had been in when they'd first met. She had a feeling that his father's good opinion meant a great deal to Luck.

"I like to let my old man think that he's in charge. Easier that way." He winked at her.

Well, maybe his father's opinion didn't mean that much. She let out an inaudible sigh of relief. Luck was pretty tough, when all was said and done, or he would not have survived the loss of his wife, or been able to pull his life together for Toby's sake.

"He's setting me up as head of a new division, specialty lumber. We subcontracted to raise a barge-load of old-growth timber that sank in Lake Superior a hundred years ago. Probably worth at least two million," Luck was saying.

"Wow," she said automatically.

"Nothing like it now. Straight and strong and clean, coming up from the bottom of the lake looking like it was milled yesterday. The silt preserved it perfectly."

He went on about the ins and outs of the discovery, veneer versus planks, while Eve listened, feeling a little guilty that she couldn't sound more interested. Toby let out a loud yee-haw on his final swing back into the barn and jumped off the rope, stumbling and landing on his knees. Luck turned to him in alarm.

"You okay?" Eve asked.

"Yeah. I'm fine." His voice was shaky. The boy brushed off his knees, and Eve saw that one was scraped and bleeding.

"Come on," she said cheerfully, letting him preserve his pride. "Let's wash that and get a bandage on it. Guess you're too old for a Pooh Bear bandage, right?"

"Right," he said fiercely.

Like father, like son, she thought with an inward smile. Just tough enough.

She put on a bluegrass CD, a mix of tunes that she'd put together on her computer. Eve hummed along with a twangy melody while she and Toby fixed dinner.

"Béla Fleck. Great banjo player. One of the best, in fact," Luck said.

Eve looked at Luck with surprise. "Yeah, that's him. But this CD is my mix. How'd you know?"

"I have all his music. Kind of funny that a New York City guy with a Hungarian name could play great bluegrass but he does."

"So you like Béla. Anything else?" Eve tilted her head and glanced at him inquisitively.

"What else do I like? Chocolate chip cookies. Strawberries," Luck said. He took a juicy one from the basket on the table and popped it into his mouth, then looked her up and down. "And girls in shorts."

"Those are for dessert. And I was talking about music," Eve said.

"What's so special about girls in shorts?" Toby wanted to know.

Embarrassed, Eve began to chop celery, inspired by the complex rhythms.

"I want to do that," Toby said.

"Not with a sharp knife, you don't," Eve answered him. "Tell you what. You can improvise on the big pot. Pretend it's a drum."

Toby grabbed the pot and went to sit by his father. The little boy pounded out an interesting counter-rhythm and Luck joined in, humming off-key but enthusiastically. Eve put down the knife and applauded them both.

"Welcome to our family hoedown," Luck said, listening intently to the music on the CD, which had changed to a new track. "With a special guest appearance by Wisconsin's own Bill Jorgenson."

"You really do have a good ear. That's good old Bill," Eve said. "I remember seeing him perform when I was a kid."

"He's playing at a festival in southern Wisconsin in a couple of weeks. Want to go when I get back from Duluth?"

"Sure."

"I wanna go too," Toby chimed in.

"Of course," his father said. "We'll bring everybody. The cows. The cat and her kittens. The whole happy circus can hit the road. Summer's almost over and I'm ready for anything. How about you, Eve?"

"Same here." She rested for a moment, bracing her hands on the counter, looking from Luck to his son and wondering how she'd ever got so . . . lucky.

* * *

Fall arrived, bringing a cold snap that froze the last few melons on the vines. Eve spent most of the morning practicing Chopin pieces on Mrs. Gunderson's piano. Their melancholy beauty seemed ideally suited to autumnal weather. But by noon she was feeling depressed—and she couldn't ignore the garden forever.

She changed into work clothes to tackle the task and strode outside, taking deep breaths of the bracing air. The shriveled leaves on the vine didn't conceal the ruined melons, which she picked up and tossed onto the compost pile along with a couple of mega-long zucchini that weren't worth saving. Then she pulled out the dying plants with gloved hands, clearing and mulching the garden per Mrs. Gunderson's detailed instructions.

Eve left one section untouched that the old lady had devoted to pumpkins. Toby inspected them every time his father brought him over, laying claim to the biggest for his jack-o'-lantern this Halloween.

Her teaching sessions at the elementary school kept her busy four days a week. Her one precious free day during the week was devoted to her music. She was already planning the Christmas chorale for the school and the nativity pageant for the church, wanting both events—sentimental favorites, especially in a small town—to go off without a hitch.

And the weekends were all about Luck. Sometimes he brought his son, sometimes not. Toby went on sleepovers a lot now, even though they left him tired and cranky, according to his dad. The boys played video games and raised hell in their eight-year-old way. Another huge advantage to being a girlfriend and not a wife, Eve knew. She wasn't expected to host sleepovers. Strictly speaking, she was a fiancée, but without a ring, no one thought of her that way.

And Luck hadn't lately mentioned buying one. She didn't much care. Between playing piano, conducting the little kids in chorus, and gardening, Eve used her hands a lot. A ring would be . . . sort of distracting. And that diamonds-are-forever business was just an advertising slogan.

Her girlfriend Michelle had breezed back into the town of Cable only two weeks ago with a big diamond solitaire, set in platinum, on her left hand. Eve wondered what had happened to make Michelle say yes to someone at last, especially when she'd been kicking up her heels during spring break in Florida like they were still all in college.

But Eve supposed Michelle was entitled to a final fling. *Not what I want,* she thought. *My heart got stolen by a great guy and his kid.*

She stepped between the rows, going over to look at Toby's pumpkin. He'd tied a piece of red ribbon around the stem to mark it as his, even though it was already twice the size of the other pumpkins and no one else was planning to claim it. She patted it. "Grow," she said softly.

"Talking to pumpkins?" The very male voice held rich amusement.

Eve whirled around. "Luck! I didn't hear you drive up."

He grinned, eyeing her as if she were wearing a bikini and not grubby gardening clothes. "Your mind was obviously elsewhere."

"Toby has dibs on this one." It wasn't much of an explanation but it would have to do. Eve pushed her hair out of her face with her gloved hand.

"I know. He told me about the red ribbon. By the way, you just got dirt on your face."

Eve put her hands on her hips and glared at him. "This is a garden. It is made of dirt. Therefore, I am dirty. What are you going to do about it?" She looked over his shoulder, thinking she shouldn't have given him an opening line like that. "Is Toby with you?"

"Nope. He's going to stay with his friend Brendan tonight."

"But he has school tomorrow."

"Spoken like a mom," Luck said with a grin. "Brendan's mom is pretty strict and they have a science project to finish."

"Oh, okay. What's it about?"

"The Effect of Moonbeams on Worm Growth. He put Squirmy's can in the moonlight for a week and measured him before and after."

Eve raised a doubtful eyebrow. "So what happened?"

"Squirmy got a couple of millimeters longer. But that doesn't prove anything. Could be the enriched dirt. Could be the power of positive thinking."

Eve laughed. "Go, worms!"

"Something like that."

She walked out of the garden, closing the gate behind her and latching it. Then she brushed the loose dirt from her clothes and pulled off her gardening gloves. "Whew. I'm going to take Mrs. Gunderson's recommendation and head straight for the hammock. Care to join me?"

He took her hand in his. "Don't mind if I do." The late afternoon sun provided little in the way of warmth and she snagged a quilt from the wicker sofa on the porch along the way.

It was machine-made and nothing special but it was big enough to line the hammock and cover them as well. Eve carefully spread it out over the knotted diamonds of rope, letting half of it hang over one side.

"What are you doing?" Luck asked.

"There's a trick to it," she began, "you have to hold the sides, then jump in. Then you fold yourself into it like a taco. But we're going to make a two-person taco. I get in first."

"Have you done this before?"

"Not the two-person taco. But let's try it. Ready . . . steady . . . here I go." She jumped, landing more or less in the middle and making the hammock swing wildly until he steadied it.

"Scooch over," he instructed her. Eve did and he hesitated for only a few seconds before jumping in, rolling against her and trying to hold still at the same time.

"We did it," she said happily. "Now for the quilt." She reached over the side and dragged it over both of them, keeping out the cool fall air. Eve snuggled close to his chest, clad in a plaid flannel shirt with a long-sleeved thermal top underneath. "How's that?"

"Works for me."

He planted a kiss on the top of her tangled hair and smoothed it a little with one hand. "So . . . . do I get a sleepover with you?"

Eve unbuttoned his plaid flannel shirt and pushed the sides apart, nuzzling his thermal undershirt. In autumn, love in Wisconsin didn't mean you had to get naked. "Sure." She ran a hand over his hard muscles, feeling them tighten even more at her light touch.

Luck drew in his breath. "I have never fooled around in a hammock. I understand it has been done, though."

"We don't have to do anything. This is really nice." She wriggled around until she was able to see his face, pressed against his folded arm and looking down at her.

He extended a leg very carefully over his side, touching a boot to the ground and setting the hammock in motion. Then he brought his leg back up and slid it between hers, drawing her against his chest once more.

Beautiful, Eve thought. To lie suspended between heaven and earth with Luck, warmed by his body and his nearness, swinging gently in the afternoon glow of autumn, was as good as life got.

Several weeks later, the big pumpkin was ready to be rolled out of the patch and into a wheelbarrow. From there it was going to be strapped into the back of Luck's SUV and driven to his house outside of Cable.

Eve and Luck handled the pumpkin with care, resisting the temptation to drag it by the stem. He got his arms around it and she gave a little boost as he heaved it into the wheelbarrow, thickly padded with straw.

"Toby's going to be overjoyed. This monster has put on quite a few pounds since the last time he saw it. I don't think he's ever had such a big one."

Eve patted it. No matter what, a pumpkin had to be patted. "It's a beautiful color. And it doesn't really have a bad side."

"Nope. Bet it has about a million seeds."

She folded her arms across her chest. "I'm not scooping out the insides. Pumpkin guts are too squishy."

"We can leave that to Brendan and Toby. Boys don't mind squishy stuff. They'll probably end up throwing it at each other."

"Did your father let you do that?"

"Hell, no." Luck picked up the wheelbarrow handles and trundled the pumpkin toward his car. "He was authoritarian about pumpkins too. Made us wash the seeds and then Mom roasted them. Waste not, want not. But I hated them. Still do."

Eve cast him a curious look. "They taste okay."

"Yeah, but it was Halloween. All we wanted was the candy, just like all the other kids. And it wasn't as if we were in imminent danger of starvation. But he insisted." His tone was light, as if he knew that complaining about having to eat pumpkin seeds was a little ridiculous. But she knew he had a sweet tooth; she'd seen him devour the desserts she made often enough for that.

Eve only nodded in response, falling into step beside him. They soon reached the car and hoisted the pumpkin into the back seat together. "Hang on—one more thing." She ran back to the house, picking up the quilt from the porch. She wrapped it around the pumpkin, leaving the stem poking out. "Just in case you have to make a sudden stop."

"I think you're getting a little carried away, don't you?" he said, laughing.

"Nope. Not at all. I can't wait to see Toby's face. He gets bragging rights. That's his pumpkin." Eve climbed up into the front seat and fastened her own seat belt, ready to go.

* * *

Toby and Brendan dashed out of Luck's house when they pulled up, keeping a safe distance until the SUV was parked and Luck had opened his door. "Check out the back seat," he called to his son.

Eve unclipped her seat belt and turned to face Toby, who shouted with glee when he saw his pumpkin. "Cool! We're gonna have the biggest pumpkin on the block!"

His father hoisted once more and lugged it onto the porch, setting the pumpkin in a plastic chair that held it snugly and kept it from rolling. "Here it shall stay," he intoned, "and here we will carve. The Dad has spoken."

Brendan whispered into Toby's ear and the boys ran into the house, coming back with markers to draw a face on it and serrated, odd-looking cutting knives with orange handles, made just for Halloween.

"Supposedly they can't cut themselves with those," Luck informed Eve. "But you know kids. I laid in a supply of bandages and antibiotic cream just in case."

"Very good. Five out of five dad points for you."

The boys kneeled in front of the pumpkin, one drawing a gap-toothed mouth and the other, scary eyes. Luck cut the lid first and gave them big serving spoons to scoop out the tangle of pulp and seeds, which they did enthusiastically, throwing globs of pumpkin guts onto the newspaper spread open for that purpose.

He made the first cut on the face and the boys hacked at the rest of it, letting Eve take over when

they got tired. She stuck faithfully to their drawing
and they were thrilled with the result when Luck
put a lit candle inside. He let them ooh and aah,
then blew it out. "All right. Finish your homework,
you guys. Halloween is tomorrow night."

Eve drove into Cable from the Gunderson farmhouse the next night, invited by Toby to go trick-
or-treating with him and his dad. He charged up
every porch that had Halloween decorations and a
few that didn't, hoping that the holdouts might be
persuaded to part with a handful of change in lieu
of candy. The night was moonlit and quite cold.

Toby had refused to wear a storebought costume for babies, as he called it, fashioning a costume of sorts out of layered sweaters, the last one
being gray with a hood. He'd attached round pink
paper ears to his hood, and drawn whiskers on his
face.

"What are you?" Eve asked, poking his bulging,
woolly belly.

"A gray mouse!" he declared. "You were a brown
mouse, so I get to be a gray one."

The note of pride in his voice gave her a funny
little thrill. It was all in how you looked at yourself,
Eve realized. To an eight-year-old boy with a secure
sense of himself, being a mouse could be a big
deal.

She held Luck's hand as they strolled up and
down the quiet streets to follow Toby, their footsteps rustling through the fallen leaves on the side-
walks. Little bands of trick-or-treaters, accompanied
by watchful parents, charged past, bent on filling
plastic bags with as much candy as possible.

Last year she had been handing it out, admiring

the originality of the homemade costumes and acting properly scared by the littlest monster in a paper mask, his round, innocently blue eyes shining through the eyeholes as he asked for a treat in a muffled voice.

When it was all over, she'd felt the way she always felt on holidays. More than a little lonely. And somehow on the fringes of life, not in it. But not this year. This year she had Luck.

Toby seemed turbocharged. But Luck knew instinctively when his son's enthusiasm would fade, and he called it quits before the boy got too tired. They were going up the porch stairs of Brendan's house when a friend of Toby's shouted from the sidewalk, where he was flanked by his parents. "Hey, Toby! Wanna sleep over? My mom and dad says it's okay, tomorrow's Saturday!"

"Can I go?" Toby said pleadingly to his father. "That's Eddie Rivera—you know the Riveras from church. Please? Can I—may I—can I go? Please?"

Luck looked at Eve and she didn't miss the gleam in his eyes.

"He can sleep in my pajamas, Mr. McClure!" Eddie shouted.

"It's Halloween. He can sleep in his costume. Okay, Toby. I'll pick them both up at ten and take them out for pancakes," he called to Eddie's parents. "You're going to need a break."

"Sure, no problem," Tom Rivera called back. Toby dashed off to join their family, waving to Luck and Eve. "Bye, Dad! Bye, Mom!"

Luck stared after him, then turned to face Eve. "Well, what do you know. He called you mom."

Eve nodded. "I heard. I'm not sure I'm ready for that."

Luck tipped her chin up and planted a tender

kiss on her lips, just brushing them with his. "Don't take it too seriously. He's just a kid. C'mon, let's go back to my house. No tricks. Just treats."

Once they'd arrived after the short drive out of Cable, he led the way and took her coat when they were standing in the hall, sliding his hands over her shoulders warmly and possessively.

She didn't shrug him off but leaned back against him, enjoying his sensual caress. Being alone with him on a bewitched, moonlit night was an unexpected pleasure. He made growly noises in her ear that made her giggle, and bit her neck, playing a wolfman in honor of the holiday for a few minutes.

He set her away from him so he could take off his coat and got it squared away inside the coat closet, then kicked off the hiking boots he wore, dropping them on the floor of the closet with two loud thunks.

Eve eased her feet out of her low-heeled pumps and padded into the living room, closely followed by Luck, growling louder. She scampered to the sofa but he caught her around the waist and swept her up in his arms. "Gotcha. Want a glass of wine, beautiful lady?"

"Sure."

"White or red?"

"Um . . . red." That sounded a little more blood-thirsty and right for Halloween.

He set her down carefully on the sofa, kissing the tip of her nose. "Be right back."

She nestled into the cushions, watching him stride away into the kitchen and admiring the length and muscularity of his legs. The thick wool socks he wore made his steps almost noiseless, and his dark sweater fit his powerful chest and shoulders to perfection. He could well be a wolf.

He returned with two wineglasses and a bottle of something good, judging by the label. Eve didn't know much about wines but she had heard of that one. He'd uncorked it in the kitchen and filled a glass for her first, then one for himself.

He raised his glass. "A toast."

"What are we toasting?" She raised hers.

He clinked it. "Things that go bump in the night, what else?"

"I see. Well, I'll drink to that."

They drank and chatted, sitting fractionally closer until she was in his lap, sipping a second glass, and munching on the cheese and crackers he'd brought out. Eve had skipped dinner, figuring she would fill up on mini chocolate bars instead, but all Luck had in the house was candy corn, which she hated.

He eased her off his lap, reaching for the bowl but not quite able to reach it. She wrinkled her nose. "None for me, thanks."

"Do you hate candy corn? So do I."

She gave him a wondering look. "Then why did you buy it?"

"So I wouldn't eat it. Does that make sense?"

"In a really weird way . . . yes." She watched as he slid off the sofa and sat in front of the coffee table, taking a handful of candy corn. "What are you doing?"

"Sending you a message." He placed the orange and yellow kernels to make letters. I LOVE YOU.

"Aww."

Luck looked a little disappointed. "Is that all?"

Eve didn't want to make an automatic response

and didn't want to hurt his feelings either. "You know how I feel about you," she said, realizing that she sounded prim and polite. But she couldn't take the reply back once it had been said.

Luck shrugged, gathered up the candy corn and began to write another message, which took forever. She watched him form the letters of the first two words, noticing absently that a single kernel of candy corn made a perfect apostrophe. LET'S MAKE, she read. Feeling a little sleepy from the wine, she closed her eyes—and opened them a minute or two later to read the whole thing.

LET'S MAKE LOVE ALL NIGHT LONG. WHAT DO YOU SAY?

He had used up all the candy corn in the bowl. Luck beamed at her.

Eve reached out and swept up the first word into her hand. Then she replied, kernel by kernel, setting them down with elaborate care and making him wait for it. YES.

Then she added an exclamation point.

Chapter 13

Late November . . .

Eve could feel the change in the air. The gloomy day seemed to herald winter weather. At least it put her in the right frame of mind for planning the Christmas chorale at the school and the church pageant. The traditional favorites were easiest for the kids to sing—most of them had been humming along to the music they heard in stores since Thanksgiving.

Which had been a semi-disaster. Luck had brought her to Duluth to meet his father and un-married aunt, and the McClures hadn't exactly warmed up to her. After a routine dinner, his father had retreated to the den to watch football and that was about it for family interaction. Eve had regretted her choice to be with Luck and not her own mom and dad.

But they'd driven back that night, with Toby asleep in the back seat, and talked all the way home—about everything and nothing. The memory of being by his side as the quiet country roads unrolled before them made her smile to herself.

She scrolled through music choices on the computer she'd set up in Mrs. Gunderson's sewing room, humming along with a few of the carols herself. The principal was happy to have Eve take over this year—there was no money in the budget to keep a full-time music teacher on staff and the teachers had managed as best they could. The kids looked forward to the time they got to spend out of the classroom and were well behaved, except for one.

Eve shook her head, thinking about Lurleen Caldwell's son. The hairdresser, a single mom, had told her that Jimmy was a handful and it was true. She'd moved closer to Cable to enroll him in the accelerated program and Jimmy's teacher, Vivi Brody, had told Eve that accelerated was the right word for him.

Vivi said Jimmy was a nice kid, just . . . bouncy. And talkative. And curious. The first was worst, Eve had discovered. Getting a group of children to stand in size order on risers was tough enough without Jimmy deciding to jump down from the third tier. He had tried her patience on the first day, but he had known it—and apologized by pressing the leftover change from his lunch money into her hand and telling her with an engaging grin to buy herself something nice.

It was awfully sweet of him, but she couldn't take the money. Still, Jimmy made it hard to be stern with him for very long. She had made sure to keep him and Toby far apart, even though their voices harmonized well. Eve didn't want two mischievous boys egging each other on while she rehearsed a group of better behaved children.

Toby's grandfather, who was as authoritative as Luck had indicated, got along well with his lively grandson. But he hadn't seemed thrilled by the idea that Luck was seeing someone who might replace his first wife one day. Yes, Grant McClure had been courteous—but underneath his good manners she sensed a coldness that made her uneasy.

She'd chosen her clothes carefully: a conservative wrap dress in burgundy and garnet jewelry. And thanks to Lurleen, her highlights had been redone, adding subtle depth to her hair. Eve still wasn't confident about wearing makeup and stuck to the bare essentials: eye pencil and eyeshadow in a shade that really could be called Brown Mouse, and a dash of blusher and lip gloss.

But she couldn't tell from Grant McClure's appraising look whether he approved or not, and Luck's aunt didn't indulge in girl talk. She asked Toby about his grades and talked to Luck about the lumber business, and Eve had felt left out.

Still, Toby had chattered almost nonstop, covering the lulls in the conversation. The food was very good. Turkey, gravy, mashed potatoes, sweet potatoes, cranberry sauce, and the pies had all come from a good local restaurant—Luck's aunt hated cooking and refused to bother with it, even on holidays.

Eve had expected to help out in the kitchen, which was an easy way to get to know people. The Rowlands had always opened a preliminary bottle or two of wine, and invited their Thanksgiving guests to don an apron and chop vegetables or stir a sauce. The domestically disinclined were assigned to cheer the others on, but Luck's family didn't do either. The mood in the McClure house—a man-

sion that had once belonged to a lumber baron—
was much more formal, and so was the table, set
with fine china, antique silver, and glittering crystal.

But Luck seemed happy enough. He took the
time to explain to Toby about the Pilgrims' journey from England and how the Indians had invited
them to a harvest feast. He'd gently encouraged
his son to say grace before the meal, and Toby got
through the simple blessing he'd memorized without a hitch, much to his father's pride. But Eve
had been glad when it was over.

She saw Mrs. Gunderson's orange-and-white cat
leap onto the sewing table and walk to the keyboard.
China settled down, her furry belly covering her
back paws, and favored Eve with a golden-eyed
stare.

"What's up, China? I fed you."

The cat certainly looked plump enough, though
her mothering days were over. Eve had had China
spayed, then given away all of her litter but one.
Toby had named the frisky little female Heidi, because the kitten was so good at hiding.

Luck's son was just as good at finding her and it
was still their favorite game. Even though Heidi
was nearly grown, she still had a kitten's playful-
ness. Every time the boy came over, Heidi dashed
away somewhere new, but Toby always figured out
where she was in the end.

Luck hadn't wanted him to bring Heidi to their
house outside of Cable, and Eve hadn't minded.
She suspected that it was just another reason for
both of them to visit often, which they did.

The Gundersons' farmhouse was a snug place
to be now that the days were bleak and cold. Mrs.
Gunderson had called from Milwaukee with in-

structions about draining outdoor water fixtures
and so forth, and Eve's dad had come over to see
that all was ready for winter.

Arvid had brought the Gunderson cows over to
his barn, since there were vacancies, as he put it,
after the fall slaughtering. She missed their low
mooing—the sound was comforting and musical
in its way—and sometimes went over to his place
to visit them.

Eve switched to a software program for composing music and jotted down a few bars of a melody
that had been running through her head. She
saved it as a work in progress, adding a title after
some thought: *When the Cows Come Home.*

She didn't hear the knock on the door, which
she generally left unlocked during the day, nor did
she hear Luck come in. But the cat jumped down
from the table when he entered the room.

"Hello, Eve."

She jumped a little in her swivel chair. "Luck—I
wasn't expecting you."

"Just thought I'd stop by."

Eve got up and put her arms around his neck,
returning the kiss he gave her. His hands slid down
from her waist over her hips, pulling her against
his front. "I'm glad you did." She arched against
him when his mouth moved lower, kissing her
neck.

He finished off with a friendly but sensual nip
on her earlobe, then looked over her shoulder at
the computer. "How busy are you?"

"Not that busy. Noodling around with the music
selections for the Christmas chorale and the
pageant."

"Toby wanted to know if he has to wear a white
shirt and tie."

Eve laughed. "He sure does. They all do."

"There's nothing he hates more." Luck let her go. Somehow even talking about Toby made them both feel slightly self-conscious, as if he were in the room. "But since his grandfather and great-aunt are coming to see him sing, he'll have to make the best of it." Her smile vanished and he noticed it. "What's the matter?"

Eve moved away from him, not meeting his concerned gaze. "I don't think your relatives like me very much."

"They have to get to know you," he replied evenly.

She nodded. "That answers that question."

"Huh? You didn't ask a question, did you?"

"I don't have to," she burst out. "What I said is true. They don't like me. You didn't exactly deny it."

Luck held up both hands. "Whoa. You are really jumping to conclusions. My folks aren't very demonstrative people and they're still getting used to the idea that there's someone I really care about in my life."

Eve wasn't mollified. She wasn't sure why. Of course, when Luck had swept her off her feet and asked her to marry him, the last thing on her mind was how complicated the holidays would get. His family and her family weren't necessarily a match made in heaven. The McClures and the Rowlands were likely to expect both Luck and Eve to show up for the really special celebrations—and how to balance all that and still end up equal wasn't going to be easy.

Maybe Luck had faced similar problems with his first wife; Eve had no idea. It occurred to her that

Toby probably went to see Lisa's parents at Christmas too. It was almost too much to think about. She took the shawl off the back of her swivel chair and put it around her shoulders, feeling suddenly cold.

Eve looked at Luck, who was watching her warily. "What?" she said in a tense voice.

"Don't bite my head off."

"I didn't mean to. Sorry."

He came over to her and rubbed her shoulders. Eve drew the shawl more tightly around herself. "It was only one day. Thanksgiving isn't always great, especially with a football fanatic in the family. Christmas is a lot more fun. I can't wait to hear Toby sing. He's so happy that you're directing the chorale."

She had the feeling he was trying to distract her from worries she wasn't about to put into words. But Eve didn't mind. Talking about the upcoming holidays was easier than discussing the entire rest of their lives.

"He's memorized all the lyrics to ten songs," she offered.

"Yeah, he's a bright kid. I hope he doesn't drive you too crazy."

She shook her head. "I only have him for an hour each day. And the chorale kids are really pretty good. Singing is physical—they aren't as restless as you might think."

"You're directing the church pageant too, right?"

"Uh-huh. With Reverend Johnson. So far, so good. We have a little Mary and Joseph for the nativity scene, and a whole lot of shepherds. But we're using cardboard sheep." She warmed to her subject, and her expression became animated. "First the audience will see the star—someone will shine

a flashlight on it when everything else is dark.
Then the shepherds come on, singing 'O Little
Town of Bethlehem' and carrying their sheep."

"Isn't Eddie Rivera a shepherd? Toby said he
was in the church pageant."

Eve nodded. "He sings like an angel."

Luck drew her into the circle of his arms. "So do
you."

"Aw, shucks." But his fond compliment pleased
her. Eve rested her head against his chest, enjoying
the warmth of the plaid flannel against her cheek.
There wasn't a man in Wisconsin who didn't wear
plaid flannel shirts in winter, but somehow they
looked particularly good on Luck. Must be the
muscle, she thought.

"You oughta play the part. 'Behold, I bring you
tidings of great joy' and all that."

"Nope," she said, laughing. "Lurleen Caldwell is
our angel this year."

Luck looked momentarily taken aback. "Interesting choice. You sure about that? But hey—you're
in charge."

Eve grinned. "She's tall and she looks great in a
long white robe and wings. And you should hear
her belt out hallelujahs. She's going to rock the
church."

"Is that a good thing?"

"Why not? Christmas is supposed to be all about
joy."

Luck sighed suddenly and shook his head.

"What's the matter?" Eve's gaze searched his
troubled face.

"I just remembered. Toby is supposed to visit
Lisa's parents in Duluth this year. We're going to
miss the pageant. He's their only grandson. I can't
say no."

Just as she'd thought. "Are you—are you going with him?" she asked hesitantly.

"I usually do," was all he said.

"But what about your dad?"

Luck shrugged. "He goes through the motions but only if Toby's around."

She understood what he wasn't saying. Evidently there wasn't much reason for Luck to stay around Cable if his son was elsewhere. Most likely Lisa's parents invited him too, even though he hadn't said that in so many words. She got the picture: he was going to be away on Christmas. Luck's expression was impassive.

All the good feeling of his unexpected visit vanished. Eve only nodded and took the few steps to her swivel chair, turning it around with a brisk motion of her hand and sitting down. "Okay. Not a problem. I'll be fine on my own. And I'll be really busy anyway."

"Lisa's parents are going to come see Toby in the chorale," Luck said quietly. "So if you—"

"I'd rather not meet them," she snapped. She hated to sound so rude, but she knew without a doubt that she definitely wouldn't measure up in their eyes.

Luck thrust his hands into his pockets and studied her for a long moment. Eve turned away and tapped a key on the keyboard, bringing the monitor back to life. The music program she'd been working on reappeared.

"Whatever you say, Eve. I don't want to argue."

Eve felt a paw tap her ankle. Heidi, living up to her name, came out from where she was hiding under the sewing table. "Oh, stop it, you—not you. I'm talking to the cat," she said to Luck. She reached down and got a grip on Heidi, lifting the cat into her lap.

Luck ventured a smile. "I figured."

Afraid she would cry, she didn't want to look him in the eye. Of course there would be other Christmases but she had thought of this one as their first and she resented it being taken away from her. She would spend a lot of time with her mom and dad, get invited to a few sedate parties hosted by local families because she'd worked on the chorale and the pageant, maybe see her friend Michelle if she was coming back. Nothing magical or romantic about that.

Chapter 14

One week later . . .

Winter had set in and the rolling landscape that surrounded the Gunderson farmhouse was bleak and brown. Eve looked out the kitchen window at the mulched garden and the light frost that covered it. Hard to believe, she thought, that it had been bursting with vines and vegetables throughout the summer or that it ever would bloom again.

Mrs. Gunderson had called just that morning to tell her where the Christmas ornaments were, in case she wanted to decorate. Eve had perched on a ladder to take the box down from a cabinet used only for seasonal storage because it was so hard to reach. She'd peeked inside the box before setting it on the kitchen table—everything was wrapped in tissue.

The timer on the coffeemaker beeped to let her know the brewing cycle was done. Eve poured a cup, then looked in the refrigerator for half-and-half. Just the sound of the door opening was enough to bring China and Heidi running, hoping for a taste of their favorite treat.

"All right, pussycats," she sighed. Eve took a teaspoon from the silverware caddy and poured in a few drops for the mama cat. Heidi tried to get there first but shrank back when China hissed at her. The older cat licked the spoon in a dignified way. Her greedy offspring, who wasn't quite her size, got her turn with the second spoonful.

"Doesn't take much to make you happy, does it?" Heidi licked her whiskers with a satisfied expression and Eve felt more cheerful. She put the spoon into the dishpan. Then she added half-and-half to her cup of coffee and took it to the table, sitting down in front of the box of ornaments.

Holding the cup with both hands, she sipped thoughtfully, enjoying the richness of the brew as she studied the box. She didn't have a tree, didn't plan to get one. But Mrs. Gunderson had explained that many of the ornaments were old and handmade, and Eve had wanted to see them. Just stringing them on ribbons over the many-paned windows would be pretty, though perhaps not as pretty as a decorated tree.

If Luck and Toby were going to be somewhere else for the holidays, she didn't have to do anything special. Leave that to her mother, who turned into a cookie-baking, ornament-making maniac every Christmas. Eve finished her coffee and set the cup aside. At least looking at someone else's ornaments wouldn't put her in a sad mood.

Amazing how sentimental a person could get over little plastic reindeer and things like that. Her mother insisted on keeping every ornament that Eve had ever crafted for her in school, from the

cotton-ball snowman to the angel made of pipe
cleaners and beads.

She imagined Mrs. Gunderson's grown sons
making ornaments for their mom in grade school
and had to smile. They were all in their forties
now, their farmboy muscle turned to fat, married
and comfortably settled in the nearby area.

With one hand, she flipped open the lid of the
box and took out several tissue-wrapped items, un-
wrapping the first of five with care. It was a tiny,
red-painted wooden horse, brushstroked with folk-
loric Scandinavian designs. The others were as like
it as handmade things could be. Eve lined up the
little herd in a row, and set the box on the floor before she dug into the next layer.

She unwrapped bearded tomtens with red felt
caps, and fuzzy reindeer, and straw stars on a string.
Then came a cotton-ball snowman, missing a nose.
Awww. So the Gunderson boys had made them too.
And their mom had kept them. She held the snowman in her hand and spruced him up a bit, pat-
ting the wisps of cotton back into place.

Luck probably had a box of ornaments like this,
proudly made by Toby out of glitter glue and pop-
sicle sticks and other unbeautiful things that added
up to something very beautiful indeed: family memories.

The three of them, when they were together,
were almost like a family but she wondered what it
would be like to be a mom for real—to Luck's son
and, someday, another son or daughter. Eve wasn't
sure she was ready for either. Blithely, she had said
simply said yes when he'd asked her to marry him.
They should have just eloped, she thought. Given
in to their overwhelming feelings. Acknowledged

their mutual loneliness. And their passion for each other.

That hadn't changed. When she and Luck got behind closed doors, it was all about passion. Something else that made her nervous. As much as she craved his touch, his physical mastery, and even just the sound of his low voice, Eve was uneasy about how much she wanted all of that— wanted *him*. Once upon a time, for most of her life, in fact, she'd been the cautious type. But no other man had ever made her feel the way Luck did.

Eve sighed. Her mother and father had married as soon as they could and had never been alone in their adult lives. She'd expected them to object to her wish to live independently but they had both supported her decision and continued to, which surprised her.

Once wed, her mother had stayed home, then raised Eve, her only child, volunteering in the school, and being a constant, comforting presence in her life. But Eve wasn't sure she was ready to make a commitment like that. Looking back on her childhood, she'd never thought about what it would be like not to have a mom.

Toby had turned out fine, but that had a lot to do with his dad. No matter what, she admired Luck for that. It was still hard for Eve to believe that he had been essentially alone for so long. Obviously he hadn't wanted to replace his wife. The worry nagged at her still—that she didn't really measure up to Lisa and never would. But Luck had told her one night, holding her in his arms after they'd made love, that he'd been waiting for her— his beautiful brown mouse.

He didn't talk about Lisa as a rule and neither did Toby. Was that a good sign? Eve had no way of knowing. But if Luck was talking his son to spend Christmas with Lisa's family, the season was bound to bring back a lot of poignant memories for him.

Eve set the cotton snowman on the back of one of the little red horses and watched it topple off. Heidi jumped up onto the table and batted at it with her paw. "Hey, stop that." The cat gave her a who-me look and jumped down, strolling across the kitchen to join China, who was napping on the rag rug. The cats curled up together, purring happily.

She rested her chin in her hand and watched them for a moment. There was a knock on the door.

Luck, her heart whispered. She went to the kitchen window to peer out and saw her mother's cheerful face framed by a fake-fur-trimmed hood. "Yoo-hoo! Anybody home?" Mrs. Rowland called.

Eve summoned up a smile and opened the door. "Hi, Mom. You must be psychic. I was just thinking about you."

"Well, isn't that nice," Mrs. Rowland said, bustling in. She brought the sunshine with her, Eve noticed when she looked outside. The bleak day was brightening, although it was still cold.

Her mother's gloved hands clutched see-through plastic bags filled with flour, sugar, butter, food coloring, and other baking supplies. Uh-oh. Eve realized that her mother was prepared to make cookies.

"You can hang up your jacket by the back door," Eve said, taking the bags from her mother's hands and peering inside. "Looks like you're planning to stay awhile."

Mrs. Rowland chuckled. "How did you guess, honey?" She pulled off her gloves and stuffed them into a pocket of her jacket before hanging it up. "Got any cookie sheets?"

"Are you kidding? Mrs. Gunderson has three different kinds." Eve rolled her eyes. "And a Swedish cookie gun. She's a domestic goddess. Pickles and preserves. Quilts. Crocheted thingies on the furniture."

"You could learn how to do all that if you wanted to," her mother replied.

Setting the bulging bags on the countertop, Eve grinned and started unloading. "No thanks. I mean, I like her homey touches, but I'd rather make music."

"I'm glad. We spent a fortune on all those lessons." Mrs. Rowland settled herself onto a tall, barstool-style chair by the kitchen counter and pulled out a rubber-banded set of old index cards with handwritten recipes on them from one of the bags. "I stopped at our house after I went to the store and threw these in, just in case."

"Mom, you know these recipes by heart."

"Yes, but you don't."

"Toby might like looking at something from olden times." Eve took off the rubber band and looked through the yellowing cards. "He thinks everything comes off a computer. These are practically historical artifacts."

"He's a nice boy. How are you getting along with him?" Mrs. Rowland's tone was light but Eve sensed an undercurrent of significant interest.

"Just fine. When he's around. Like most kids, he's got a full schedule."

"That gives you and Luck more time alone."

"Yes. But his schedule is pretty full too. Business trips to Duluth and Eau Claire, family obligations, et cetera."

Mrs. Rowland put on her half-glasses and inspected the expiration date on the baking powder, as if she didn't hear the slight edge in her daughter's voice. "Oh. Well, you two have a lifetime ahead of you. And it's nice to know that he's working hard—"

"I can support myself, Mom. I'm not marrying a meal ticket."

Her mother heard it this time. She looked at Eve with mild surprise. "I never said you were."

Eve conceded the point with a nod.

"Is anything the matter, honey?"

"No."

Teresa Rowland studied her daughter's mulish expression. She knew better than to press the point. She set up the baking ingredients in the order in which they would be opened and measured out, and looked around for a warm place to put the butter to soften.

Unfortunately, the sunny windowsill was occupied by the two cats, which had moved up there from the rag rug.

"Aren't they cozy. Mother and daughter, right?"

"Yup."

Mrs. Rowland took down a plate for the butter and set it over the pilot light on the gas stove. "So do you and Toby do things together? He must like having a mom in his life."

"I'm not his mom yet," Eve said quietly.

"But I know how much he likes you. He must be looking forward to Christmas, when all of you can be together."

With one foot Eve pushed the box of Christmas ornaments under the table but she didn't have time to put away the ones she had taken out. Her action brought her mother's attention to the small things on the table.

"Aren't those precious. I love the traditional ones and those red Swedish horses are sweet. I had one just like this when I was a little girl." She picked up one and admired it. "I wonder where it is."

"Probably in the attic. Along with everything else."

"Memories are important, honey. I'm so glad that you're about to start making some of your own with Luck."

Eve made a wry face. She didn't feel like sharing her doubts on that subject with her mother, especially since her doubts had everything to do with her and not much to do with Luck, who seemed to know exactly what he wanted. She kneeled down to open the cabinet where the cookie sheets and other awkwardly shaped items were stored, banging and clanking the metal bakeware as a diversionary tactic as she took out several and brought them to the counter.

Humming, Mrs. Rowland found an assortment of bowls, and measured out the flour, sugar, cocoa, and spices in different amounts for each.

Her mother had an assembly-line system that seldom varied. She started with a basic butter-cookie dough that could be shaped into stars decorated with colored sugar or rolled up with chocolate-flavored dough to make pinwheels—whatever took her fancy.

Eve watched her for several minutes, comforted by the sight of her mom in an apron, absorbed in a task that would soon fill the kitchen with good smells. She looked over at the butter softening in the sun just when Heidi jumped up to investigate it, about to lick the wax paper.

Eve shooed the cat away and poked one stick of butter. Good to go. She unwrapped the wax paper and let the softened stick drop into an empty bowl, creaming it vigorously with a fork. Mrs. Rowland smiled. "Good work." She smiled encouragingly and handed over a cup of sugar to add to the fluffy butter.

"Oops—forgot to preheat the oven." Eve took care of that and then rubbed the butter wrapper over the cookie sheets.

Cookie production began in earnest and the kitchen counter disappeared under bags and bottles and little drifts of flour. Her mother offered a taste of anise-flavored dough on a spoon, and Eve opened her mouth, feeling ridiculously like a baby bird. "Mmm. Mery good," she said thickly.

The door opened and a whoosh of cold air heralded the arrival of Toby, with Luck right on his heels. "Surprise!" he shouted. He ran to Eve and wrapped his arms around her knees, giving her an exuberant, little-boy hug that made her smile.

She swallowed the dough and bent down to hug him back. "How nice to see you."

Luck stood behind his son and leaned forward slightly to kiss the tip of her nose when she straightened up. "You have flour on your face."

"That's my mother's fault. This is all her idea."

"Moms get blamed for everything," Mrs. Rowland said, laughing.

Toby spun away from the counter and noticed the ornaments. "Wow, look at these!" He picked up a wooden horse and made it gallop across the table. "Are we going to have a Christmas tree this year, Dad?"

"No, son. Don't forget the visit to your grand-parents."

"But that doesn't mean we can't have a tree."

"Well, if you really want one—"

"I really do. Really, really, really."

Luck looked down and ruffled his son's hair. Toby wasn't wearing a cap and his cheeks were pink.

"You mean Lisa's parents, don't you?" Mrs. Rowland said politely, not looking at Eve. "That's very thoughtful of you, Luck."

Eve tipped her chin up, feeling a sudden wave of emotion hit her. No matter what, she wasn't going to convey the impression that she was upset, not with Toby listening.

"I'd rather be with Eve and my dad," she heard Toby say.

"Oh, I'm sure your grandparents will enjoy see-ing you, young man," Mrs. Rowland said. "You can bring them a box of homemade cookies for a gift. Tell you what. I'll show you how to use the cookie gun and we can make different kinds. We'll deco-rate them when they've cooled."

"Okay! I've made chocolate chip cookies with Eve but I bet you're an expert."

"You're right," Eve said. "But I'm not sure we should be encouraging a cookie habit."

"I don't hafta eat them. I just like making them." Toby dragged over another tall chair and scrambled up it, his jacket sliding off his shoulders and down over his hands.

"Better take off the jacket," Mrs. Rowland chided him gently. She took his hands and turned them palms up for inspection. "These need a wash." She helped him with both tasks and winked at Eve.

"Why don't you two go in the living room and talk? Toby and I have a lot of work to do."

Smooth move. Eve had to hand it to her mother. "Uh—okay. Thanks. Would you like some coffee, Luck?"

"Sure." He smiled encouragingly and she felt a flash of guilt, remembering the mood of their last meeting. She hadn't wanted to discuss her mixed feelings about the upcoming Christmas, but there might be no avoiding it today.

Chapter 15

They exchanged awkward small talk for about twenty minutes until it was clear from the noise in the kitchen—an electric beater that her mother had finally found—that Toby was fully occupied.

Settling himself in an armchair, Luck cradled his cup of coffee in one big hand. "Sorry we didn't call first. We just happened to be driving by," he said offhandedly.

"You don't have to be so ceremonious. I seem to remember we got engaged not too long ago," she said dryly.

"Even so. You looked like you were having a pretty good time with your mom."

Eve held up a hand. "Who thinks you were sent by God to rescue me from the ranks of single women."

Luck sipped at his coffee. "Considering how independent you are, you don't seem to mind my rescue efforts."

"I appreciate your help with everything." She waved a hand, indicating the house in general.

"It's different being on my own and suddenly responsible for all the things my parents used to do."

"Do you like it?"

"Sure. It's a great little place. Very cozy."

"I meant being on your own, Eve."

"Yes, I do." She tried to sound nonchalant, because she did like it.

"I'm glad. And it is a great place for one person. Some houses would be just too big." He stopped talking and Eve heard the wind kick up, blowing around the eaves. Luck seemed to hear it too. "Here comes trouble. Feel that chill in the air?"

"It's December," she said flatly.

Luck set his coffee cup aside and looked at her steadily. "You know I'm not talking about the weather." He rested his elbows on his thighs and clasped his hands together as he leaned forward.

"What are you getting at?" Eve had poured herself another cup before they left the kitchen but she didn't want it. She held it all the same. The lingering warmth of the thick china mug was comforting.

"The second I told you that I usually went with Toby to his grandparents' house, you just shut down. I could see it in your eyes."

Eve felt numb. "Funny. I could say the exact same thing about you."

Luck let out a long sigh. "So where do we go from here?"

She thought that one over, but not for long. "I think we need to discuss how your past marriage is going to fit into this one."

"My marriage to Lisa has nothing to do with our relationship."

"It does. It will."

He unclasped his hands and touched his fingertips together. "Did I tell you that I put her picture
away?"

"No." Eve felt a wave of despair. A framed photograph was one thing, but Luck was still emotionally
bound to a memory. He'd had a whole separate life
with another woman, who had given him a son. His
ties to Lisa's family were important to Toby and
she could not—would not—get in the way.

But that didn't change the fact that she hadn't
expected to spend Christmas without Luck.

"Ta-da!" Toby burst into the room with Mrs.
Rowland in back of him, waving a spatula in the
air. Eve looked and saw the first batch of just-out-
of-the-oven cookies in the platter in his hands. Her
mother had let him improvise—the pinwheels
were a freeform amalgamation of brown and white
dough, and the rest were covered with so much
colored sugar and sprinkles she really couldn't tell
what they were made of.

"Those look great, son," Luck said warmly.

"Have one." Toby proffered the plate.

His father selected a pinwheel, handling it gin-
gerly because it was almost too hot to hold. He
took a bite. "Delicious. I don't think I've ever had
a better pinwheel."

"How about you, Eve?"

"Sure. But it'll taste better when it's cool." She
took one to be polite and balanced it on the rim of
her coffee cup, too upset to eat. Her mother, the
mind reader, noticed and persuaded Toby to go
back to the kitchen with her.

A long silence followed. "So where were we?"
Luck said at last.

"I wish I knew."

He rose and walked to the window, looking at the bleak landscape outside. "When I first met you, do you know what I thought?"

Eve didn't answer.

"That winter was over. Cold as it was that night, it felt like spring. And now . . ." He thrust his hands in his jeans pockets. "It's winter again."

She knew exactly what he was saying in his understated way. In a flash of unwelcome insight, Eve understood just why the holidays could be so treacherous. If all was right with the world and the people you loved were around, then they were great.

Of course, she'd been alone on Christmas before—comparatively alone. Her parents and her friends always made the holiday special, and whenever she'd felt sorry for herself, there was always music to listen to or create.

Falling in love had changed everything. The last thing she wanted was to be emotionally dependent on Luck or anyone else. But she was. She couldn't deny it.

Before he had come into her life, she'd been lonely—but busy enough not to feel that way very often. And good enough at daydreaming to imagine a future with some perfect man she hadn't met yet.

Daydreams were easy to control. Life wasn't. She couldn't find the words to tell Luck that and she was afraid of sounding immature if she did. If only he would take her in his arms and just hug her sadness away . . . but he seemed so remote. And her worries were small stuff compared to the loneliness and grief he'd endured.

So she didn't say much more, besides suggesting that they rejoin her mother and Toby in the kitchen. Luck, who seemed disinclined to go deeper into the matter at hand, agreed.

He brought his coffee cup and sat down at the table, looking curiously at the row of tiny horses and the other ornaments. "Do these belong to Mrs. Gunderson?"

"Yes," Eve said. "She called from Milwaukee to let me know where the box was. I think she hoped I would do a little decorating. From the looks of it, she's been collecting them for years."

"Once a mom, always a mom," said Mrs. Rowland. "You keep thousands of things in the hopes that your grown children will take them along when they—"

She broke off, looking from Luck to Eve.

"When they marry," Eve finished the sentence for her.

"No. That wasn't what I was going to say. When they move on, was all," her mother said.

"Speaking of that, I think Toby and I had better get going." Luck stood and went to get their things. "He's got homework to finish this weekend. C'mon, pal." He held out his son's jacket as Toby gave the pile of fresh-baked cookies a regretful look and dusted the flour from his hands.

"Do we hafta go?"

Luck nodded. "Thanks for the coffee, Eve. Call me later, okay?" He placed a perfunctory kiss on her lips. Eve had a feeling he was doing it more for her mother's benefit than hers. "Take care, Mrs. Rowland."

"Nice to see you again, Luck."

"Mrs. Rowland, can we freeze those for my grandpa and grandma?"

"Sure, honey." She waved the spatula over the

cookies. "I hereby declare these cookies the sole property of Toby McClure."

He seemed satisfied with that official-sounding declaration. The little boy zipped up his jacket and headed for the door, followed by his father.

Mrs. Rowland waved good-bye from the kitchen window, then turned to Eve. "Mind telling me what that was all about?"

Eve sat down at the table and put her head in her hands. "Oh, Mom. It's just that—well, I don't know if either one of us is ready to get married."

"So don't," her mother said softly. "Take your time."

"Is it just me?"

"No, honey. Most couples have second thoughts. When you first fall in love—" she hesitated, looking at her daughter.

Eve picked up on the undercurrent of nervousness in her mother's voice. "You mean you and Dad went through something like this?"

"I was younger than you are now. And I was sure, so sure that I loved him. There wasn't any other man I ever wanted. But marriage was a big step. So when he went off to Minneapolis for middle-management training, I got to sit around little old Cable and wonder if I wasn't supposed to be doing something else."

"Like what?" Eve asked curiously. She had never thought of her mom as having ambitions—or even a life apart from motherhood and being a wife.

Mrs. Rowland shook her head. "I never figured that one out. The truth is, your dad made me so darn happy that no one else and nothing else mattered as much—and then you came along."

"Did you ever want another kid?" That was a

question Eve had never asked, but it came out before she could stop herself. She knew that some of her mixed feelings had to do with becoming a real mother to Toby and the possibility of having a child of her own someday. As an only child, and a somewhat sheltered one at that, Eve had grown up with parents who were devoted to each other and her.

"It didn't happen, put it that way." Her mother's voice held a faint sadness. "But we treasured you. Our beautiful dreamer who loved music and books."

"C'mon, Mom. I wasn't ever beautiful. Just your basic . . . mouse." With chagrin, she realized that Luck's description of her had always fit.

"No, Eve. You always had a very special quality— your shyness was part of your charm, honey. But your dad and I saw right away that Luck brought out the best in you. You changed so much over the summer and fall. He adores you and so does Toby."

Eve sighed. "Is it selfish of me to want him to be around over Christmas?"

Her mother patted her hand. "Not at all. That's only natural. But he strikes me as the kind of man who doesn't break a promise once he makes it. And he most likely told his first wife's parents last Christmas that Toby would be with them this year."

"You're probably right. I was so upset I didn't think to ask him." The Rowlands' holiday plans scarcely differed from year to year. Where they were and who they saw almost never changed.

"You can't expect Luck to read your mind, Eve."

Eve frowned at her mother. "You could give him lessons in that."

Mrs. Rowland suppressed a smile. "It's not as

easy as it used to be. You're out on your own, your music teaching is turning into a real career, and you're almost grown up."

"I heard that 'almost.' You think I still have some growing up to do, at least where Luck is concerned."

"Now you're reading my mind."

Eve slouched in her chair, kicking the table leg. The only thing worse than feeling like a lovelorn teenager was being treated like one. Her mom's sense of humor wouldn't let her indulge in self-pity much longer. "Thanks for listening to my moaning and groaning, Mom," she said at last.

"Do you feel better?"

"No."

Her mother snorted. "Well, you will. Now sit up straight and stop sulking. Luck honors his commitments and he puts his son first. That's the kind of man that makes a good husband."

Luck stuffed a hastily assembled sandwich and a sports drink in his backpack, and headed for his car. He planned to take the trail he'd hiked with his son in early spring and see if he could walk away his blues.

He hadn't expected Eve to react so emotionally to his telling her he would be away on Christmas, but looking back on their two conversations, he wished he'd said more. It wasn't as if she'd pitched a hissy fit or acted like he had to be with her.

She'd just looked miserable. And she'd been so quiet he hadn't known what to say. Something about her mood made him wary, as if her emotions had the power to cast a spell over his. He had felt a sadness come over him at the sight of her woebegone face.

When they'd been alone, he couldn't bring himself to explain why he thought it was so important for his son to be with Lisa's parents. And it had been impossible the second time with Toby there and Mrs. Rowland too.

Inwardly he castigated himself for showing up with his son in tow, although he had hoped to catch her alone and figured, vaguely, that they would send Toby out to play.

Seeing her baking cookies with her mother underlined something he tried to forget: that Eve was younger than he was. A lot younger. He had ten years on her. But the significant issue that separated them was his loss of Lisa. Eve knew nothing of how the experience of a loved one's death changed the survivor. It wasn't anything he would wish to have happen to her. Asking her to marry him—well, he was having second thoughts.

Luck had to admit, if only to himself, that Eve had very little idea of what she was getting into. In fairness, Luck couldn't ask her to deal with so much: one set of ready-made grandparents, and his irascible father, who was nice to Toby but not anyone else. A stepson. A guy like him, who just didn't have it all figured out yet and had been emotionally shut down for years. Plus all the responsibilities of a family that really wasn't hers, when it came right down to it.

Wanting her was understandable. Wanting to claim her for his own might just be selfish. He had begun to resolve his grief, he reminded himself. Putting Lisa's picture away was only the beginning. Maybe he had asked Eve to marry him too soon, but being with her accelerated the healing process. The sensual tenderness she showed him had brought him out of a long, dark era of his life, Luck thought. And damn—she had no real idea of how sexy she was, and that made her all the more irresistible to him.

Loving her—and that included making love to her—had brought him back to life. The thought of her naked in his bed, pulling up the sheets to cover herself, with that sparkle in her eyes, made him hot for her every time. Totally hot.

Thinking along those lines sometimes made him forget how intelligent and sensitive Eve was. Of course she was correct about his first marriage affecting his relationship with her, although he hadn't wanted to admit it.

He hadn't been brave enough to agree and say she was right when it came down to it. Maybe actually loving someone new was taking all the courage he had. It sure as hell was confusing him.

Luck looked for his cell phone, wanting to bring it in case Toby called, even though he knew his son was having a great time over at Brendan's house, supposedly doing homework but more likely sliding down the stairs on Brendan's mom's exercise mats. A personal trainer with two other sons, she'd long ago grown used to the antics of noisy boys.

He found it, stuck it in his pocket, and turned to leave when the phone rang. Out of habit—the habit of a solitary man who'd wanted to be left alone for far too long—he checked the caller ID.

Eve.

He steeled himself not to answer. He needed to be alone for just a little while longer.

* * *

Reaching the road that led to Lake Namekagon made him think of the glorious summer day when they'd taken his boat out on the lake. Only the pines were green now and there were patches of ice where there had been only water dancing with the sun. But the scenery was appealing in its way. At least it matched his mood.

Luck drove to the trail head and parked, grabbing gloves and scarf, and slipping the backpack straps over his shoulders. The recent frost and the resultant heaving had torn up the trail but he could follow the blue blazes painted on the trees. Slogging through frozen mud would work up a sweat, and he hoped the cold would clear his mind. He locked the car and set off.

Two miles out, he turned back when Toby called to say he was invited to the Riveras' and could he go? He was surprised to hear that his dad was out in the middle of the woods and impressed by the clarity of the satellite connection.

Worth the money, Luck thought absently, as he trudged back to the trail head. The weather channel had issued a storm watch, information that his son had added as an afterthought.

Dark clouds had rolled in and covered the sky. Luck slid behind the wheel and fired up the engine, checking the forecast one last time. The weatherman predicted a lot of snow, but he seemed to be hedging his bets and didn't say how much or exactly when it would start. Luck figured he had time to get to the big supermarket a few towns over and stock up. Toby was bouncing on the seat beside him, talking about going to the Riveras'.

"Eddie has the new Xbox, Dad. And some really cool games."

"Oh boy. Try not to rot your brain too much, okay?"

"I won't. His mom makes us do something else after a while. She'll probably throw us out in the snow. When is it going to start?"

Luck put the car in reverse and backed out of the driveway. "Pretty soon, which is why I was rushing you."

"I figured." The little boy stopped fidgeting after a while and looked out the window. "Let it snow. I wanna build a fort and have a snowball fight and make a humongous snowman."

"You have a whole weekend. The Riveras asked if you could stay until Sunday night."

Toby nodded. "Eddie's parents are really nice. His mom's going to have a baby soon. Maybe by Christmas."

"I noticed."

"She looks like she swallowed a pumpkin."

Luck grinned and shook his head. "Just don't tell her that. Every pregnant woman worries about getting her figure back."

"Are you and Eve going to have a baby, Dad?"

He glanced at Toby. "We haven't discussed it."

"Do you want to?"

The boy's eager question was asked in all innocence. But Luck felt a pang. "I don't know, son. We aren't married yet, anyway."

Toby seemed content with that answer and sat back, twiddling the straps on his backpack. Luck looked at him and smiled. His son seemed truly happy, more interested in his friends than his father these days. Which was as it should be.

They reached the Riveras' house, a modest two-story with—incongruously—a huge snowplow parked in the driveway. Tom Rivera worked for the local road crew and it was more efficient for him to start a run from his house than from the giant shed out by the county line that housed the big rigs. He was allowed to bring it home when bad weather was forecast.

"Wow! Look at that!" Toby slid over as far as his seat belt would let him and rolled down his window to admire the snowplow, which was new and bright red. Even under the overcast sky, the paint gleamed.

"Pretty impressive. But not a toy."

Toby rolled his eyes. "Like Mr. Rivera would let us play on it. I'm just looking, that's all."

Leaving it open, Eddie rocketed out the front door without a jacket, followed—slowly—by his pregnant mother, who waved to them. Tom Rivera came out next and caught his son by the collar, bringing him up short. "C'mon in," he shouted.

Luck rolled down his window. "Gotta make a supermarket run," he shouted back. "Thanks, though."

"Bye, Dad." Toby unbuckled his seat belt and grabbed his backpack. He got out of the car, slamming the door, and ran to the Riveras, accepting a slap on the back from Tom and an awkward hug from Eddie's mother.

Round as she was, she still looked beautiful. Luck thought of Toby's question and imagined Eve looking like that. Carrying his baby. The thought

made him get a little misty but he rubbed a gloved
hand roughly over his eyes, dismissing it. He was
glad he had an excuse not to visit with the Riveras.

Luck waved again and reversed out of the driveway, barreling onto the highway ramp not far from
their house. The wind had picked up and the first
flakes were beginning to fall. He went over what
they needed from the market, trying to remember
where everything was so he could dash in, find
stuff, and dash out again.

Milk, meat, butter, eggs, bacon. Bread, muffins,
bagels. Apples and oranges. Canned soup and stew.
Carrots and broccoli, which Toby ate unwillingly.
They didn't need cookies. While he'd been out in
the woods, Mrs. Rowland had dropped off a nicely
wrapped box of the ones Toby wanted to give his
grandparents, and another box with the broken
ones for them to eat.

He got off the highway and swung into the supermarket parking lot, dismayed to see that a lot of
other people had had the same idea. Once inside,
he shopped systematically, glancing occasionally
through the plate-glass windows at the front of the
store. The snow was coming down but not too fast.

Luck paid for the groceries, which he bagged
himself to save time, earning a smile from the
pretty cashier, and made another stop next door
for beer. Loading up the trunk, he slammed it
shut, sending about a half-inch of soft snow flying.
Luck brushed it off his jacket and got behind the
wheel once more.

Driving much more slowly through the crowded
lot, he took a back road to the highway to avoid
the line at the on ramp and got on two miles
ahead. Within a few minutes, the snowstorm hit in
earnest.

The windshield wipers could barely clear the soft, thick flakes from the glass and as soon as they swiped it away, more snow covered it. Keeping extra distance and going slow, Luck oriented himself by the red taillights ahead of him and what he could make out of the cars and trucks on either side.

There weren't many. Or maybe that was just because he couldn't see them. Visibility was close to zero. He kept his speed below thirty and tried to read the road signs through the swirling snow. He knew he was only minutes from his turnoff—but whether he was going to be able to get to it, he didn't know. Like everyone else, he crept along, hoping to avoid an accident.

He didn't see the semi that slammed into him from behind. And he wasn't conscious when the paramedics got him out of the car and took him to the hospital.

"And how are you tonight, Mr. McClure?" a friendly voice said. Luck opened his eyes and looked at the nurse's name tag. The letters were blurry and he squinted until they came into focus. MARY PICARD. MEMORIAL MEDICAL CENTER.

"I feel like I was hit by a truck," he groaned.

"You were," Mary said. "A semi."

Luck nodded weakly, not able to lift his head off the pillow. "So you tell me how I am. I don't remember a thing. What happened?"

"Your car went into a guardrail. The truck driver was okay. He came by to ask how you were doing. We told him you were going to be all right."

"Glad to hear it," Luck said. "Nice of him to visit. Unless it was his fault."

"The cops said it wasn't. Gosh, no one was prepared for that storm—we weren't. Good thing it blew in and blew out in less than six hours. The ER was jumping. No fatalities, thank goodness." She checked his vitals and made notes on the clipboard at the end of his bed.

Groggy as Luck was, he tried to sit up. "Glad to hear that too. How long have I been here?"

"Seven hours." Mary checked her watch. "You got a bad bump on the head that knocked you out when you went into the side window but the air bag worked."

"Does my son know what happened?"

Mary Picard patted his hand. "Your father thought it was best not to give him too many details of the crash, but yes, Toby does know you're in the hospital. He's still staying with the Riveras."

"They're good people."

The nurse inclined her head in agreement. "I met Tom Rivera. One of the other road crew guys helped the paramedics get you out of the wreck, and he happened to mention the accident to Tom. He stopped by to see you too. You can call Toby if you like." She pointed to the bedside phone with the eraser end of her pencil. "Everything's taken care of. We might discharge you by tomorrow, depending on your tests. All you need to do is rest."

"Okay." Luck sank back into the pillows and closed his eyes. "Sounds like a plan. But one more thing."

Mary Picard gave him a bright-eyed look, ready to answer questions.

"The car?"

She winked. "Totaled. Now go to sleep."

"Yes, ma'am."

* * *

Several hours later, he awoke to hear the sweetest sound in the world: Eve's voice.

"Hey," he murmured, focusing on her worried face. "When did you get here?"

She leaned over to kiss him on the cheek, giving him an impression of warm flesh and sweet-smelling woman that shot right to his—well, not all of him was limp. Down, boy, Luck thought. So this was what it meant to be a man. You could get hit by a semi but some things still worked, no matter what. Feeling ridiculously happy to be alive, he smiled at her.

She smiled back, tremulously. "About an hour ago. Mary Picard thought you might be waking up. She sent me in."

"Nice lady."

"Yes, she is. She made sure to notify everyone. Your dad's here—he's waiting down the hall. Mary said we had to come in one at a time."

Luck nodded. "My dad let you go first, huh?"

Eve looked a little surprised. "I didn't think of it that way. But I guess he did."

"Then he likes you."

"Maybe so."

Luck yawned and looked around the room, realizing that he had it all to himself. "Private room? My insurance doesn't cover that."

"Your father paid for it."

"Oh. Nice of him."

Eve sat up straight, looking almost prim. "Should I leave so he can come in?"

He reached out a hand and pulled her a little closer. "Not yet. Give me a kiss first."

Her lips were soft and the kiss was infinitely tender. Luck enjoyed it more than any other she had ever given him. She broke it off, though, looking down at him, fondness and worry in her eyes. He didn't want her to worry but he loved having her so close.

"So what happens next?" he murmured.

"You get to take the rest of December off. I don't think your father would even let you work."

"Fine with me."

The doctor and a neurologist confirmed what Mary had said: he was basically fine. They discharged Luck that morning, although he griped about the wheelchair ride to the hospital door.

Bundled up, sitting in the front seat of the Rowlands' car, Luck looked through the window at a transformed world. The snowstorm had left more than two feet of snow that covered the countryside in pure white drifts, dotted with dark green pines.

"Wow. Look at that. A classic Wisconsin winter wonderland."

"Our first big storm of the season and December's just beginning." Eve kept her eyes on the road. "Toby and Eddie built a huge snow fort. And school's closed today—too many kids out and a lot of the teachers couldn't get in. The crews are still plowing the back roads."

"How's he doing? Does he even miss me?" Luck asked wryly.

"We didn't want him to freak out. Once we knew you were going to be all right, we kind of downplayed the accident. I hope you don't mind."

"No." Luck fell silent for a minute or so. "Considering that he lost his mother so young, I wouldn't want him to worry about losing me. You did the right thing."

"Well, it was all of us. The family. Yours and mine, I mean. And we agreed that you should take it easy. Your dad thinks you've been working too hard."

He shot her a sidelong glance, thinking about what she'd just said. Interesting. So he'd been knocked out cold and they—the McClures and the Rowlands—had come together as a family. Very interesting.

"I won't argue," Luck said.

"Funny you should say that." She pointed to a folded sheet of hospital letterhead stuck in her purse. "Moodiness and argumentative behavior sometimes follow a head injury. The doctor briefed us on what to watch out for. I took notes."

"Thank you, nurse," he teased. "Right now I'm way too happy to argue about anything. Hospitals are not my favorite places. But they took good care of me."

"I know," she said. "Mary Picard let me sleep on a cot next to you."

"Really. She didn't tell me that. I'm touched." He was more than touched. Somehow, that was all the proof he needed of her love for him. He wanted to jump for joy and kiss her senseless the second he got out of the car. He wanted to ask her to drive to Duluth and pick out the biggest damn diamond ring in the first jewelry store they came to. But she would think he was crazy if he did anything like that. His worries about Eve, his depressed mood—in fact, all of the dark emotions that had surfaced before the accident seemed to have been knocked clear out of his head, although he did remember them.

"Here we are." She turned into the driveway of his house outside of Cable.

He looked at the pure white snow atop it and a delicate trimming of icicles along the gutters that caught the light. "This old place never looked so good, Eve."

She motioned to the high banks of snow on either side. "Tom Rivera plowed your driveway."

"Perfect job. I wish I had a rig like his. Considering how pregnant his wife is, it's a good thing the county lets him park that snowplow at home. They won't have to worry about getting her to the hospital on time no matter how bad the weather gets."

"Silvia doesn't ever seem to worry about anything. She's a sweetie. I forgot to tell you—she was all set to bring you dinner in the hospital so you wouldn't have to eat applesauce and rubber chicken, but then they let you go home. She packed everything up in a cooler. It's in the trunk."

"Lucky me. Toby says she's a great cook."

"Yeah, he really likes her. He's going to stay there again tonight."

Luck nodded, hoping that meant he was going to get even luckier. All he wanted was to sleep in his own bed, and hold her in his arms all night long.

"So. Uh, are you staying?"

Eve gave him a tentative smile that grew wider and wider. "If you want me to."

She dealt with the cooler and a few other things she wanted to bring in without letting him help. Luck stepped carefully on the cleared pathway to the front steps, not wanting to end up in the ER again with a sprained ankle or broken wrist. He turned the key in the lock, and the sound was almost magical.

It meant he was home. Safe. With Eve.

She came up the porch steps behind him, her handbag swinging from her wrist, clutching the small cooler filled with food. The sheet of paper from the hospital with her notes on it fluttered down on the doormat, and he picked it up, straightening to push the unlocked door open for her.

Eve headed for the kitchen and he turned on the living room lights, quickly scanning the paper for what she was supposed to watch out for.

Severe or unusual headaches.
Visual disturbances.
Numbness in one or both sides of the body.
Partial or complete paralysis.
Dizziness, vertigo, disorientation.

So far, so good. He hadn't experienced any of those.

Moodiness. Argumentative behavior. She'd mentioned that. Nope. *Despair.* Nope again. He was feeling the exact opposite.

Exhilaration.

That fit. He could add *joy* and *relief* and *gratitude* that his accident had no lasting ill effects to the list. But if feeling glad all over might mean he had to go back to the hospital, it was probably best not to share that feeling with her.

Luck took off his jacket and warm things, and went into the kitchen to help her. She'd already taken her coat off and slung it over the back of a kitchen chair. He handed her the list. Busy peeking under the foil of a see-through plastic container that held saffron rice and braised chicken, she waved it away. Luck stuck the list on the refrigerator with a magnet.

"Wow, this smells good. Ready for dinner?" she asked.

"Sure. Am I allowed to have wine?"

Eve shrugged. "The doctor didn't say you couldn't."

"I'm asking you, nurse."

She shook her head. "Stop it. I am completely unqualified to dispense medical advice."

Luck was glad to hear it. He got out two wine-glasses, uncorked a bottle of good burgundy, and began to set the table. Eve microwaved two plates of the rice and chicken, and while the seconds counted down she dished up the salad that Silvia Rivera had made.

When she went back into the kitchen for their main courses, he pulled out her chair and poured the wine. Then he lit a candle.

She came back in, using pot holders to bring two plates filled with steaming food. "Isn't that romantic."

Luck favored her with a wicked grin. "We have something to celebrate. So let's do it right."

Later that night, after they had made tender love and Eve had fallen asleep in his arms, Luck switched on the bedside lamp, moving with care so as not to waken her. Dreaming, she nestled deeper into the crook of his arm, her silky hair covering one flushed cheek. He reached up a hand to brush the hair back behind her ear and Eve stirred slightly.

"Hush," he whispered. "Go back to sleep. My turn to watch over you."

Chapter 16

"Lurleen, stand still," Eve said around a mouthful of pins. She removed them one by one, sticking each in the unfinished hem of Lurleen's white robe. "Do you want your wings to fall off?"

"Mercy me. Certainly not." The tall hairdresser looked down at Eve. "Now tell me how you got to be director, caterer, and costumer for this pageant."

"Just lucky, I guess," Eve grumbled. "But I don't know if bringing a box of doughnuts in could be called catering."

"You're doing a lot of work," Lurleen insisted. She shifted a little on platform shoes that made her even taller.

"Love those. I didn't know angels wore platforms." Eve sat back on her heels.

"This one does. But I'll wear my white slippers for the show, of course. Just thought these would make it easier for you to pin the hem."

"They did." Eve took the edge of the robe between finger and thumb and inspected her handiwork with satisfaction. "You won't trip."

"Good. I'd probably take out all the shepherds and the wise men too if I did." Lurleen twirled around in the full-skirted robe when Eve let go, and warmed up her voice with a few la-la-las.

"Save it for the rehearsal," Eve instructed her.

"Yes, ma'am. Us divas have to pamper our little old vocal cords."

Eve shooed her away. "Next up," she called. Five small shepherds appeared, two boys and three girls, dressed by their moms in big pillowcases dyed brown and belted with cotton rope. Their jeans and sneakers peeked out below. "You guys look pretty good. Where's your sheep?"

"My dad made some out of cardboard," a girl piped up. "He's over there with my little sister."

Eve looked to where she was pointing. A flock of two-dimensional sheep lay flat on a dropcloth, already painted white. The girl's sister and a couple of her friends were carefully dipping cotton balls in glue and sticking them on the sheep.

One girl, a little older than the others, had been entrusted with the task of painting eyes and noses and hooves in black. She put a dollop of black paint from the end of her brush on a sheep face and made a big, funny-looking nose as Eve watched.

Eve nodded approvingly. "Great work, sheepsters. Send in the wise men."

The girl who'd spoken up waved her pals over and three older boys in wigs and beards made from string mops came over. The effect was comical, considering that they were wearing team jerseys sponsored by Cable's only barber.

"My beard itches," a boy complained.

Eve loosened the string that held it on and he treated himself to a soothing scratch. "Think you can sing in them?" she asked.

The boys looked at each other and launched into the first stanza of "We Three Kings," more or less on key. Eve applauded. "Very good! You memorized that perfectly."

"We memorized the other version too," one of the boys said, "the one about rubber cigars and stuff."

Eve waggled a reproving finger at them. "But you're not going to sing that on stage, right?"

The boys shook their heads, giving her solemn looks. The annual Christmas pageant at the church was a much-loved tradition, and all their relatives would attend. She knew they would behave. Eve had decided to begin rehearsals for the pageant first, ahead of the school chorale, even though it would be performed later.

The school kids were all in the same class and used to doing things together—and they only had to sing, not remember lines or entrances and exits, and they didn't have to deal with costumes. The pageant kids were different ages, and some were very young.

But she'd figured out a role for everyone who wanted to participate, grateful for the other adults who'd volunteered their time. Even Silvia Rivera, a few weeks away from her due date, had come to help out. She'd brought a platter of healthy snacks for the kids and was sitting on a folding chair in one corner amusing the littlest ones with quiet games.

Eve walked over to collect them—the children were villagers and all they had to do was sit quietly as part of the onstage tableau and try to remember not to wave at their proud moms and dads. "Hi, guys. Are you being good?"

"Yes, Eve. Just look at them." Silvia Rivera

stretched out her hands to the circle of children gathered around her and beamed at them all.

"Is our Mary here today?" Eve didn't see Nyree, a gentle girl with an angelic face, among the group.

"No, she has the sniffles," said one of the children. "Joseph has strep."

"Uh-oh. Think you can be good villagers without Mary and Joseph?"

The children nodded eagerly. Eddie came over and touched his mother on the shoulder. "My mom can be Mary for today," he said. "Just so long as she gets to sit down."

"Would you mind, Silvia? That really is all you'd have to do. We're just doing the preliminary staging today, getting the kids used to going on and off stage at the right times and things like that."

"Sure. Why not?" Silvia said. She got to her feet with a helping hand from her sturdy son and asked the group of children to line up two by two. It occurred to Eve that the real Mary on her way to Bethlehem had probably looked a lot like Silvia did today: luminous dark eyes and a face that was happy and a little tired at the same time, very pregnant and rubbing her arching back under the blue dress she wore.

"Right this way." Eve led the small villagers and Silvia, as Eddie folded the chair and carried it for his mother. The parish house meeting hall was just big enough for a Christmas pageant and the small stage at one end had a few of the players wandering around it already.

Lurleen clomped up the steps at the side, pulling up her angel robe so that her platform shoes and purple jeans showed, ready to boss the kids around for all she was worth. Her wings, slightly lopsided, banged against her back with every step.

Eve took Silvia's hand and they went up next. Eddie followed, unfolding the chair on the spot where the stable and manger would be set up. Silvia settled into it with an appreciative sigh. "Thanks, m'ijo." The little kids gathered around her again and sat down.

"Places, people," Eve called. She picked up a clipboard at the front of the stage and read what she'd jotted down. "When I call your part, say 'here'. Three wise men?"

"Here. Here."

"Where's the third?"

A bearded boy galloped wildly up the stairs and joined the other two. "Here!"

"Okay. Shepherds?"

The brown-clad shepherds replied as one.

"Okay. Sheep?" she asked mischievously. The lad coming up the stairs with them under his arm baa-ed. He leaned the sheep against the back curtain one by one, and not a single cotton ball fell off. The girl who'd painted their faces had given each a unique expression, although they were otherwise identical.

"Angel?"

Lurleen was flicking the switch of the flashlight that was supposed to illuminate the star over the nativity scene. "I think we need to put new batteries in this thing . . . .whoops. No, we don't." She shone it by accident into her own eyes and blinked, scowling in a way that made the three wise men snicker behind their beards.

"Angel?" Eve asked again.

"Most definitely here," Lurleen said loudly. She lifted up the flashlight with a grand gesture. "Behold! I bring you tidings of great joy! The flashlight is working!"

"She looks like the Statue of Livery," a little vil
lager whispered, loud enough for everyone to hear
Everyone laughed and Lurleen joined in. Good
thing their angel had a great sense of humor, Eve
thought.

Reverend Johnson, who'd poked his head in the
door to see how everything was coming along
laughed too. Then Eve saw Luck coming down the
aisle, a few sheets of unpainted plywood tucked
under his arm. Wearing a barn jacket and a red
muffler, he looked like the picture of health—and
ruggedly handsome. But she had to do her duty
and give him a lecture, even if she would much
rather have kissed him.

"You're supposed to be resting," she said with
mock sternness.

"I watched TV for a while. But I got bored. So
Tom came over and we jigsawed some scenery
Here's some of beautiful downtown Bethlehem."
He separated the pieces of plywood and leaned
them against the row of seats in front of the stage
"They need to be primed and painted, but I think
they'll do fine. Like 'em?"

Eve smiled her approval. "They're really nice."

"Gotta do something to get your attention these
days. I don't see enough of you."

She felt instantly guilty. Directing two productions
was taking up way too much of her time. But . . . if
he wasn't going to be around this Christmas . .
she had to do something to keep from thinking
about it. "Thanks, Luck," was all she said. But she
gave him a discreet kiss on the cheek when she
thought no one was looking. "Where's Tom?"

"He went over to the county shed. Said not to le
Silvia stay on her feet too long—but I see you've

aken care of that." He pulled off his glove and waved to Tom's wife.

Eve looked onstage and caught Lurleen's inquisitive glance at Luck. She must have seen the brief kiss—and Eve was going to have to answer a lot of good-natured questions in the near future.

She assessed the number of people on the stage and looked around the auditorium for any stragglers. A few more kids divested themselves of jackets, mittens, and scarves, aided by their moms and dads, then made sure the hockey skates they'd brought in were stowed away and raced to join their friends.

"Looks like hockey practice just let out," Luck observed, resting an affectionate hand on Eve's shoulder. Lurleen didn't miss that gesture either.

"It's amazing how enthusiastic they are about participating in the pageant," Eve said.

He nodded. "Toby really wanted to be in it, but since the chorale is scheduled a week earlier than the pageant, he had to stick with that. Lisa's parents bought his plane ticket months ago. He's flying out right after school closes for the Christmas break."

Eve stiffened under his touch. That said it all, if not in so many words. Even though he was fully recovered from the accident, she'd thought—maybe better word was hoped—that it might motivate him to remain in Cable. With her. But more than ever, she didn't want to press the point. The decision was his to make and Christmas was still a few weeks away.

She nodded and turned her attention back to the stage. "Places!" she called again. "Everybody get where you're supposed to be—and stay there."

* * *

Luck was enjoying the gift of time more than he'd thought possible. His guess: Grant McClure thought of his son's accident as a wake-up call. He'd talked only briefly to his father at the hospital, but Grant had called frequently since—and not to discuss business.

As usual, his father was a stickler about keeping his word. Luck handed most of his business responsibilities over to a capable subordinate that both McClures trusted, and didn't intend to look at a profit-and-loss statement or balance sheet until January rolled around. His dad insisted that Luck had been working too hard, and Luck had a feeling that the older man thought his preoccupied state of mind might have contributed to the crash.

It was unusual for his dad to discuss emotions at all, and he wasn't exactly eloquent about it. Just issued blunt orders and expected them to be followed, as usual. But this time, his businesslike approach had brought Grant McClure closer to his only son—and Luck had a lot of extra hours to spend with Toby as a result.

Luck had given a lot of thought to his relationship with his own son. In its own odd way, it had worked for both of them for a long time. But he couldn't say now that everything about it had been healthy for Toby. Luck had managed on his own for too long, withdrawn into grief that seemed to have a permanent lock on his heart. His boy hadn't had the freedom to just be a kid—a happy kid who didn't have to worry about his lonely father. The memory of Toby's tactless attempts at matchmaking still made Luck smile—and wince a little.

And then along came Eve, when and where he least expected to find someone he could care about. Shy and sweet. But with a mind of her own—and everything else he wanted in a woman.

No wonder he'd rushed her into saying yes to marriage. When he thought about it, he'd rushed things from the night they'd met, when he'd bumped into her on that cold street outside the tavern. Couldn't blame himself for that. But a woman like Eve was worth waiting for.

He returned his mind to the task at hand: painting the scenery for the Christmas pageant. The primer coat had dried and he sketched on it lightly in pencil, adding details he remembered from Sunday school books with colored illustrations of the Holy Land.

Nothing grand about Bethlehem came to mind, just houses with clay walls and thatched roofs. He sketched in windows. It would be fun to paint in faces—and jigsaw some openings so kids could peek at the audience if they stood behind the scenery. Might be nice to add a few palm trees, he thought. Easy enough to build those, and they could create palm fronds out of green posterboard cut with scissors.

Absorbed in his work, he only half-heard the school bus pull up outside and Toby slam the front door behind him. "Anybody home?" the boy called.

"Yeah," Luck called back. "I'm building a city. Come on down and see."

The thunk of a backpack hitting the floor in the hall made the basement ceiling reverberate. "You mean like Sim City?" Toby asked as he galloped down the stairs. He glanced at the computer in the corner and saw a blank, dark screen. It wasn't even on.

"No, son. This is real—well, not exactly. It's scenery for the Christmas pageant. The little town of Bethlehem."

"Oh," Toby said. "But how come it's all white, Dad? Did Bethlehem look like that?"

"No one really knows. Anyway, that's just the primer coat. We can paint it any colors we want."

"Cool." Toby studied the light sketching on the flat plywood. "Is that a window? Can you cut it out so kids can look out?"

Luck grinned at his son and ruffled his hair. "Great minds think alike. Let's get to work."

Eve pulled into the driveway of the Gunderson house, in between the snowbanks neatly piled on either side. Thank goodness for Arvid Bergen. He mounted a snowplow blade on his tractor to clear his way to the main road and he'd made a stop to do her driveway after the big storm.

She'd offered to pay him but he'd refused with a smile, saying something about just being neighborly. One of these days, when she wasn't so busy, she would stomp through the snow with a pie or a box of cookies for him.

But between the church pageant and the school chorale, she barely had time to breathe. Both were coming along nicely—Toby's classmates had learned every word of every song in the chorale program by heart.

Jimmy Caldwell was going to be the star of the school show, according to his mom, Lurleen. Eve knew that the hairdresser set aside time to help her son rehearse, complaining about his lack of stick-to-it-iveness. But Jimmy had a promising tenor

voice, high and clear. Eve had assigned him a solo:
the opening lyrics of "Silent Night." She could just
imagine the hush in the school auditorium when
the boy began the beautiful song . . . she could
hear it in her head right now.

A loud honk interrupted her reverie and Eve
looked over her shoulder to see who had pulled
up behind her. A purple velvet glove waved merrily
out the window of an old station wagon and Eve
caught the glint of light on multiple earrings. But
it took her a second to recognize who it was:
Lurleen was wearing wraparound sunglasses and a
hooded parka.

She got out of the station wagon, looking ready
to hit the slopes, and came over to Eve's car.
Rather than roll down the window and keep the
engine running, Eve got out, grabbing her teaching materials, sheet music, and handbag. She wasn't
all that eager for company but there was no saying
no to Lurleen.

"Hiya! Mind if I come in? Jimmy lost the sheet
music he needed and I was hoping you might have
an extra copy somewhere—"

"Sure. Come on in," Eve said brightly. If that was
all Lurleen wanted, Eve would find it in a hurry
and then have the rest of the afternoon to herself.

They went in through the mud porch, kicking
off snowboots there but keeping their jackets on
until they were inside the kitchen. Lurleen pushed
her wraparound sunglasses back over her hair before she took off her jacket and arranged it over
the back of a wooden chair. "Now isn't this cozy,"
she said with an appreciative look around Mrs.
Gunderson's kitchen. "You live here all by yourself, I hear."

Eve wondered what else Lurleen had heard. She figured she was about to find out. "Would you like some coffee?" she said, resigned to her fate.

"Sure. Thanks so much." She fluffed up her exuberant ringlets with both hands, making the sunglasses fall back down on her nose. "Oh, my. Dark in here. These sunglasses really work."

Eve had to smile. Lurleen's zany sense of humor was contagious. She set about making coffee and brought out the cookie jar, looking inside. A few of Toby's cookies were left at the bottom. She fished them out and put them on a pretty antique plate.

"Reminds me of my grandmother's china," Lurleen said, taking off the sunglasses and looking closely at the plate. "She had a whole set just like this."

"Mrs. Gunderson probably had the same pattern," Eve said. "Everything you see belongs to her. I'm just renting this place while she looks after her sister in Milwaukee."

"Oh, I see," Lurleen said. She picked up a cookie and bit into it, licking colored sugar from her lips. "I just bet a kid made these. When Jimmy helps me bake he puts on so many decorations you can't see the cookie underneath."

"Good guess," Eve laughed. "So does Toby McClure."

Lurleen nodded sagely and finished the cookie. "That's Luck's little boy. His dad is sweet on you, I can tell. I remember the day you came in for highlights and said you had a new guy. So he was the one, huh?"

Eve only nodded. She didn't feel as if she knew Lurleen well enough to go into the details of her relationship with Luck. Eve didn't doubt that a hairdresser was used to women letting their hair down, literally and figuratively, but even so—she wasn't going to gossip.

"He sure is handsome," Lurleen said eagerly.

"Yes, he is." Eve stood up when the timer on the coffeemaker beeped. "How do you like your coffee?"

"Half-and-half, three sugars," Lurleen said. "Not counting calories."

Eve opened the refrigerator door and Heidi bounded into the room, meowing. Lurleen sneezed.

"Bless you."

China followed the smaller cat, waving her tail in an imperious way. Lurleen sneezed again. "Mercy! I may have to skip the beverage service—I'm allergic to cats—oh!" She sneezed a third time.

"I'm so sorry," Eve said politely. "I could make you coffee to go. I have the paper cups with lids."

"Th-that's all right." Lurleen was collecting her sunglasses, handbag, and slinging her hooded jacket over her shoulders. She sneezed again. "I'll see you at the church, Eve." She walked out to the mud porch and got her boots on in record time, then headed out.

"Bye! Call me—I'll bring in that music you said Jimmy needed!"

Too busy sneezing to reply, Lurleen only waved.

Eve turned to the cats with a smile. "Thanks, you two." She took out the half-and-half and found a teaspoon. Once they had their treat, she poured herself a cup of coffee and relaxed. She crossed one leg over the other and her foot touched the cardboard box of ornaments that she hadn't moved from under the table.

She reached down and pulled it out so she

could see inside it. Someone, probably her mother, had put the little red horses and the tomtens and the straw stars on top.

What with one thing and another, Eve hadn't thought about them since. She wondered what Luck was doing right now, and whether she should call him. Then she wondered why she was being such a wuss about it.

Because you might have to do without him this Christmas, she reminded herself. But it was best not to give him the idea that she couldn't get through the holiday without him. Because she could.

Eve picked up the straw stars and untangled the string that linked them. It looked long enough to decorate the head of her bed. And she could put other little things along the top of the white wainscoting, just for fun. The cats might knock them down, but Mrs. Gunderson had wanted her to use her treasured decorations. She could set aside the breakables and just put up the straw items and wooden toys instead.

She finished her coffee and found a bag to carry the decorations upstairs in. It was something to do. Especially since Luck hadn't called.

Eve kneeled on the quilt, stringing the stars over the headboard and sitting back on her heels to admire them. They looked just right in the old-fashioned room, and the sight cheered her up a little.

Then the phone rang. There was only one and it was downstairs, since the frugal Mrs. Gunderson didn't believe in extravagances like extension phones or cordless models.

She wondered if she should ignore it. There was an insistent quality to the ring that made her think it might be Lurleen. Eve told herself to stop imagining things and unfolded herself from her kneeling position. Her legs were a little stiff and she didn't rush down the stairs. But the phone kept ringing.

Okay, it had to be Lurleen. Luck wasn't that patient. She picked up the receiver. "Hello?"

"Hi." Luck's warm greeting sent a thrill right through her.

"Oh—hi," she replied, trying to sound nonchalant.

"Toby and I are building Bethlehem. It's coming along but we're ready to take a break. So what are you up to?"

Missing you, she wanted to say. "Nothing much. Doing a little decorating."

He was silent for a few seconds. "So you bought a tree."

"Did she, Dad?" she heard Toby say excitedly. "Can we help her trim it? I really, really want a tree this year."

"You're going to your grandparents," Luck reminded him.

"But you're not," Toby said. "So we could have a tree, so you have something to look at in the living room, and we could decorate it. After we decorate Eve's tree."

"Are you listening to all this?"

Eve could hear the laughter in Luck's voice, but she was too startled by what Toby had just said to be polite. "Yes. Why didn't you tell me you weren't going with Toby?" she demanded.

"Ah, I was waiting for the right moment. There

was something else—well, I wanted to surprise you with that."

What surprise? Was he buying her an engagement ring? That question moved to #1 on the List of Questions She Didn't Want to Ask.

"Dad, don't tell her about the croquet set—" she heard Toby whisper loudly before his father clapped a hand over the receiver.

Eve was taken aback. She had fretted and fussed, and told herself that she shouldn't come between him and his son at Christmastime. She hadn't said one word about it after his accident—it just didn't seem right. And she was getting a croquet set, not an engagement ring.

She heard his hand come off the receiver. "Are you there?" Luck asked.

"Yes."

He must have sensed the mixed emotions in that one little word, because he told Toby to go watch TV upstairs.

"Want me to come over? I don't have to bring the scenery pieces or anything, I'll just take some digital shots of it and you can see if it's what you had in mind."

"I'm sure it's fine," she said tonelessly.

"Well . . . then I won't. Want to come over later? Toby and I will cook for you."

"No. I mean, no thanks. I have a lot of work to do." She just couldn't put any warmth in her tone. "Maybe we can get together on Sunday," she added.

"Okay. Whatever you want. Call me. I'm not going anywhere."

Maybe not today or tomorrow, she thought crossly, after she managed a polite good-bye. But soon enough.

A knock on the door brought her downstairs

again, in a very bad mood. Why was it that when you didn't want to see people, they started showing up in droves? She looked out the window and recognized her mother's car. With a Christmas tree tied to the top of it.

Vowing to be perky if it killed her, Eve opened the door and smiled brightly.

"Hi, honey! You know, I was thinking about all those pretty decorations in Mrs. Gunderson's box. It seemed like a shame not to use them. So I bought you a tree."

Eve's eyes widened. "You mean that's for me?"

Her mother nodded. "Uh-huh. I bought a tree stand too. They're very inexpensive. Just in case there wasn't one here."

"But Mom—" Eve stopped herself. No matter how bad her mood was, it wasn't her mother's fault. And it wasn't as if Eve could tell her to take the tree back.

"Your dad went with me," Mrs. Rowland went on, going back to the car to untie the tree. Eve threw on a jacket and slipped her feet into clogs, following her outside.

Her mother opened the side doors and released the slipknots in the twine that ran behind the seats and up around the roof of the car. "He pinched the needles all over it to see if the tree was fresh. Then he had the guy stand it up so he could look at it from all sides and make sure it wasn't lopsided. You know how he is."

Eve nodded. Her father had inspected every tree for sale on the lot during the holidays, taking his time to select the one he deemed perfect. Left to her own devices, Eve would have picked the most forlorn-looking one, feeling that it needed to be loved just as it was.

She stretched out a hand to grab the trunk and felt the cold pitch smear her palm. Gloves would have been a good idea, but it was too late now. Her mother had taken the trouble to bring her a tree and the least Eve could do was help her get it in.

Mrs. Rowland grasped it near the top. "Ready?"

"Yup."

They lifted it off easily and marched into the house with it between them, setting it in the kitchen temporarily. The cats went ballistic, sniffing it and biting at the needles.

Her mother shooed them away. "Naughty kitties. Stop that. They'll throw up if they eat the needles, Eve."

Eve picked up China, holding her around her soft middle and made a grab for Heidi, who dodged her. She put China behind the cellar door and closed it. "One down, one to go." She knew that the younger cat would lead her on a merry chase and she wasn't in the mood for it.

Mrs. Rowland went back outside for the tree stand but Eve took off her jacket and kicked off her clogs. She folded her arms across her chest, looking the tree over. Even leaning against the kitchen counter it was taller than she was—and its piney fragrance filled the air.

She took a deep breath and let it out. Her irritability went with it. Her mother came back in, humming a Christmas carol. "Do you like it, honey? Where shall we put it?"

"Hmm. We could leave it right where it is."

"I know you don't mean that. Don't you think it would look nice in the living room?"

That had to be the oldest mom trick in the book: making your kid think that they had arrived at a decision you had actually made. Still, her mother's innocent smile left no doubt in Eve's mind that arguing would be a waste of time.

"Sure. The living room would be great. Let me put down a waterproof cloth before you fill up the tree stand and we'll wrestle it in there."

"Okay." Her mother took off her warm things and bustled around the kitchen, filling a pitcher with water for the stand, and sitting down to assemble it.

She fumbled with the pronglike legs and the screws that attached them to the part that held water. "I wish your father were here. He could get this together in a jiffy."

"Please don't call him," Eve said. "I'm sure we can figure it out." For someone who didn't want to be alone at Christmas, she realized that she was being fairly surly about anyone other than Luck coming over.

She took the partially assembled tree stand from her mother, and tackled the task herself. "Righty tighty, lefty loosey," she said under her breath as she fiddled with the bolts and nuts.

Her mother laughed. "Your father used to say that. You two had so much fun building things together way back when—do you remember?"

With a flash of guilt, Eve remembered what Luck had said. He'd been working on the scenery for the Christmas pageant with his son, and she'd sounded totally uninterested. "Yes, I do." Her voice was subdued.

"What's the matter, honey?"

Eve didn't answer right away. She scrubbed a hand over her face to get rid of the moisture in her eyes and the prickly feeling in her nose that signaled the onset of a good cry. "Nothing."

Her mother sighed. "This is your first Christmas

on your own. We just wanted to make it special for you. I'm sorry. Maybe we should have let you pick your own tree—"

"It's not that, Mom. It was really nice of you and Dad to pick it out for me. I know you got me the best tree on the lot. I was just—feeling sentimental, I guess. I do remember those days . . . and all the good times."

"I'm glad," her mother said softly.

"Do you think we can get the tree to stand up without him sitting in the recliner giving directions to us helpless women?"

Mrs. Rowland's eyes twinkled. "Quite probably."

Chapter 17

You're a big girl now, Eve told herself as she watched her mother drive away.

And you really are alone.

She let China out of the cellar and the cat meowed plaintively until Eve picked her up. Might as well enjoy the tree in its natural state, she thought. She carried the cat into the living room and sat down with her, recalling her mother's advice to let the branches relax before she hung ornaments on them.

Eve plopped down into the sofa, keeping China in her lap. The cat purred contentedly as Eve stroked her, inhaling the glorious pine smell of the fresh tree. She could feel herself relaxing too, little by little.

The dark green of the tree seemed to absorb the light in the room and it looked much bigger in here than it had in the kitchen. But Mrs. Gunderson's kitchen was a lot larger than the parlor, as the old lady called the living room. Eve wondered how women managed to do it all back then, cooking and canning and washing and tending to large families and the field hands too. She would bet anything that farmwives didn't miss all that back-breaking labor.

Lost in reverie, she thought about how pretty the tree would look with all the ornaments in the box and colored lights—which she didn't have. Driving back to town to buy some at the hardware store just seemed like too much effort.

Oh, geez. In honor of Mrs. Gunderson, she decided, she was going to get up off her duff, quit feeling sorry for herself, and get Christmas back on track. She lifted the drowsy cat out of her lap and settled her into the cushions of the sofa, then got up.

Eve collected jacket, car keys, and handbag on her way out. A quick look in the mirror told her that she looked utterly unglamorous, with pine needles in her hair and no lipstick, but it was too late now. The day was drawing to a close and she needed to get into Cable before the store closed.

The road unrolled ahead of her, fringed by tall, dark pines. The snowstorm that had blown through northern Wisconsin had left deep drifts in the wooded areas that showed no signs of melting. It was definitely going to be a white Christmas, but you could count on that around here.

Eve switched on the radio, choosing a classical station that was playing something undemanding to listen to. It never took long to get into town, especially not in the evening, and she parked in front of the store. Grabbing her things, she swung out of the car and pushed through the door.

The jumble that was Moore's Hardware was something she enjoyed. The store owner attempted to organize the stock every so often, but basically,

hat meant he knew where everything was and the
customers didn't. She asked John, the owner, for
he location of Christmas lights, and he directed
her down an aisle. Humming along with the piped-
n carols on the sound system, she proceeded down
t—and ran smack into a very familiar, plaid-flannel-
clad chest. Luck McClure's chest.

"Hello, Eve."

She was completely flustered for a moment.
"Wh-what are you doing here?"

"Needed a few things to finish the scenery.
What about you?" His smile was broad and warm,
making her wish she hadn't been so rude to him
when he called earlier.

"I was hoping they still had Christmas lights
left." She looked around on the lower shelves and
didn't see any.

If he thought that her buying a tree and decorating it herself was rude, he didn't mention it, just
nodded as he said, "I think they do." He reached
for the last package of lights, way up on a high
shelf, and handed it to her. Eve had to fight the
impulse to put her arms around his waist and give
him a big hug.

I can't stay mad at him, she thought. I just can't.
She clutched the package, an off-brand she had
never heard of. But beggars couldn't be choosers.

"There you go." He beamed, like he had per-
sonally invented Jewel Many Color Tiny Twinkle
Nitey Lites just for her. Eve ventured a tentative
smile.

Luck looked down the aisle, then up the other
way. Automatically, she did the same, seeing no
one. His big hands came up to caress her shoulders and draw her into his embrace. Then his
mouth came down on hers for a brief but wickedly

sensual kiss. The package she was holding kept him from pressing into her, but even so. The kiss just about knocked her emotional socks off.

He broke it off and looked around. They were still alone. Luck stroked her hair, picking out a few pine needles. "Sure you don't want me to come over and help you decorate?"

"Ah . . ."

John Moore chose that moment to enter the aisle, helping a customer, but he didn't give them a second glance. Luck moved away from her just the same. Eve felt a sense of aching loss, missing the warmth and strength of his big body, and wanting another kiss more than she'd ever wanted anything in her life.

It hadn't been all that long since they'd spent the night together, but her overactive imagination and tendency to worry made it seem like forever.

"Toby went over to a friend's house, just in case you were wondering. Kid has quite a social life. He doesn't need his old man like he used to. And that's good. Anyway, I'm free." He winked.

That did it. "Sure. Come on over," she said weakly. She held the package of twinkle lights close to her chest and floated toward the door, past the cash register.

Luck was right behind her, and he took her arm. "Don't you want to pay for those?"

"Huh?" Eve turned scarlet. "Oh, yeah." She turned around and looked for John, then dug into her purse for the money.

Luck walked into the Gunderson kitchen, shutting the door to keep the cold out. "Whew. I think

he temperature dropped about twenty degrees
between the hardware store and here."

If it had, Eve wasn't feeling it. She was warm all
over. Colliding with him in the store aisle—and
yielding to his bold kiss—was the perfect way to re-
connect. Finding out that he would be around this
Christmas was, very simply, what she had needed
to hear. What she had been longing to hear. Luck
couldn't help it if Toby had given the surprise
away. Hadn't she gotten what she wanted?

Not everything. And not just yet, she thought
with an inward smile. But soon. Very soon.

He took off his heavy jacket, shrugging it from
the breadth of his shoulders and tucking the thermal knit shirt he wore back into the waistband of
his faded jeans. Eve took a deep breath. Nice. Very
nice. He looked great.

He didn't seem to see anything in the kitchen
that interested him and he strolled into the living
room while she was hanging up her coat. "So that's
the tree. Big one. How'd you get that here by yourself?"

"My mother helped me. Actually, she bought it
for me. My father picked it out. I'm hoping that
they're going to do the math one of these days and
figure out that I'm twenty-six years old."

She heard him laugh. "That's still pretty young.
Sometimes you make me feel kinda old, did I ever
tell you that?"

"No. You're not that much older than me, Luck.
Only ten years."

He turned around and watched her adjust her
rumpled clothes. "So long as it works for you, Eve,
I don't care. You look beautiful."

A glimpse of herself in the mirror she'd passed
told her that she looked awful.

"No, I don't."

There were still pine needles in her hair and her nose was pink from the cold. Eve looked at him nervously, then excused herself, a little awkwardly, to go upstairs. She could make necessary repairs to her appearance in the bathroom. She was sure Luck could amuse himself for the next five minutes.

She pulled a brush through her hair, fluffing it frantically, then dashed on a little raspberry pink lipgloss. Eve peered into the bathroom mirror. So far, so good. But her eyes could use some . . . something.

This wasn't the time to learn everything she didn't know about eye makeup, especially when there wasn't anyone to teach her. Eve settled for bringing out her eyes with soft dark pencil, drawing a delicate line that did wonders when she examined herself again in the mirror.

She'd made big, brown, doe eyes. How cool was that? Beginner's luck, she told herself lightly, but don't knock it.

Eve yanked a knit dress in a rich sienna color off a hanger and took off what she had on, slipping the knit dress over her head. Bad move. The static in the indoor air made her hair rise in delicate wisps. Eve ran the hairbrush under the faucet, and dragged it, slightly damp, over her hair. She looked in the mirror again. Good move. In fact, she looked good all over, even to her own critical eyes.

She wanted to dash back down the stairs but she forced herself to go down slowly. Luck must have heard her coming, because he walked out of the kitchen and waited for her at the bottom of the stairs.

"How does that song go?" he said quietly. "Step
by step . . ."

"I fell in love with you." Eve finished the sentence.

Luck's face lit up. He took his hands out of the
pockets of his jeans and raised them up to bring
her into the circle of his strong arms when she got
to the last step. Eve went willingly. Her mixed-up
emotions melted into one as he brought her
roughly against his body and kissed her hard at
first. Then he kissed her again, exploring her mouth
with a sensual tenderness that made her want to
beg for more.

"I want you, Eve," he said huskily. "I know you
went upstairs to get all dolled up for me, but that
dress is coming off all the same. You ready?"

Breathlessly, she said yes.

Chapter 18

As they lay sleeping, the snow began to fall. And
t didn't stop. By morning, when Eve stirred in
Luck's arms, the edges of the curtains were trimmed
n brilliant white light. Through a wider space, she
aw a lump of snow, probably from the roof, fall
oundlessly past the window glass.

"Hey." She patted him on the chest. "I think
omething happened last night."

A blissful smile appeared on his face but he didn't
•pen his eyes. "Oh yeah. You and me. I remember
very incredible minute. Ready for more?"

She giggled. "Um, not just yet."

Luck still didn't open his eyes, but he kept her
lext to him, wrapping a muscular arm around her
houlders. He pulled up the covers a little higher,
naking sure she was warm, since they were both
•aked.

"Aren't you curious?"

"Right now . . . I'm perfectly happy," he mur-
nured.

"But I think it snowed. A lot. It's so quiet out side."

She was silent, so that he would understand what she meant. The muffling effect of a heavy snowfall gave the room the feeling of being wrapped in a giant, cozy cloud. Eve listened, then realized that Luck was snoring very slightly. "Wake up," she said

"Huh?" He rolled over on his side and got her in a full-body hug, sliding his leg between hers and tucking her head under his chin. Eve laughed, a muffled sound that made him give her room to breathe, and she seized the opportunity to wiggle free.

Shivering a little, she ran to the window and opened the curtain. "Nooo—not the light—please no," Luck groaned.

"Holy cow! How beautiful!" Knowing she couldn't be seen from outside in this particular window Eve rested her hands on the deep windowsill and looked at the snow that had engulfed the country side.

Her car had disappeared under it and Luck's SUV resembled a gigantic marshmallow. She could see the taller pine trees, laden with puffy snow up to the topmost twigs. The deciduous trees had an easier burden to bear: their hollows and forks were filled with white but their branches were only out lined by it.

She heard Luck thrash the covers and punch his pillow. He was probably going back to sleep. She didn't turn around. In the near distance, the county snowplow appeared, big and red and shiny, break ing through the drifts and spraying snow high in the air on either side of the road. "Hey, maybe that's Tom Rivera. I can't see who's at the wheel, though."

Instinctively, Eve moved her body behind the curtain but kept looking out.

The approaching snowplow scraped along, making a fair amount of noise. She wasn't aware that Luck slipped out of bed, as naked as she was, until he pounced.

"Gotcha!" he roared, sweeping her up in his arms.

Eve shrieked and laughed, pummeling his chest. But she didn't want him to put her down.

Luck sat down on the edge of the bed with her, then reached out a hand for the tangled covers, dragging them around her until she felt blissfully safe and contented, like a little kid on a snow day. That thought put her in mind of Luck's son.

"What about Toby?"

Luck made whooshy sounds in her ear until Eve giggled. "We can call him later. I don't think he'll see a day like this as a hardship. More like a gift from on high."

It was too. She really didn't want to leave her warm cocoon but she wanted breakfast. "How about some coffee? Bacon and eggs?"

Luck nodded. "Caveman hungry. Woman make food for him. Caveman eat. Then him and woman fool around some more."

She stroked his scratchy chin. "At some point, caveman is going to have to shovel."

"Okay, okay," Luck sighed. He rose from the bed with her still wrapped in the covers and walked to the window. "Wow. Looks like three feet on top of what we got last time."

"That makes five feet."

He set her down and Eve pulled the covers around herself. "Woman good at arithmetic. Woman has to help caveman shovel," he said.

She let the covers fall and stood in front of him in all her naked glory. "Maybe later."

He walked her backward to the bed and they forgot all about breakfast and coffee for the next forty-five minutes.

The arduous work of clearing a path to the cars and then removing the drifted snow from both consumed the better part of the early afternoon. Fueled by an enormous breakfast, they moved what seemed to be a ton of snow. Eve saw Arvid riding his tractor, coming down the narrow back road to plow them out as far as the main road.

She waved and hallooed and he waved back, then made short work of the snow before riding on to help another neighbor farther along.

"Guess we can get out now," she said.

Luck shook his head and leaned on his shovel. "The road to town might not be completely clear. Let's call Toby and see if his friend's parents know what's going on."

They went back inside, stomping the snow from their boots and shaking it off their jackets and gloves outside before it melted. He settled himself in a chair, looking brawny and sweet and good enough to eat, Eve thought appreciatively. She listened to his side of a conversation with Toby, occasionally overhearing the boy's replies, breathless and excited. His friend's dad had taken both boys out to do some sledding and the check-in call didn't last long.

"Nice that Toby has so many friends," she said.

Luck nodded. "Yup. I'll have to reciprocate, of course. Maybe I'll invite them all over at once and let them play video games until the sun comes up."

"Their parents will never forgive you."

"That's the idea, Eve. Then I won't have to do it again."

"You are truly terrible," she said with a smile.

"When I want to be." Luck looked into his coffee cup, then up at her with a pitiful expression.

She grinned. "Don't start that caveman routine again."

"Hey, that was my best puppydog face, not the caveman," he said. "Any more coffee?"

She patted him on the head. "Sure thing. Coming up."

Luck stretched out his long, jeans-clad leg and bumped a foot against the box of ornaments. He looked down. "I seem to remember that we were going to decorate your tree."

She shrugged. "It's not going anywhere."

"Neither are we. Got any doughnuts to go with that coffee?"

She flipped open the lid of a rectangular cardboard box. "Two glazed. One jelly."

Luck helped himself to the jelly doughnut while she poured the coffee. "Doesn't get any cozier than this, babe." He munched and sipped and looked at her adoringly. "So when are we getting married?"

"Huh?" Eve set down the coffeepot, grateful it was nearly empty and wouldn't slosh. "Where did that come from?"

He grinned. "My heart of hearts."

"Oh. Well. Sooner or later, I guess." Her diffident tone masked a sudden excitement. So she really did have a guy who didn't think great sex and true love were mutually exclusive propositions. And he wasn't going to disappear over the holidays. Eve thought about that, and studied the loving look on his face.

"Do I get my druthers?" he asked softly. "Could we get married sooner?"

"I don't even have a dress yet."

"Wear the one you wore last night. We'll find a justice of the peace."

"Whoa." Eve held up her hands. "What happened to waiting?"

"Why do we have to wait?"

"Luck, does this have anything to do with your car accident?"

He finished off the jelly doughnut, and brushed the sugar from his fingertips. "Maybe. I don't feel like waiting any more. So . . ." He picked up the glazed doughnut and clasped her wrist, sticking the doughnut on her thumb.

"What are you doing?"

"With this ring," Luck intoned, "I thee wed."

"Luck, be serious," she laughed. "Besides, that's the wrong finger."

He took the doughnut off and began to eat it. "I'll resize it for you."

"You do that. We still shouldn't rush into getting married. There's Toby to think of, and your folks and mine, and all that . . ." Eve trailed off, not wanting to think of what *all that* entailed. Especially not with nine zillion things to keep track of for the school chorale and church pageant.

"All right," he said amiably. "Whenever you're ready."

No matter what he said, the accident had changed him. Or maybe she was seeing the effect of taking a month off. If only she could do the same.

Maybe in January. After her Christmas commitments were over, and the last little singer and shepherd went home humming.

Of course, Luck wouldn't be happy doing nothing indefinitely. But once in a while, it was clear that he loved it—and it was good for both of them, Eve thought. Sitting here with him in the sunny kitchen, energized by the hard work they had just done and warmed by the good, strong coffee felt like heaven on earth to her.

Why not make it permanent? Eve didn't know. She felt like she needed just one more little push and where it would come from—well, she didn't know that either.

"Let's decorate the tree first."

"Okay." He got to his feet and hoisted the box of ornaments, taking it into the living room. Eve cleared away the remains of their snack, and put the cups into the dishpan, running the hot water into a stream of detergent to make it froth up high.

"Don't come in yet," he called from the other room.

"Okay," she called back. "I might as well do these dishes."

He didn't answer and she got busy, scrubbing plates and sluicing more hot water over them, then stacking them in the drainboard. She wiped the counters and tidied up, then said loudly, "How about now?"

"Yes. Enter." He appeared in the kitchen doorway and stretched out a hand to take her arm. Eve let him guide her to where the tree stood. He'd managed to get the lights on it, somewhat haphazardly, but not much else. "I think I need your help."

"You bet." She kneeled by the box, looking through the tissue-paper-wrapped ornaments for wire hooks, which she found and set aside. Then she began to unwrap more, finding a set of blue glass moons from Czechoslovakia with painted man-in-the-moon faces.

She exclaimed over each old treasure in the box, not stopping until all were unwrapped and set out on the rug, ready to be hung on the fragrant tree. Luck looked in back of her. "Here comes trouble."

Eve looked around to see China pad noiselessly into the room. "Oh, she's used to the tree by now. But if Heidi shows up, watch out. Maybe it's best to put her in the cellar until we're done."

"That's the Christmas spirit," Luck said approvingly.

They got busy, taking the rest of the afternoon to trim the tree, from the red Swedish horses to the last straw star, touching each other's hands now and then through the thick tangle of narrow branches and needles. When dusk had fallen outside, Eve led him to the sofa and they both fell back into the cushions, exhausted.

"Wow. Look at that. But we forgot to turn on the lights."

"Go for it," she encouraged.

He got up and kneeled to flick the switch on the light cord. The tree came to life, a brilliant, magical thing that made the whole room glow.

"Oh my." There was soft wonder in her voice. "That's my first Christmas tree. I mean, those are someone else's ornaments but—"

"It is your tree, Eve. It looks fantastic."

"Thanks." He came back and they shared a long kiss that held more feeling than they could possibly put into words.

Luck broke it off and sat back. He looked at the tree again, then at her, and slipped a finger into his shirt pocket and pulled out a folded piece of paper. "And now for the surprise. I think I made you wait too long for this."

She shook her head. "No. You only just told me that there was a surprise, remember?"

"You'll understand in a minute. Here you go." He handed her the piece of paper. "I wrote you a poem,"

"Aww."

"Go ahead. Read it aloud."

Eve gave him a puzzled look and unfolded the paper, murmuring the simple words.

Where horses are red
And moonlight is blue
Look for a gift
That says I love you.

She looked at the tree, trying to understand the clue and got it at once. A blue moon was hung directly over a red-painted horse. And next to it was a small velvet box.

"Go see what it is," Luck said, pride and pleasure mingled in his low voice.

Eve rose and took the box, turning to him as she opened it. A diamond ring twinkled back at her, brighter than any star she'd ever seen.

"Like I said, I made you wait too long."

Her eyes filled with tears. "N-no. I think your timing is just right."

"Come back here, Eve. I want to put that ring on your hand myself. Do you know how much I love you?" He opened his arms and she went to him without another word.

Chapter 19

The children stood in orderly rows on the small stage of the school auditorium, staring out at the crowd that filled the place. The girls wore lace-collared velvet dresses in deep colors, delighted with an opportunity to be beautiful. Demure and well-behaved, they didn't fidget much, except to touch their brushed and shining hair, or fold their hands together as they waited to begin. As for the boys, their pressed white shirts had been pulled halfway out of belted pants and their ties were already loosened from the knots. Every parent in town had done what they could to get cowlicks to lie flat—most of the boys had a scrubbed, uncomfortable look, except for the few lucky ones who were allowed to sport spiky haircuts.

Eve looked them over from where she stood, just in front of the stage, with Mrs. Alstrom, the church organist, to her left at the magnificent new grand piano, a Christmas gift to the school. Black and glossy, the piano gleamed, reflecting the tall floor vase filled with green-and-white holly and red

roses that had been set near it. But the audience
couldn't see the discreet brass plaque over the key
board that bore the donor's name: Grant McClure

He'd come to see one of the chorale rehearsal
and observed Mrs. Alstrom struggling to coax
something that sounded like music out of the old
upright that had been in the auditorium forever
Out of the blue, Luck's father had insisted on re
placing it and the school administration couldn'
very well refuse. Grant hadn't offered much in the
way of explanation to the principal or to Eve, only
said something about having a lot to be gratefu
for this holiday season. But Eve hadn't missed the
twinkle in his eye.

Outside the tall windows that graced the audito
rium walls, she noticed the light snow falling
steadily. For the most part, the concert attendees
had shed their outerwear before sitting down and
the hallway coat closets were crammed full of
boots and parkas. But a few of the younger kids
were skating over the polished floor in their socks
working off excess energy under the eye of the
kindergarten teacher.

They went back to their seats when Gene Chase
the math teacher, switched off the bright overhead
fluorescents from a panel in the rear of the audito
rium and switched on the stage illumination. The
open doors to the hallway let in some light so the
latecomers could find seats, and the people in
the auditorium settled down, shushing the littlest
children who'd come to see their big brothers and
big sisters on stage.

Eve signaled Jimmy Caldwell to come forward
from the ranks for his solo. She saw him search the
faces in the crowd for his mother and then smile,
but Eve didn't turn around. She knew without

looking that Lurleen was waving to him, proud of her son.

Somewhere behind her sat Luck, equally proud of Toby, who looked a little lost among the many other children on stage. He had a lot of friends at the school, but no siblings to watch him perform, of course. But Mr. and Mrs. Freitag, his grandparents on his mother's side, had come to the show, and so had Luck's father and her parents.

The Freitags would be leaving with Toby and driving back to Duluth, since the Christmas concert officially marked the beginning of the winter break for the Cable area school system. And Luck would be staying with Eve.

She raised her hands to get the children on stage to direct their attention to her, and the diamond on her left hand caught the light from the hallway and flashed. Eve felt loved every time she looked at it.

Lurleen had spotted the ring in seconds at the last chorale rehearsal, crowing over it as if she hadn't been married three times already and counting, as she put it. And she'd spread the news. But Eve didn't mind. It seemed that everywhere she went, she got quizzed about their marriage plans, and everyone insisted it was meant to be. Even Silvia Rivera had asked shy questions, folding her arms atop her very pregnant middle and looking starry-eyed at the prospect of a hometown wedding for her son's music teacher and his best friend's dad.

Just in case he would be called away from the concert to plow, Tom Rivera had driven the snowplow in. Eve and Luck had volunteered to bring Silvia and her son Eddie home, and Toby was eager to show off Luck's new SUV to his friend. But the snowplow had gotten all the attention when Tom pulled up in the school parking lot. The county crew had decorated the top of the cab with eight plastic reindeer and hung sleighbells on the doors.

Mrs. Alstrom played a few notes and the people in the auditorium fell into a respectful hush. The math teacher had managed to rig a spotlight for Jimmy and the boy stepped into its glow, blinking a little, no longer able to see his mother, Eve knew. Which was good, because he would have to concentrate on performing.

Eve nodded to Mrs. Alstrom and the first chords of "Silent Night" filled the air. Then Jimmy's sweet tenor soared above the music, giving life to the beloved carol and renewed meaning to the story it told.

Afterwards, as families and friends filed out into the hallway, calling out wishes for happy holidays, Eve saw Luck with Lisa's parents and his father. Luck waved her over and drew her to his side, and Grant McClure proudly introduced her to the Freitags. There was nothing but warmth in their eyes as they met the woman who would become their grandson's stepmother, and the last remaining doubt Eve had had vanished forever.

Her parents came over and they exchanged small talk, waiting for Toby, who rocketed out from the backstage area and took Eve's hand and his father's, swinging between them for a moment, then wrapped himself around his grandmother's knees.

"Easy, kiddo," Luck said, smiling down at him until the boy let go and shook both his grandfathers' hands one by one.

"What do you think?" Toby asked excitedly, looking at his mother's parents. "Isn't Eve nice?"

"She sure is," Mrs. Freitag said. "And that was a wonderful concert. Thank you for inviting us, Toby."

"Eve made us rehearse everything a million times."

"Of course. Her music teacher made her rehearse everything a million times when she was a little girl," Teresa Rowland said. "That's why she's so good at what she does."

"Yeah, but you're better at baking cookies, Mrs. Rowland."

"I like that," Eve said indignantly.

"But it's true," Toby protested. He stifled a yawn.

His father ruffled his hair. "Tired? Good. You can sleep all the way to Duluth. Your suitcase is in the trunk of Grandma and Grandpa's car, and there's blankets and snacks for you." He thought for a moment. "Oh, did I tell you they have a new car?"

"Is it nicer than ours?" Toby asked.

"That's not a very polite question but the answer is yes," Luck said. "It has a backseat DVD player."

"Cool!"

"Sorry to take him away for Christmas," Mr. Freitag said to both Luck and Eve.

"That's all right," Luck answered. "He thinks I'm finally old enough to manage. But I'm not allowed to unwrap a single gift until he gets back on New Year's Day."

"Sure you can stand it that long? You were the kind of kid who handed me a list weeks ahead and tore into the pile of presents in five seconds flat," Grant joked. "Just to make sure you got what you wanted."

"Gotta plan for the future and hope for the best. You taught me that." Luck clapped his father on the back. "This year I got everything I wanted." He took Eve's hand to show off the beautiful ring that symbolized their love. "The lady said yes."

Of course the Freitags and the Rowlands and Grant McClure had been told of their engagement the day after Luck had given her the ring, but hearing Luck say it with so much warmth and emotion in his voice meant the world to Eve. She nodded shyly at the smiling faces around her, but she didn't really hear what everyone was saying. The small talk continued for a few minutes more, then good-byes were said as the last of the people in the auditorium got ready to leave and the teachers began to fold up the chairs, talking quietly.

Side by side, Luck and Eve waved good-bye to their family and to Toby, holding his grandparents' hands and talking animatedly as he left with them.

Mrs. Alstrom put away the music, calling to Eve, "I'll take care of this, honey. You must be tuckered out. And I just bet you and your young man have better things to do."

Luck grinned at the older woman. "You're right about that, Mrs. Alstrom." He guided Eve down a side aisle to get out of everyone's way and they stood before one of the tall windows, looking out into the dark. The snow had stopped and the clouds had cleared swiftly in the winter wind.

"Look at the stars," she said softly.

He touched a hand to her chin and turned her

ce to him. "I'd rather look at you. All night
ng."

Then, as if there were no one there at all be-
des the two of them, Luck brought his bride-to-
e within the loving circle of his arms and kissed
er.

Buy These Calder Novels by

Janet Dailey

Shifting Calder Wind   0-8217-7223-6   **$7.99**US/**$10.99**CA
Chase Calder has no recollection of who he is, why he came to Fo
Worth...or who tried to put a bullet in his head the night that a cowboy name
Laredo Smith saved his life. Laredo recognizes him as the owner of Mor
tana's Triple C Ranch—but according to the local papers, Chase has just bee
declared dead, the victum of a fiery car crash. The only person Chase ca
trust is his level-headed daughter-in-law, Jessy Calder. Helping Chase bring
Jessy into conflict with headstrong Cat Calder, and into an uneasy allianc
with the mysterious and seductive Laredo. And when another family men
ber is found murdered on Calder soil, Chase resolves to come out of hidin
and track down a ruthless killer...before the killer finds him first...

Green Calder Grass   0-8217-7222-8   **$7.99**US/**$10.99**CA
Jessy Niles Calder grew up on the Triple C ranch, six hundred square mile
of grassland that can be bountiful or harsh, that bends to no man's will—ju
like a Calder. As Ty Calder's wife, Jessy finally has all she's ever wanted. B
even in the midst of this new happiness there are hidden enemies, greedy fc
the rich Montana land, and willing to shed blood to get it. Not to mentio
Ty's ex-wife Tara, causing trouble wherever she goes. And soon Jessy wi
be faced with the fight of her life—one that will change the Triple C for
ever...

Calder Promise   0-8217-7541-3   **$7.99**US/**$10.99**CA
Young and beautiful, Laura Calder isn't content to live on a Montana ranc
Touring Europe with her "Aunt" Tara brings her into contact with the sc
phisticated world she's craved...and with the two men—and ultimat
rivals—who will lay claim to her heart. Boone Rutledge is the son of a Texa
billionaire and used to getting what he wants. He wants Laura...and so doe
a Sebastian Dunshill, Earl of Crawford, a handsome, sexy Londoner with
few secrets he can't share.

Available Wherever Books Are Sold!

Check out our website at **www.kensingtonbooks.com**